CRS

THE
LOVE STREET
SCHOOL
MURDERS

BOOK ONE
STRANGERS

Not to Know Me Argues Yourself Unknown,
John Milton, Paradise Lost (1608-1674)

Copyright © C R Searle July 2024. All Rights Reserved.

First print edition

The right of C R Searle to be identified as the author of this work has been asserted in accordance with sections 77 and 78 of the Copyright Designs and Patents Act 1988.

In this work of fiction, the characters, places and events are either a product of the author's imagination or they are used entirely fictitiously. Any resemblance to actual persons, living or dead is purely coincidental.

This book may not be reproduced or transmitted or stored in whole or in part by any means, including, graphic, electronic, or mechanical without the express written consent of the author except in the case of brief quotations embodied in critical articles and reviews.

Cover design by C R Searle, composited by Ryan Ashcroft, bookbrand.co.uk
Formatting by Ryan Ashcroft

Also, by C R Searle

The Rebus and the Parrot, Book One:
The Bottomless Well of Time

The Rebus and the Parrot, Book Two:
The Secret of the Château Tollendal

The Rebus and the Parrot, Book Three:
The Battle of the Stones

The Rebus and the Parrot, Book Four:
The Children of the Ankh

The Rebus and the Parrot, Book Five:
The Totem of Tarhuhiawaku

The Rebus and the Parrot, Book Six:
The Masters of Time

The Rebus and the Parrot, Book Seven:
The End Game

The Love Street School Murders, Book Two:
Reminiscence

The Love Street School Murders, Book Three:
Denouement

Prologue	12
Chapter 1	17
Chapter 2	37
Chapter 3	70
Chapter 4	80
Chapter 5	87
Chapter 6	92
Chapter 7	103
Chapter 8	111
Chapter 9	115
Chapter 10	121
Chapter 11	139
Chapter 12	152
Chapter 13	174
Chapter 14	184
Chapter 15	192
Chapter 16	197
Chapter 17	208
Chapter 18	228
Chapter 19	244
Chapter 20	262
Chapter 21	270
Chapter 22	288

Book One

Strangers

Prologue

Once Upon a Time
Wolfgang Amadeus Mozart: Clarinet Concerto in A Major, 2nd Movement

They stood beneath the domed, snow-white, pavilion in a sun dappled woodland glade echoing to the trill of birds waking to a day barely begun and the sweetly tinkling babble of the stream tripping over gentle falls of polished stones into the pool of crystal-clear water below them. Their reflections in its limpid surface as deceptively real as the proud Narcissus saw when the goddess Nemesis lured him to his death; his sin to love himself without care for others. The sun bright on its nine, fluted pillars, the alter stone that separated them and warm on their faces, a young man; a boy, but grown tall, lithe and muscular in his teenage years and as beautiful as only boys of that age can be, and the woman, more beautiful still, dressed in a clinging, white diaphanous shift, belted at her slim waist with a braided cord of gold its, tasseled ends falling to her sandalled feet, her lustrous raven black hair, which fell to her mid-back dressed in a garland of flowers; red anemone, purple withy, pink and white asphodel and a yellow narcissus.

'Is this trial you have set yourself finished?' She asked, her voice loving, but no less impatient.

'Yes, today,' he answered, with a smile, the searching fingers of his right hand finding hers in an apologetic coil she drew to her lips and brushed with the softest kiss. What he had done, and what he now did, already forgiven, but though they were, transgressed their sacred duty.

'You have suffered too much, and the error was never yours; not really,' she gently scolded, knowing in her woman's heart it was. That all that followed that first kiss was his mistake; one he should have refused. But how could he have known it would end as it did; he was a boy no older than her? It was unforgivably cruel. A cruelty borne of man's vulgar passion for woman. But he knew their love was doomed, could never be the love she hoped and dreamed it was, but though it was, she has loved him with a constancy enough to make her weep.

'It was never hers.'

'No, it wasn't,' she agreed, turning after him to look at her face in the pool. A young woman grown to beguiling beauty, but too much thinking herself the match of any man and once again, enamoured of a faithless lover careless of her tender heart, but with friends to protect her now, as she never had before. AA, Tomon and Brian, who would protect her as he couldn't.

'And I have not suffered, as you and your servants have made sure I didn't and *Euphrosyne* and *Thalia* most of all, who are all the time ready to help me if danger threatened and when it did, I was no more hurt than if I was an actor in a play my part an illusory shadow as empty of feeling as those that stretch beneath our feet. Though, Arthur, as he insists, we call him until this business is done,' he smiled, his fondness for the man who was his Nemesis, 'too much enjoys his part and *Aglaia,* too much encourages his intemperate excesses with her unseemly behaviour. Which I know confuses his simple, soldiers mind as it confuses mine.' He laughed. 'The character she plays so cold and darkly enigmatic she startles all who look upon her, but though she does they look upon her all the more; cannot help but look upon her. A veritable *Medusa,* but her head forever wreathed in smoke and not the snakes that grew from hers.'

'Yes, he does, and I have told him, as I have told her, to be more careful of what they do, but you are also to blame wearing your part in this drama like a hair shirt and enjoying it better than they do; *Léandre.* But mine,' she shamelessly intrigued, 'a crooked backed and ugly crone is a caution to all women the beauty of their youth will one-day fade, but though it does, and old age is a trial we must gracefully endure, and more than any man knows how, it is a carapace, an illusion; is not who we really are. But even so, I am every day met with spite and cruelty by those who fear what they must become and, in their vanity, hate me, and the men more than the maids you so endlessly tease with your tragic mask. But far worse,' she gestured abstractedly, gazing at the flat spreading branches of the gnarled old cypress tree that grew out of the root bound cleft of the butter-yellow rock on the low green hill above them, 'they have abandoned themselves to the vulgar and ignore the divine; desire only the desire of men and lose themselves in lust. Have,' she deeply sighed, 'abandoned the Goddess we must dutifully serve to be their creatures, when they are base in every way and hardly deserve the love, we give to them.'

'You are too hard.'

'Maybe I am, but the hurt I caution you against is not of the flesh, which is easily mended, but of the soul, which isn't,' she scolded, again, her right index finger pressed to his lips.

'She has suffered more hurt and more heart ache than I ever will, and I can do nothing to make amends, but let her know I love her still, as I have loved her from that first time we met.'

'You know you cannot ....' She left the words unsaid.

'I know,' he glumly answered, his eyes turned again to her smiling face as she greeted her class, as she would later greet him, but would not know him for who he was, though she was ever sweet and kind, 'but had we that one time when she wanted me, and I, in my duty to you, refused her?'

'It can never be. Not *that,* so leave her now this last time and let her know by some secret sign you love her still. That the wrong you think you did her was not your fault, but was the fault of others' she said, picking a small posy of flowers from the garland she wore as crown.

'You like her?'

'I very much like her,' she smiled. 'As she likes me and suspects, as no one else does, I am not who I pretend to be, but like her or not, this must come to an end; today.' She smiled her tender reproof, as he took the posy and kissed her on her cheek and in the instant he did, she saw in the pool he was already gone to her. Changing by degrees from light of the boy he was, to shade of the death he long ago suffered, to be reborn anew in the light of the boy he must now be, as he hurried through the snow towards the building where they had these last few weeks met.

Chapter 1

Monday December 17, 1962
Alma Cogan: The Story of My Life

The boy came like a shadow out of nowhere and hurried on nervously scampering, red chapped, athletically slender legs into the cold annex building to the crackling, high-pitched, fiercely whining sound of the nine o'clock bell chiming its thunderous alarm over the school's newly installed, only last Friday, 15-inch, corner mounted in every classroom, cloakroom, corridor and public space, *GRF Tannoy* system. A Heath-Robinson contraption so hurriedly assembled over the last two weeks by Valeria's coarse and careless lover, Dylan Lloyd-Thomas and diminutively comic, but despite he was, sinister and rather frightening, friend, Terry Mack, she suspected it was an elaborate practical joke, a vicious payback on the headmaster they both hated.

Though a not very funny joke, she sighed, not for the first time that horribly cold winter morning, her luminous, soft blue eyes lifting to the antique *RCA s*peaker box sitting askew like a battered old shield on the small plywood shelf they had erected above her still open classroom door last Friday evening. Which trembled and vibrated and moved so alarmingly on its flimsy pedestal she feared it would fall onto one of her snows flaked, red nosed, adorably sweet, first year pupils as they hurried into the second floor, annex classroom she had these last three months occupied to the temporary exclusion of almost every other member of the schools teaching staff. As she hoped she might be soon excluded until the now stalled building work that littered the ground floor was completed; a vain hope, she concluded, knowing how mean the headmaster was.

The exception being her Head of Department, Mr Arno de Roy, a fat bellied, taciturn Anglo-Dutchman whose execrable French hardly deserved the title, a man who never failed to remind her of Charles Laughton's, *Quasimodo* in the 1939 film, *The Hunchback of Notre-Dame.* But sadly, without the gentle care he showed his companion in petty tyranny, *Esmeralda,* played by Maureen O'Hara, whose desire for the handsome, *Captain Phoebus,* was, perhaps, a little like her own irrational desire for Dylan. A man like him, she suspected, as so many men are; self-regarding, dominating and dangerously cruel in their primitive passions towards the women who love them. But who so thrilled and aroused her with his greedy lust, his conceited charm and his masculinity she had to have him? Did, if only to dream the sweet love of her youth, Pascal. Her beautiful, Pascal, her *Iphis,* as AA so gently called him, though he was no girl, and she his, *Ianthe,* a boy she loved better than life and still did, the measure of all the men she had ever known, but betrayed and lost in a thoughtlessly silly moment, as she deserved, she did.

As she didn't deserve Arno's irrational, bad tempered jealousy, so typical of her stuffy male colleagues, his ill-disguised scorn, which was so at odds with the liberal, easy going, emancipated Dutch character she knew so well. Knew and loved from several memorable weekends she had spent in Amsterdam, where she never failed to visit the Stedelijk Museum to see their collection of Cézanne, Monet, van Gogh, Braque and Kandinsky, who died in Neuilly-sur-Seine, just a few kilometres far from where she once lived with her mother in Saint Germain en Laye. And, of course, the incomparable Rijksmuseum for Rembrandt and Vermeer, who is surely the best of the Dutch masters. His magnificent *Woman in Blue Reading a Letter* one of the most evocative paintings of a woman she had ever seen, the last time, just last year, though she had spent rather more time in the Oude Kerk with Etienne and Madeleine than was good for any of them, their first and last holiday together and so drunk every night on whiskey and weed she hardly remembered anything, she sighed, it was the last time they were happy together.

And sighed again Arno was such a tedious bore. But so big and so tall and so draped in a luxuriance of unfashionable floppy, brown hair so at odds with his porcine nose and opulently slack and sensual lips, the effect of him rather frightened her, as it did the children, he so little cared about, she thought. Eyeing his empty classroom across the now puddle wet corridor with a mixture of sadness and regret he thought himself so grand, so above her, he now mostly ignored her, something in his repressed, English homosexuality, she supposed that hated all women.

That and his bristling annoyance she taught French the way she did; far better than he did, as French, the language of culture and romance should be taught, with passion, verve and colourful example, she smiled her classroom looked so wonderfully gay and inviting. A language so alive with meaning no empty grammar, rote learned by straight-backed, frightened children can do it justice. A strange man by any measure of their complicated breed who just two afternoons every week, was her only teaching companion in that lonely outpost of the school's cramped estate. Mr Eldred, the schools waspishly indignant, seemingly much-put-upon caretaker and Mrs Wiśniewski the hook nosed, watchful cleaner being her only other visitors, but he so rarely, she hardly ever saw him and then only to see him scurrying away like a frightened beetle, ignoring she had a dozen times asked him to empty the dangerous clutter he had made of her store room, now piled so high with boxes, chairs and desks, she could hardly get in.

All of it coming from the now almost empty building beyond her and Arno's still relatively busy corridor, carried there, she knew, by the randy gang of workmen, who so teased her when she passed, whose labours had come to such an abrupt and quarrelsome end last Wednesday afternoon. Its hastily abandoned, untidy squalor the perfect metaphor for the heartache she now everyday felt. A soulless, haunting emptiness made worse by the biting chill that blew through the gable-roofed, portico entrance below her windows with a moan like a banshee, which even now rattled its temporary, plywood door on its hinges, left open by Clifford when he came in a minute ago. A place so unlike the Lycée Louis-le-Grande in the Rue Saint Jacques in Paris, where she had taught psychology and philosophy for most of the last four years, she found their comparison utterly impossible, bewildering and absurdly ridiculous.

And her leaving in such a desperate, if understandable hurry the school she so loved, a terrible mistake, not least the view from her third-floor window, she groaned, she so missed it. Which unlike the one she now saw, her knees rested against one of the barely warm cast iron radiators that hugged the wall beneath the windows, overlooked the soft-brown, limestone facade of Haussmann's second empire architecture and the blossom filled, box gardens and walks they contained in the Cour d'Honneur. A mistake she deeply regretted, but a mistake she was resolved she would soon put right, though she would miss dear, AA more than she could say; if miss him she must? Something she must soon tell him; tonight, perhaps when they met, as they often met after school, in his elegant sitting room to drink and smoke as she knew she shouldn't?

'Yes,' she sighed, yet again, her upraised wagging finger a gentle, if distracted scold to the three girls in wet raincoats who squabbled, as only girls can squabble, to have the two seats in front of her own, neatly piled desk. A view so unlike the one that now greeted her through the ice rimed, snow dappled, horribly dirty windows that since before she woke that morning had seen the first determined, growing heavy

fall of snow that winter, but a snow now here to stay.

The deeply slanted roof scape of the school's red glazed, brick buildings already a thick mantle of frosted white, which despite she so hated the place looked quite lovely; as it never truly had before. As snow, in that truly magical way it always does, so remarkably changes our perception of the world, turning the everyday bleak, mundane and discordantly ugly into something astonishingly, wondrously beautiful. It's cloistered, tight packed, sharp-edged buildings so horribly pierced at the top, middle and bottom by thick bands of yellow glazed brick, grey stone lintels and pigeon pooed, heavy sills in the fashion of a Dickensian prison, factory, workhouse or railway station, now softened and rounded to deceive the eye it was other than it was.

A woolly softening of virgin white snow that extended without fault or jar to the city which enclosed it, which pressed its claustrophobically high, iron spiked, boundary walls in a tight embrace. Its haphazard clutter of ancient and modern buildings drawing her eye in an endlessly fascinating search of its pleasing, but sometimes oddly, incongruous panorama. A panorama which began with such bright optimism in the Italian design garden of cone, box and sphere trimmed shrubs, which hugged the slate grey river bend in the park, directly behind the annex. Just visible to her far right, if she pressed her nose hard to the window and just then shrouded in a pretty, sun dappled mist nowhere else seen that morning, which framed the church and spire it almost hid to sublime perfection. Only to end in sad disappointment with the three, lime-green, rust speckled, gas tanks, which stood on the far side of the racecourse beside the soot blackened railway arches to her left. And with a backdrop of snow topped low hills in between which seemed contrived by God's artistic hand to hold the pressing weight of the sullen grey sky in its place, a scene so picturesque that morning she sighed it might have been painted to its dreamlike perfection by Mesdag or Mauve, such was the surreal, canvas-like quality of the world she now looked out upon. A city scape turned to wistful, dreamy illusion.

A city in so many ways reminiscent of some of the older French towns and cities she knew so well, Rambouillet, Chartres and Rouen, where *Madame Bovary* met her ruin, she smiled she should think of her just then, but why not, she loved her, though AA unkindly said she was, at the very least, shallow, predictable and naïve, and at worst a scheming, heartless harlot of the very worst kind? Troyes and Lyons, which also boasted a proud Roman history, though the Amphitheatre des Trois Gauls at the foot of La Croix-Rousse Hill and the ruins of the Odeon near the summit of the Fourvière were perhaps far more impressive than its modest collection of sandstone ruins, and with an amphitheatre so buried and neglected it shamed the city it was.

And of course, the historic Paris she now so longed to see again. Notre Dame, Le Marais, Montmartre, Montparnasse, Les Halles and of course the Quartier Latin where she had so long roomed and studied at the Sorbonne and then worked barely half a mile away, at the Lycée she now so heart achingly missed; the alma mater of a hundred great names. A place she so loved it thrilled her heart to think of it again and with an aching that longed to return there in the New Year.

To walk in Le Jardin du Luxembourg, where she often ate her lunch beside the palace, to see again the Panthéon where the inimitable Voltaire lies buried alongside Rousseau, Victor Hugo, Émile Zola and Marie Curie - such an indomitably brave woman, where she had spent many happy hours reading on its always crowded steps or just watching the world go by. The bohemian Paris of boulevards; the Boulevard Saint-Germain, the Boulevard Saint-Michel, the Rue de Rennes, the Paris of narrow, cobbled streets and even narrower bistros, bars and cafes, where writers, painters, poets, actors, philosophers and their hangers-on would meet to drink and brag they were so famous. Where she and her many friends would every weekend meet to drink wine and cognac and smoke far too many strong French cigarettes and endlessly talk the night away.

The Prince Paul Bar and Harry's American Bar on the Rue Daunou, being two of her favourite haunts, where all the American writers and tourist hung out and where the Irish poet Brendan Behan honed his writing skills to their Gaelic perfection and Les Deux Magots in the Place Saint-Germain-des-Prés and Le Café de Flore, which he scathingly referred to as the twin cathedrals of existentialism, though he boasted he never prayed at either. Disliking the pompous intellectualism of Sartre but liking Camus's philosophy of the absurd; but who didn't like Camus; everyone liked Camus, though he was never a philosopher in the tradition of Sartre, who was his friend until they famously fell out. La Coupole, on the Boulevard du Montparnasse, where she met her husband, Étienne, despite he and her sister, Madeleine said they didn't and the nearby La Closerie de Lilas, where Gertrude Stein held court, where they said they did.

The Paris of Picasso, who she once saw in Nice, though neither she nor Madeleine dared to speak to him, as he pushed Matisse, his old friend and the only rival he would admit, in his wheelchair not ten feet from where they stood rooted to the spot, their pretty mouths agape. Of Becket, Joyce, Piaf, Genet, Lacan, Merleau-Ponty and Simone de Beauvoir, whose writings were both a love and an inspiration to her, not least her *Le Deuxième Sexe,* which every girl and every boy should read before they are too much grown. Should be forced to read and understand before they look longingly at each other, who she had a score of times met and talked, too. Of F Scott-Fitzgerald and Ernest Hemingway, *w*ho AA was astonished and a little angry to hear, she had also several times met during the war and was jealous she had, though not of her; but of him. That's when she knew he loved her knew she loved him and a rather a lot!

The past, she smiled, turning on her heels, she was oddly and so sensuously alive that bitterly cold December morning. The end of the school's Michaelmas term, as the headmaster grandly called it, now just five long days away, as she looked at every changed feature of the city with an enchanted eye. A city of so many contrasts from spires and ancient castle walls to modern offices and apartment blocks, their windows ablaze with yellow lights or reflecting shards of iridescent colour in the faint sun that pierced the sky above the cramped huddle of its roof tops.

Flat, gabled, domed, hipped, arched and skillioned, like the brash and gaudy garage that stood beside the art deco, ABC Regal Cinema to her left where she every week bought her petrol and where two months earlier a traffic accident forced her to buy her little car; a car she had grown to love and would terribly miss. Each rising and falling in snow-capped crenulations towards the cathedral's flag topped tower, which to her playful, growing more winsome eye appeared to pull them like a draw string to its centre. Perhaps by the force of its historic, deeply inspiring past, its stirring, unashamed beauty; its majestic power their shame and their aspiration.

The hypnotically slanting, heavy fall of snow adding to this odd illusory effect and seeming to ripple the scene in front of her into a drape of curtain-like furrows of muted light and shade, hinting the tower could, by some impossible means, lift to emptiness everything it encompassed. An emptiness she had known since she was a teenage girl of fifteen lies beneath the surface of our irrationally naïve, sensible perceptions. An emptiness our unconscious minds contrive in ways yet unknown to fill the world we perceive, or *think* we perceive, though we might equally know another, perhaps many other worlds and all of them very different from our own.

That this, every day familiar scene could, in the blink of an eye, be so easily lost to her and made anew in the play of bewitching light and shadow that now fell upon her eyes to trick her mind to see the world as it truly is; an artifice, a deception, a pretence that waits upon moments like this to reveal itself. A world, a reality that was no more than Plato said it was all those years ago, the flickering, illusory dance of light on the walls of the prison cave we inhabit. A two-dimensional projection conjured by the camera obscura of our minds, which devoid, as it now was, of its everyday guiding referents, hints, but no more than hints, the invisible that lies beyond our grasp. The invisible made visible by an unconscious mind that is both the beginning and end of reality. A reality which is so much more than the one we think it is, that speaks to us without we hardly know it does in dreams, illusions, fantasies and fleeting intuitions.

As the painters she so adored have a thousand times tried to show us, Monet, Renoir, Sisley, Pissarro, Degas, Manet, Bazille, Cassatt and so many others besides, not least the English painter, Turner, perhaps the best of all of them, whose work she had lately come to know. Though dear AA would laugh to hear her say such a thing and scold her she did, but so kindly she never took offence, never truly believed he didn't feel what she felt, glimpsed what she glimpsed.

'Mmm,' she sighed to the mild amusement of her now keenly watching, excitedly expectant class, who adored her without exception, a teacher so unlike any other they had ever known. Young, French and so beautifully exotic she was as glamorous as any film star they had ever seen on the television and with lips so fabulously red they shone. 'Mmm,' she sighed again, ignoring the heavy stamp of someone's wet feet on the floor behind her, the noisy, impatient chatter of children anxious to say hello, the quite unnecessary thump of a desk lid and that *bloody* bell, which relentlessly chimed on and on. Her mood, despite her want to hurry back to

Paris, made hopeful, frivolous and daring by the tryst she and Dylan, had, last Thursday planned; if he remembered they had? After all he was very drunk and perhaps a little out of sorts by the news the headmaster was planning to sack him. Which she didn't believe! Nor the absurd reason he gave for doing it and of course the news Barbara was about to divorce him, which made her feel less guilty she had so easily and against her better judgment become his lover.

Though she must first run the gauntlet of 3C before that delicious treat would again unfold, she smiled, he eyes turned toward the quarter open, storeroom door at the back of the classroom and the table she would soon prepare, perhaps the last time they would be together that way, she blushed she was so wanton and so wickedly shameless she didn't care a fig she was. And so very confident she could change him; make him the lover she knew he could truly be.

But first 3C! A socially inept, disinterested, delinquent, aggressively quarrelsome and educationally retarded group of children, as so many children were in The Love Street Secondary Modern School for Boys and Girls. Children she had to her shame and regret grown to dislike in the few months she had known them, except for Hilda, Fay and poor little Clifford, all three of them so very sweet and kind, though none of them the *fairies* slightly bonkers Pauline Fisk insisted they were and certainly not, Greta, a strange girl who both perplexed and intrigued her.

But not half as much as the three girls she now saw sauntering across the net ball court below her window towards the gymnasium to her left, careless they were late by several long minutes. The two buildings and the main school building between them, with its black and white painted, cupola clock tower with its father time weathervane perched on its top, forming a tight U shaped, rectangular quadrangle that stretched to the open back gate to her right. One of the schools three concrete playgrounds and wherein, nestled beneath the steps of the gym was the school folly, an open to the weather, ridiculously impractical, ice-covered swimming pool.

The three of them careless of the cold wind that blew their skirts to a daring display of shapely, suspender stockinged legs and bright coloured knickers as they strolled in a conspiratorial, tight hugging link to their first lesson of the day; netball, she had earlier heard Miss Langford say it was with a zealots' fierce pride the weather, no matter how bad it was, or might become, would not put her off. A young woman just turned twenty-one she rather liked, though they had never spoken more than a very brief and friendly hello, their paths rarely crossing in school time and her earnestly sensible Head Girl manner being a little too perky and off putting for her liking, but always sweet and amiable in that sporty way girls of her *sort* are.

And all three of them loudly giggling and brazenly smoking a shared cigarette as they did, careless, Cod-Eye Turner, the schools Head of Sport was watching them from the top of the gymnasium's broad, sweeping steps in weather defying blue shorts and singlet vest so tight about his muscular body he looked like Milo of Croton the ancient Greek wrestler and almost as naked as Charles Meynier painted him. Their school banned high heels dancing over the snow, their school blazers sensuously open to his watchful gaze and their grey pleated skirts hitched, *Courrèges*-like to their mid-thighs in an attractively lewd display he couldn't fail to notice.

Nor did he; by the jaw-slack, wide-eyed look on his pock-marked, ugly scarred face, which was speechless with frustrated rage and impotent indignation. But no less than the knot of snow wet boys who watched them pass with grinning smirks and ribald comments all three of them laughed to hear and who could blame them, they were young, careless and gorgeously sexy.

But though they were, and she admired they were she truly did, they were without a doubt three of the cheekiest, vulgar and tediously disruptive girls she had ever met in her entire life. Though, Ronnie, the middle of the three, and the least pretty with her stiff and shapeless hair, who she had lately come to know and like for the lonely, rather innocent girl she was beneath the shallow bravado she pretended, was all too easily led astray by them, as naïve, sexually inexperienced girls often are in the company of girls who are very definitely not. If girl was an appropriate soubriquet for those blatantly provocative, confidently beautiful, sexually alluring, Nabokov *nymphets* - did ever a man better describe their type? Demonic, feline and predatory, and she doubted it was girl implying an innocence of youth they had long ago lost.

Though the tall, athletic, strikingly attractive and curvaceous, Judy Dowd with her perfect hair, perfect skin, perfect white teeth and perfect makeup was the most mature of the three of them and with a quick and ready acid wit that spoke of a sharp if entirely wasted intelligence beneath the surface of her twinkling eyes and *Bardot* pouting lips. And she shamelessly knew she was cleverer than she cared to admit, turning on her four-inch heels as she passed the far side of the swimming pool to wink, she had seen her watching her from the window.

But irrepressibly rude and exasperating though they all three undoubtedly were, they were pussycats compared to Hussey and Lomas, two thoroughly wicked and heartlessly cruel boys from the same class she had come to hate and dread as she had never hated and dreaded anyone in her life before. Boys who were immune to every kindness she had shown them, who worse by far, saw her kindness, her tolerance and her gentle forbearance as a weakness to be exploited, to be undone by any means possible. Boys so mockingly insolent, so shamelessly threatening, so preposterously stupid, so arrogantly blind to instruction, so vulgar and intimidating she had lately begun to wonder if they were insane and visibly blushed and shivered, they were. Much to the amusement of the two little girls now seated in front of her and so close she might have touched their neatly ribboned heads with her barely outstretched hand, who sheepishly giggled she was cold, as the rest of the class thought she was. The thought that anyone could be so vile without just cause, hinting something dark and diabolically forbidding in the world, something horribly primeval that perhaps lurks in the shadows of all our lives.

*

'Jeldi, jeldi,' yelled Cod-Eye, working his one-time career soldiers' mouth to a donkey grimace, as Judy, Ronnie and Gerry ducked beneath his muscular arm and found the open door to the gymnasium in a fit of defiantly hysterical laughter that almost brought them to their knees. Much to Miss Persephone Langford's glaring disapproval, his deputy and, to those who knew them, as few did, his friend, who knew the words he used, and too often used, she sighed, were of some low, vulgar Indian origin and hated he did. Had several times told him she did, but mostly with the boys, who were now noisily changing into their gym kit, their mood already cowed by his famous temper.

'Where is Clifford, Persephone, have you seen him this morning? I haven't?' He asked, sure no one was listening, his one good eye scanning the now empty, snow churned quadrangle, the small building site that was the half-finished, seemingly never to be finished swimming pool he so detested and the now almost empty and forlorn annex building where Valeria looked out.

'No, Tiro?'

'Arthur, Persephone, someone will hear you,' he replied, pretending a worry he didn't feel.'

'Tiro is better, but if you insist?'

'I do.'

'He will come, Arthur,' she smiled, her finger lightly touching the back of his hand. As they both knew he would and so changed from the boy he was, they barely recognised him beneath the mask of pimples and blackheads that scarred his face, and his hair shaved to his crusted scalp like some mangy old dog with fleas; he was truly ugly. But though he was, laughed and ignored every insult aimed at him and none were more insulting than Hussey and Lomas.

'Jeldi, jeldi, jeldi,' Cod-Eye fiercely called a second time, seeing several boys come out of the changing room and sheepishly look his way, as Hilda Dobson, a tiny, sugary sweet, if frustratingly obstinate little girl, came up the steps towards him her battered satchel so heavy on her little back she stooped beneath its weight. Who though only half the size of Judy, Gerry and Ronnie and without the least hint she was a girl beneath the oversized red woollen balaclava and two sizes too big for her, red duffle coat she wore, nevertheless returned his insult with a smile?

'You are come,' said Miss Langford, admiring her pluck, which never ceased to amaze her. But not as much as she admired Judy Dowd, who quite literally took her breath away, who she had begun to realise she loved in that special way only girls can love another girl; but dared not say.

'Gosh, will that silly, noisy bell never stop ringing in my ears,' whispered Valeria, her head half turned over her shoulder to the speaker above the door hopeful it soon would, but with an image suddenly caught in the corner of her eye she hardly dared believe. Hilda standing at the top of the steps between Cod-Eye and Miss Langford, her always, pretty, elfin face now quite remarkably beautiful and turned to look up at her and with such a knowing stare she blanched to see she did. But no longer dressed in the shapeless winter woollies she wore a moment ago, but wearing a gold trimmed, lustrously white diaphanous shift that fell from her slender, almost bare shoulders to her sandaled feet in soft, windblown pleats and her hair, normally a lifelessly stiff, vilely cut, coupé, now a lustrous plait that twisted to her slender waist and weaved with a medley of fresh summer flowers of the most vivid colours; red anemone, purple withy, pink and white asphodel and yellow narcissus, as bright as the summer sun.

'Oh, my goodness, me,' she whispered, blinking and squinting to see the vision she had inexplicably become. A nymph, a fairy, she hardly knew what to call her, but as she did, saw Miss Langford standing to her right, her left had draped on her shoulder and dressed in a white, sensuously clinging, diaphanous Greek peplos Though it was loosely fallen from her left shoulder to reveal her ample left breast and with a garland of the same coloured flowers in her hair that was surely a crown. And she too, staring up at her; her bewitching gaze watchful and concerned, as was Cod-Eye's, who looked at her with his one cyclopean eye with the same warning.

Who stood bare chested in the fierce bright sunlight that now drenched them in the summer meadow of wildflowers, butterflies and fluttering birds that stretched for miles behind them beneath a sky so blue she gasped it could be so blue, his calloused, hairy workman's hand lightly rested on Hilda's other shoulder in a protection that could not be mistaken? He would kill any man who thought to harm her, or her companion *queen;* as queen, Miss Langford surely was.

His now thickly bearded face grim, determined and watchful, as though he waited a battle he knew must soon come, his posture proud and defiant of any man who might think to raise his sword against them. His clothes the simple red leather skirt of the Hoplite soldier of ancient Greece fastened at the thick of his waist with a leather belt and sword, protection for his upper legs and waist. His boots laced to the mid-calf beneath iron greaves. On his head a white plumed helmet, the crest a thick protective bridge no sword would ever break and with cheek-plates on either side of his face that would glance any danger that struck him there, dagger, arrow or spear. In his left hand he held a wooden spear tipped with an iron point nine feet tall and at his feet a circular shield of white painted leather and wood studded with bronze rested on his leg.

'Mon dieu,' she gasped, but no sooner had she than she saw they were gone and with nothing to say they were ever there except the little yellow flower, a buttercup or was it perhaps a narcissus, Fay Cottrell now bent to pick up as she hurried into the gym and with smile that was so enigmatically sweet and knowing as she turned to look at her, she wondered if, Pauline Fisk was quite as bonkers as she believed she was? This being the second time in less than four days she had hallucinated. The first-time last Thursday night when she was with Dylan that third time and saw Terry standing in the doorway of the Greyhound Public House changed into the naked, hairy, horned monster, Pauline said he was. A hallucination so vivid she could easily recall it now and with a tremble of fear her watching class once again thought was a shiver of cold.

'Miss. Miss,' called a little voice pulling her from her reverie, 'shall I shut the door and take the register, I think we are all here now?'

'Oh, yes, Jane, take it now please, mon chouchou,' she whispered, her eyes turned from the little girl standing beside her to look again at the RCA speaker, which continued to incessantly chime the nine o'clock bell despite the hour was now fifty times struck. A joke as she had always known it was to irritate the headmaster. Well, it was irritating her now; it really was!

Chapter 2

Monday December 17, 1962
Chris Montez: Do You Want to Dance

A Joke, Dylan only last Thursday evening ardently denied it was, she reminded herself, as the bell chimed on and on, claiming it was a sincere and practical demonstration of both his and Terry's expert skills that rightly and all too worryingly, she had been surprised to learn, suspected the Headmaster was just a week away from terminating both their temporary contracts to help repay the money he owed his bookmaker, a gangster, she heard it said, by the name of Mr Sydney Plant. Linda's father, as all the school knew he was, she mused, seeing her coming out of the main school corridor towards the annex, her Prefect's mood fiercely determined. A poised and very attractive young woman with a mature self-confidence quite beyond her fifteen years, but a girl who studiously and often rudely avoided her. Who, Dylan said, had threatened to expose him for the criminal fraudster he was to the Director of Education? A fraud that for several years now had failed to paint, repair or put right any of the dilapidation that so shamed the school beyond the main corridor, purchase books and equipment more than the bare minimum, or put a roof on the swimming pool, built these last two years from the proceeds of a hundred charitable events and virtually useless without one and, just last week, brought the long planned renovation and refurbishment of the now near gutted annex to a sudden stop until he paid all he owed. Which was so much he really couldn't, not unless his wife, Violet agreed, which she wouldn't, apparently hating him every bit as much as he hated her.

And because they suspected he was about to end both their contracts and because they knew he had long dreamed of having an ultra-modern *Tannoy* system, just like the one the Grammar school across the river boasted - and he so dreamed of being a Grammar school Headmaster, it every day tormented him he wasn't, though it tormented his well-to-do wife a great deal more, they had both pretended a knowledge of electrical and acoustic engineering neither of them truly possessed in the hope he might think again his decision. Which she now seriously doubted he would, if indeed he had made such a decision, and she wasn't at all sure he had?

A spectacularly incomplete knowledge, as it turned out of valves, resistors, condensers and speakers, not to say the subtleties of signal boost, bandwidth, logarithmic gain, linearity, slew rate, overshoot and goodness knows what else, Dylan boasted he knew from a much-thumbed copy of a 1959 edition of *Practical Wireless*. An excellent and highly informative periodical for the enthusiastic and perhaps gifted amateur, he confidently informed her, but one surely never intended for the major work he and Terry had so cavalierly undertaken in the two weeks past. She groaned, gently shutting the heavy door to the corridor with an irritated resignation that dearly hoped her day would soon improve, her hand brushing the sturdy bolt lock beneath the brass forged, beehive doorknob, as her eyes once again fell on the storeroom door.

*

A *Tannoy* system, which promised the Headmaster's voice would carry with majestic gravity across the school at the turn of the second hand, much worn, *Three Way, General Electric, Lever Rotary Switch* he now held between his thumb and forefinger in a nervous tremble of anticipation that could barely contain his excitement he was about to speak into the brick-sized, recently purloined, black *BBC* microphone clamped to the arms of the chemistry stand in front of him. And with a pair of *DLR, NO. 5, Brown Bakelite Military Headphones* perched of his head, which, he fancied, gave him the debonair look of the World War II bomber pilot he had once dared to hope he might have been, had he not been so short sighted. That grovelling, useless twat, Eric Scullion, had been, as his wife a thousand times reminded him, he had.

A voice so instantly reminiscent of the sonorous, nasal drawl of Lord Haw Haw, the traitorous Reichssender propagandist of the German war when he began, if only known to his witless pupils from the *Pathé News* and Television broadcasts of his traitorous speeches and with a tedious repetition that promised they would never forget the sacrifice *our* servicemen and women had made in the face of his mocking words, the school truly thought it was him! Not that Casterbrook intended to sound like that hated Irish patriot, but he did, and with a hollow, oddly distant echo in the background that did much to convince his bemused and now growing more silly audience his transmission was coming from somewhere over on continental Europe.

No. If it was his unconscious intention to sound like anyone that cold winter morning, a morning already soured to the pit of his dyspeptic stomach by the violent argument he had had with his wife, Violet at breakfast, it certainly wasn't that Irish twat, William Joyce. Who, as a once commissioned officer in the infantry, he hated only marginally less than he hated the entire German High Command, Hitler, Hess, Goebbels, Goering and Himmler? Who, he never tired of telling anyone who cared to listen, he met at a cheese and wine reception at the 1936 summer Olympics in Berlin, where he was competing in the swimming, who he collectively blamed for all too soon end of his once remarkable sporting career as if they had jointly planned it?

No. If he hoped to sound like anyone at all it was his hero of British Radio, the inimitable, Alvar Lidell, whose peerless pronunciation and precise articulation of the English language was the epitome of speech and whose loss to the *Third Programme* was a tragedy he had yet to come to terms with; perhaps never would. An impeccable Englishman of good breeding he so admired he longed to be like him, whose grave, but balanced announcement of the Edward VIII's abdication still brought a tear to his eye, though his heart now belonged to his niece. The wonderful Queen Elizabeth, who he had the distinction of meeting in 1957 when he was a patient in the Royal Infirmary, who remembered she met him in 1948; or so he boasted she did.

*

'This is the headmaster calling,' he gravely intoned in his booming, vowel strangled Black Country accent, his irritatingly echoing headphones muffling the still incessant chime of the bells to a whisper he barely heard. 'This is the headmaster calling,' he repeated again for dramatic effect, words instantly transposed by the *Goonish* imaginations of his listening audience into Lord Haw Haw's trademark beginning to every treacherous broadcast he ever made. Not a parody or a clever play on words, as you might suppose, but an unconscious hearing that would forever think it was him; and he did, say; "This is Jairmany calling. This is Jairmany calling." That left them collapsed on their desks in near hysterical laughter and not surprisingly produced a wave of comic salutes, Heil Hitler's, toothbrush moustaches and ludicrous, goose-stepping marches that brought every class to the riotous brink of anarchy; though not Cod-Eyes, whose threatening presence in the changing rooms made every boy and girl mute with terror.

A noise that reverberated down the corridors much to the anxiety of the Headmaster's now frantic secretary, the timidly polite, dutifully diligent, extremely pretty, slim and very shapely in that twee and mumsy sort way no one ever notices girls of her apparently virtuous sort - except those with eyes to see, and there was more than one who did, porcelain fragile, Miss Carol Paget. Who indignant to hear they were making fun of all her efforts to put right what Dylan Lloyd-Thomas and Terry Mack had left undone last Friday was desperately trying to reach the stylus on the ten inch, *His Masters Voice* vinyl recording of *Big Ben's* famous chimes, whilst all the while trying to avoid any physical contact with her notoriously insatiable, predatory roué, of a serial shagging, Headmaster, whose broad shouldered bulk prevented she ever would.

'Oh, do please hurry whatever it is you are supposed to be doing with that, Miss Paget,' he seethed, ignoring he was still speaking into the microphone as his hand instinctively found the firm round of her bottom as she acrobatically stretched on a faltering tiptoe across the cluttered table. A painful gymnastic that knew he was all the while looking at her ample cleavage as she did and would surely grab her breasts so very hard if he could; soon would, as he had once before when he thought she wasn't looking. And what a terrifying fright that had been.

'I'm doing my very best, Mr Casterbrook, I really am,' she bleated, as his spade-like, swimmers hand scrunched the hem of her skirt to her bare thigh and roughly found the elastic of her black suspender. 'NO,' she screamed, as he tugged at her black satin knickers; a present from *Browns* she bought herself last week, but not for him; for Joe, if he would *have* her? 'HEADMASTER,' she squealed dropping the stylus as she scissored her legs with the force of a vice.

'HEADMASTER,' roared the school, with all the cruel amusement that is the heartless parody of the downtrodden the world over to someone else's hurt and shame, particularly those they believe to be the minions of their enemies, even if it was the romantically dreamy, convent-pure innocent, Miss Paget, who everyone liked, but Rick Taylor most of all; who loved her to distraction.

*

'What the fuck is he doing to her?' Groaned Tinker, staring in red faced simmering rage at the box free, matt black, *Dual Concentric, Tannoy Speaker* that was perched so high in the corner of the boys changing room, Cod-Eye had to spear it with a javelin. A fabulous throw from almost twenty feet that smashed it to the floor in a broken heap of tangled wires, but though it did, it still needed several good hard kicks from his size fourteen plimsolls to end its noise.

A fabulously wasted effort as it quickly turned out as a second matching speaker broadcasting from the girls changing room next door, and a third, and possibly a fourth from somewhere else, and with an asynchronous amplification that seemed to hear it louder than it ever was before, that was either compliment to the acoustic qualities of the Edwardian architecture of the school, or the invention of a High Fidelity, Quadraphonic sound system, brought his every word back to mock him with a nerve scraping resonance that got under his skin.

'Fucking her up the arse, Tink, can't you hear,' came some half-dressed wags sarcastic reply.

'Who was that?' Barked a seething Cod-Eye, searching the densely milling crowd of half-naked boys to find the culprit, but seeing no one he could blame with any certainty, saw instead, Hussey, Lomas and Robin were still missing. 'Where are Hussey and Lomas and where is that useless knob, Clifford Robin?' He demanded only to be cut off by the nerve tingling sound of the headmaster's faux *BBC* English, a cross between the whimsy of Arthur Askey's antique comedy and the petulant whine of Gerald Campion's, fat arsed and never funny, *Billy Bunter.*

'Where are the lists, Miss Paget?' He angrily groaned, his fingers snapping the urgency of his appeal. 'A moment, school,' he politely requested, his voice the calm of Alvar Lidell in a crisis.

'A moment school,' echoed one of the boys. An ill-judged jibe that hoped Cod-Eye would find it funny that earned him a punch in the soft of his stomach that bent him to his knees in agony.

'I don't know, Mr Casterbrook,' came her snuffling reply above the gales of laughter that erupted from the girls changing room next door, as he quietly asked her a second time to find the team lists for next Friday's swimming gala, the centre piece of this first school announcement.

'Waiting, my dear,' they heard him ask with the mellifluously sweet, but archly stinging threat that was the subtext of his nasty life. 'Still waiting,' they heard him call again to the drum of his fingers on the table, 'if you would be so FUCKING kind as to give them to me before I die of old age. The school, as I do, await your pleasure with bated breath, don't you know.'

'No,' she silently screamed, her backed turned to his to hide her hot tears, her steeply mounting anxiety assuming Munch like proportions of critical self-doubt and despair as she listened to the raw, giggling, expectant laughter echoing down the corridors like a whistling train in a long dark tunnel. A laughter that delighted in her flustering panic, her nervous confusion, her, self-evident misery and growing anguish as they heard her noisily rummage the three drawers of her uncommonly neat – they had all seen it, flower and photo topped, pinewood desk for the second time that morning, splitting a bright polished, carefully manicured, blossom-pink nail, as she did, to find the list, as he backwards and forwards turned in his squeaking swivel chair to watch her, enjoying her pain as he always did. A balm for his dented pride. A balm he hoped would rid him of the hurt, Violet everyday heaped upon him in bucket loads, but no less than Barbara, did, who he loved to a dizzying distraction far more than he ever loved Pauline Fisk, now gone so completely mad, he hardly knew why he ever did. 'Tits,' he sighed into the microphone, to a roar that washed the corridors with an eye watering scream of pleasure, they were ever his downfall and Violet, Barbara and Pauline had the most splendid, tits in the world, though Madame Doucet's were better by far; so perfectly formed.

List she had typed with as much precision as anyone could reasonably expect her to type on the antique, alphabet reduced – the S was a faint smudge and the E was a law unto itself, 1937, *Underwood No. 6, Master* typewriter, she was everyday forced to use, from the horribly scribbled in damp pencil, notes Cod-Eye had given her late last Friday afternoon. As the Headmaster and now most everyone else jokingly referred to him, and she to her blushing shame, now always did, if only in her head, which wasn't really a sin, and she a Sunday school teacher who ought to know better than to speak that way about anyone, least of all him. Who had suffered so horribly in the war and despite he could be so fierce was always so sweet to her, just like her father did, who the Japs had in Burma for the better part of four years and then killed him? Not literally, but soon after he got home from all the evil things, they did to him and his many friends and her mother three years after and her just ten years old in 1950 when she died.

And then, when she had typed it as best, she could, Casterbrook, knowing she was in a hurry to go home, made her copy them a hundred and fifty unnecessary times on the smelly, *Ditto Banda* she so hated, and he so loved with the irrationality of a man who thought he was getting something for nothing. A foul smelling, silver and cream, spirit duplicator of Second World War vintage, which so stained her creamy white, elegantly long fingers, a vile aniline purple it took an hour to wash and scrub them clean. And gave her such a beastly, throbbing headache behind her hazel-brown, almond shaped eyes, neatly made up in three shades of pastel-blue – which last month's *Honey* magazine said was a must for all young girls of fashion, which she hoped she was, tried so very hard to be, though no one seemed to notice she was, except young Tinker and Joe Fisher, she was left headachy and nauseous for the rest of the evening.

And if that wasn't enough to make her late for the film she had so longed to see again she could hardly wait to get home to wash and change for its seven thirty start, he then made her *Sellotape* fifty large posters advertising the gala *meet,* as swimmers call these silly, pointless things, from one end of the blooming school to the other and in a growing, very lonely, spooky bitter cold dark that made her rather frightened, not least when she found herself alone in the annex and wondered how Valeria could stand it and with only Mr Arno de Roy for company.

But finish she eventually did with the help of Madame Doucet, as she always called her, despite she scolded her she mustn't, but must call her Valeria and gave her a gift of lovely perfume to seal their friendship, but despite she did, she couldn't, well, not to her face, who was working late. And with time enough to get a good seat near the front of the Odeon cinema, which was showing the second release of *Dr No* that weekend with the gorgeously hunky, impossibly handsome Sean Connery in the starring role. Who she had adored, though he was a little more physical than the men she generally liked, since first she saw him playing *Vronski* in the *BBC's Anna Karenina* last year with the beautiful Claire Bloom, though perhaps as sweet as the men she did like when he played *Michael McBride* in the adorable, *Darby O'Gill and The Little People,* three years before. Such a lovely fairy-tale and every bit as sweet and charming as all her favourites, though one she had never read as a little girl, but must, if she could find a copy.

Rather beautifully drawn posters, she had to admit, Mrs Fisk, the flamboyant, shockingly three times married, growing noticeably odder by the day, with her whispered talk of goblins, fairies, dancing elves, woodland nymphs and Satyrs with monstrously large penises – such a shocking word for a woman to speak aloud, as she never heard a woman say such a thing before, she everyday claimed she saw, had sketched. A nonsense Valeria said was the result of the sweet smelling, *herbal* tobacco she smoked incessantly in that filthy pipe of hers. A woman she so admired she everyday wanted to be like her, to dress like her, so chic and yet so understated, to do her hair and makeup like her, to walk on impossible high heels like her, to speak like her in that gorgeous French accent, to have men look at her as every man in the school did, but in that sneering, scornful way men do when they know a woman is beyond their reach.

A woman so unlike poor Mrs Fisk, whose plump, fifty-something, once beautiful face was forever plastered in a mask of heavy makeup that tried so very hard to please, but please who?' She wondered, Casterbrook? She supposed, who was rumoured to have been her lover, before Barbara Lloyd-Thomas. A rumour she didn't believe. Her exotic, several shades of purple and red dyed hair everyday wreathed in colourful gypsy scarves, her ears dangling impossibly large gold hooped ear rings, her tie-died peasant tops, velvet waistcoats, floaty, ankle-flapping, paisley skirts and peasant sandals better than any words describing the theatrical, strangely compelling, if fragile personality, the schools extremely talented Head of Art, was.

Posters she knew were expertly copied from one of the two, Casterbrook hung in tinted glass-protected splendour behind his enormous office desk. Both originals, the first, the official poster of the 1936, Berlin summer Olympics, he never tired of boasting he competed in as a reserve swimmer, though he never swam a stroke, which showed a giant laurel wreathed *Adonis* standing above the *Brandenburg Quadriga.* The second, the one Mrs Fisk had drawn, the official poster of the 1938 Empire Games in Sydney, a *meet* he again said he attended as a reserve, though again he never swam, which showed the much more endearing figure of a Union Jack emblazoned runner hurdling over the Sydney Harbour Bridge. Which some of the older, kiss-arse teachers, said bore a striking resemblance to a younger more athletic, him; it didn't. Which she had cleverly redrawn to show a sumptuously sculpted female swimmer, who looked astonishingly like Judy Dowd, provocatively arched like a dolphin doing the same and with the date and time the meet was to begin stencilled in red, Baskerville Old Face print, beneath her delicately pointed toes. God, how utterly beautiful that young girl was, but such a wicked tart if all the stories about her and her two friends, Gerry and Ronnie, were to be believed!

And now the list and its smelly copies were lost and with only the crumpled *ditto* master petulantly vandalised by the headmaster before he went on air lying on the top shelf of her battered and bent out of shape, sickly, pea-green, antique three tier wire basket letter tray to say they were ever done.

Were done! And now she must do them all again before the practice - *meet,* she quickly corrected herself, he had scheduled in the nearby City Baths, their own little pool being far too small and far too cold that bitterly cold December morning to accommodate the children who must very soon gather there. The girls under the care of the very sweet, but still very inexperienced, Miss Langford, which he of course would supervise, and with frequent, unannounced visits to their changing room to make them squeal with panic, which were such a notorious feature of these events. The boys under the scrupulous care of Cod-Eye Turner.

And what an ironic joke that was, the poor man didn't know how to take care of himself, but how could he, he was a war damaged, angry man, like her late father was, as so many men of their unfortunate generation were, who hated life and seemed so out of step with his colleagues, who made fun of him behind his back. But mostly, it seemed, he hated that nice little chap, Clifford Robin, who he endlessly picked on. And hated the handsome, if naïvely simple, Tinker Taylor, too, who had become something of a pet of hers since the Michaelmas term began.

'Still, waiting, Miss Paget,' cooed the headmaster, his mood growing dangerously unstable.

'Sorry, Mr Casterbrook, but I can't seem to find them,' she tearfully whined.

Tears of bitter frustration that knew with an absolute certainty, she dared not say, the headmaster, now dangerously risen from his chair to leave his audience in a thrall of mounting expectation, had taken them home on Friday evening. But didn't know, he had barely an hour before, left them beside his half-eaten bowl of *Lyle's Golden Syrup* dripped, *Quaker* porridge oats. As he well knew he had, as he stared with ill-disguised lust at her athletically trim without the least effort - she was proud to say, crouched to the knee, sinewy body. So close in fact she could smell his musty old crotch barely a foot in front of her face; an earthy, rutting, primal smell that despite the growing fear she felt stirred a passion in her that was growing perilously out of control. Though she would never submit to his clumsy and brutishly vulgar overtures; but there were others she longed to feel the press of her body against, Joe, of course, but others, too.

So quickly and so violently angry had he escaped from his forever sniping her odious disappointment at his lack of career success, he was *only* the headmaster of a second-rate secondary modern school, and not the Grammar school that was a true mark of success, shrew of an impossibly ugly wife, Violet. Though only the dangerous, hypertensive swell of his jugular vein beneath his starched white, studded collar and the cyanotic blush on his puffy, irritable lips, said he was. So powerful was his silent, if growing more precarious control over his frustrated matrimonial emotions. A door-sized, Herculean woman of hirsute, lantern jaw, majestic bosom and bollard-round buttocks, whose high born, principled Welsh Chapel ways had so longed stifled his low born social pretensions he every hour of every day wanted to kill her.

But not just kill her, wanted to bludgeon her to a bloody, lifeless pulp and when he had, pull her scolding tongue from her fat slobbering gob and six-inch nail it to the second floor balustrade of their much admired, three storied, double-fronted, red brick, centrally heated, as no other house in their limited social circle, was, riparian lodge. Or was it a villa, he never knew the difference? And would have killed her there and then, had he stayed a minute longer in her maliciously sneering, forever mocking his every effort to better himself, as his mother said he must, cold hearted company. God how he hated that awful woman! Hated her to distraction.

Frigid these last twenty-two years by any reasonable estimation of its singularly apt definition, because he was sure he had not seen the inside of her tent-like knickers since he was six months escaped from the bombed out, blood spattered beaches of Dunkirk with a coward's desperate wish never to see a fucking German soldier with a gun ever again. Which thank God he never did, because her father, a lofty Brigadier General in the Western Command, made it his solemn duty no harm would ever come to the only man ever likely to propose marriage to his fright of a fat arsed daughter. A fresh faced, cringing oik of a measly lance corporal with an enviable, if sadly, unsuccessful athletic prowess from Dudley's larynx strangled wastes. As common as shit on his shoe, but a boy he quickly promoted to the rank of Second Lieutenant a week before they were married and a week after that, posted him to a search light battery at Lyness in the Orkneys. That, too his infinite relief, lasted the duration of the war and with three promotions that earned him his Majors crowns and a schooling in belligerent, self-serving arrogance before he left the wastes of Scapa Flow, far better than any book could ever teach him.

*

'Are you quite sure the lists I copied for you aren't in your briefcase, Mr Casterbrook, 'I thought I saw you put them in there before you left on Friday,' she timidly asked, stepping a foot back from his now domineering presence, her eyes half turned to the quarter open door of his wood panelled in oak, spacious office. His inner sanctum, as he was want to call it - imagining himself a modern day Robert Donat in the film, *Goodbye, Mr Chips,* a madness, as everyone knew it was, but one that complimented his vanity, where it sat open on his brass fitted, twin pedestalled, antique Mahogany desk; quite the most majestic desk she had ever seen.

'NO, I DIDN'T MISS PAGET, AS WELL YOU KNOW I DIDN'T. YOU FUCKING HALF WIT DOZY TROLLOP. CAN YOU NOT DO ANYHING RIGHT WITHOUT I SHOW YOU FIRST,' he bellowed in her face, so loud it made the whole school jump out of their skin.

Not least Madame Doucet, who could hardly believe her ears the impossibly vile man could be so beastly to poor, Miss Paget. 'Le porc dégoûtant et ignoble,' she seethed, much to the amusement of her bewildered class, who repeated it back word for word, 'le porc dégoûtant et ignoble.'

'NO, A HUNDRED FUCKING TIMES NO. I LEFT THEN ON YOUR DESK, MISS PAGET. THERE ON YOUR DESK. WHY WOULD I TAKE THEM HOME? GOD HELP ME YOU BRAINLESS TWAT CAN YOU DO NOTHING RIGHT?' He thundered, ignoring he had, and she now so afraid of him, she was visibly trembling. And he so much relished her cringing, cowering, deep blushing distress. A distress which so jacked his cock to the burning hard, growing more painful priapism, it now was, it poked the fly of his charcoal grey, sharp pressed to a burnished shine, Oxford Bags, like a tent pole. And never so hard as when she went to her knees one last time to rummage the overflowing with rubbish, buff-willow, cleverly woven, wastepaper basket - a present from Tinker, who made it for her, though it did rather wobble. Her short sleeved, tailored with care, ivory-white blouse, pulled up from her fashionably short, black pleated skirt to reveal four inches of sinuous spine above the two-inch-thick, black, patent leather belt she wore about her slender waist, so creamy white he longed to touch it.

'They're not here. They're nowhere I can see. Really, Mr Casterbrook,' she moaned, to the scornful titters of the still eagerly listening school, as she turned on her three inch heels to face him with a down cast, frightened look in her tear bright eyes that immediately saw the thick, hard bulge of his cock pressing his trousers between the open folds of his calf length academic gown and so close to her own trembling hand she almost dared to touch it. Wanted to touch it! Or one just like, it! So much did she want a man of her own! Any man! No; not just any man, she almost screeched her guilty secret, Joe Fisher, he was the man she wanted most of all. The newly graduated, English Teacher who since last September she had loved better than any man she had ever loved before, though her winsome, dreamy schoolboy admirer rather touched her lonely heart, so innocent, though growing so bold, was his three-month crush on her.

An innocent, truly wholesome, puppy love, but one that could never be anything more than it was! The first true love of a naïve and gentle boy for an older, more experienced woman, who could never be his! An experience of first love that is surely the dream of every boy and girl? Though she dearly hoped he would one day find a more rewarding love of his own? That his gentle heart would not be broken by the love he so deeply felt for her? A love she could not return, had never said she would, but like the fairy tales she so adored, would lead instead to something far better than she could ever hope to give him. A first and only kiss, perhaps, but never more than that? But not even a kiss, now! Not now Joe was nearly hers. Would soon be hers.

A loving kiss, which is how all her favourite stories ended: *Cinderella*, treated so cruelly by her step-mother and step-sisters until she found love in the arms of her prince charming, she sighed, remembering it was the first *Disney* film she saw, which her painfully strict, then newly widowed mother took her to see for a seventh birthday treat at the Gaumont Cinema in 1947 and what a lovely treat that was. As was, *Snow White and the Seven Dwarfs,* which she loved even better and saw at the ABC Regal just around the corner the following year, which was so funny and with such lovely songs she knew them all by heart: the dwarfs ever so catchy, *Heigh-ho* and *Whistle While You Work,* but best of all, yes, best of all by far, *Some Day My Prince Will Come,* which always thrilled her with expectation. Then there was *Sleeping Beauty,* of course, which she had three times seen since its debut showing at the Odeon in the autumn of 1959, which starred a prince as brave and handsome as any she had ever imagined.

And would a first kiss be so very wrong, she idly wondered? Nothing too serious of course, she mused, thinking she might yet grant him that little treat, her face taking on such a flushed and dreamy, doe-eyed look, the Headmaster, who was watching her with a growing more bewildered exasperation, thought she was about to have a fit of some terrible sort, as girls of her nervous, solitary, sexually frustrated temperament often do, but something soft and gentle he would treasure forever, as he would treasure her forever. His first, but not his last love.

He being a quietly persistent lad with a growing more daring look in his fierce brown eyes, not to say a constantly reassuringly good-sized swelling in his long grey trousers whenever she looked at him, which was most every day now. No, he must find another more suitable beau than her, she resolved, someone his own age, someone who would love him back. Someone like that pretty girl who was in here just a moment ago, Linda. Yes, Linda Plant, whose solicitor father, or was he an accountant? She couldn't quite remember, was a recent friend of the headmasters. Or perhaps the beautiful, if distant, Angela Dee, who boasted breasts almost as big as Judy's, but with a temperament so much sweeter, if somewhat remote and aloof. Who she had now twice seen in the company of Dylan Lloyd-Thomas, late after school?

'For the last time of asking, Miss Paget, will you find or kindly retype my swimming lists. MISS PAGET, ARE YOU LISTENING TO ME? ARE YOU? DO TELL ME IF YOU

ARE MY DEAR,' Shouted the Headmaster, an inch from her crimson face and with an intimately rude prod in the swollen nipple of her left breast that hurt her rather a lot as he knew it would.

'What?' She gasped his mouth so close to hers she almost choked on the fug of stale *Player's Navy Cut* and tangy malt whiskey that spilled from his mouth like a fart-like, foetid exhaust.

'Again, Miss Paget, would you be ever so kind as to retype my swimming list's, the swimming lists you have for some unfathomable reason lost, misplaced, or otherwise thrown away in your haste to be rid of them, after all it's what I pay you to do my dear, isn't it?' He hissed with a sinister malevolence. A hiss that held the school, who knew what a dreadful and dangerously bad-tempered man he was, spell bound with morbid anticipation. 'And when you have would you be so kind as to make me two hundred and fifty copies of that said lists; no make that three hundred and fifty copies, Miss Paget,' he suddenly and irrationally barked, the explosion of intemperate anger spitting flecks of angry green phlegm into her terrified, ash-grey, contorted face and starting the school to a squeal of delectable dread he might soon kill her.

Knowing very well ten would do until he retrieved the originals from his breakfast table, which he intended to do later that morning. Which, did he but know it, were just then thrown into the rubbish bin by his wife and with a dollop of creamy, syrup drenched porridge on top of them to ruin them forever. A sight their little maid, the brick thick,

Ruby thought a giggle of fun.

'And when you have Miss Paget, please be so kind as to give them to that useless one-eyed twat, Cod-Eye Turner, at morning break and tell him I want today's meet to go off like clockwork or his fat, useless arse is in the mincer.' He ranted and raved to the blistering fury of the man he had just insulted, listening, as the whole school was to his fury. Who for the thousandth time promised to kill the fuck? To shoot his bloody brains out! Would! 'And empty that fucking wastepaper basket this instant,' he pointed, 'you get sloppier by the day, you really do.

'But it's not my job, Mr Casterbrook. Mrs Wiśniewski, should do it when she does your room, but she never does, even when I tell her she must,' she tearfully bleated her annoyance. Referring to the dwarf-like, bent nosed, crooked-backed, wrinkled old witch of a school cleaner whose footsteps were just then coming to a shuffling stop in front of the frosted glass reception window above the *Ribbon Microphone,* her bony, lizard-like fingers lifted to slide it open.

*

'**I** don't care whose fucking job it is, just get it emptied and whilst you're about it, shut that bloody awful, screeching racket off and tell that randy fucking, Welsh clown, Dylan Lloyd-Thomas and that creepy little tosser, Terry Mack to fix that horse arsed cock up of a fucking useless contraption before *you* use it again,' he one last time bellowed in her cringing ear. Pointing with a ramrod straight arm at the new bought for eleven precious guineas of school funds he could ill afford - so much of it had he fraudulently stolen to finance his mistress's fickle desires, *Dansette Popular, Four Speed, Auto-changer,* trimmed in blue and slate-grey plush, record player. Miss Langford, the new to school this term, PE teacher, said was *fab.* Like he gave a fucking toss what that pert waisted, dimple-chinned, fresh-faced, country-rambling every fucking weekend, fool, thought, even if she was a friend-of-a-friend of his wife and almost as lovely as the delectable Madame Doucet, though without the least hint of her sophistication. A woman so out of place in the modern world he wondered where she came from.

'Do you really want three hundred and fifty copies, Mr Casterbrook?' She begged he didn't.

'Yes, Miss Paget, you heard me correctly the first time, three hundred and fifty copies by break-time this morning or I will know the reason why. And by-the-by, my dear,' he seethed, would you kindly switch that fucking thing off as I just now asked you, too,' he gently cooed, pointing to the rotary switch, as she darted in dizzy confusion to the half-open, gun-grey, metal cabinet that flanked the tight shut, office door beside the now slowly, ever so slowly, sliding open reception window to find the precious ream of A4, white paper she would need for that smelly dirty task. Which opened onto the splendidly domed and colonnaded in the Corinthian style, vestibule entrance to the school, its tiled in red, blue and gold mosaic patterned floor, boasting its Latin motto, *Deo Patriae Litteris,* For God, Country and Learning, as everyone knew it did, so often was it said and ignored for the pretentiously useless, Latin humbug it truly was.

'What?' She blurted, grabbing the only ream of paper the cabinet possessed.

'The fucking microphone, Miss Paget, would you switch the bloody thing off, now, before I really lose my temper with you,' he pointed, the throbbing between his legs now overpowering.

'Yes, Mr Casterbrook,' she squeaked, darting past his improbably fat, yellow stained finger to switch it off as the window opened to reveal the top of Mrs Wiśniewski's head, mop and bucket in hand, staring in. A sight that made her near jump out of her skin so fearfully ugly was that shrunken little woman. So fearfully ugly she hardly dared look at her for more than a second.

'It's on,' she said, pointing her crooked finger at the microphone, her peasant scarfed head and fierce, glaring eyes just visible above the wide wooden sill, her thick, East European accent, scrambling even these two simple words into something barely discernible to her English ear.

'No, fucking it's off,' said the headmaster. 'Miss Paget has just turned it off you fucking useless Russian twat,' an insult he knew was so much worse than anything else he could say.

'Not Russian, Polish. *Polka,* you fucking idiot fool of a man,' she angrily replied, her eyes blazing her hate filled scorn into his with a steely, unblinking nerve he so much hated, but found impossible to confront, seeing in her face something he couldn't fathom and feared. 'Everyone hears you screaming at her. Hears you from here to Warsaw.' She continued, pointing a wand-like finger at Miss Paget, whose own downcast look of horror now saw the switch was still flashing its green for on. She hadn't turned it off far enough, as Dylan said she must. Or turned it too far, she couldn't remember. 'They hear every word you say. You dumb arse fucking shit.'

'What? What did she say?' He yelled, not understanding a single word she said, so quickly had they spilled from her toothless mouth, but realising from the look of her grinning face it was every bit as rude as he guessed it was.

'I say nothing you shouldn't know, you, dirty old bugger,' she defiantly answered, pointing to the folds of his cape with careless disregard for the throbbing bulge he too late tried to hide.

'Bollocks,' whispered Miss Paget, turning the rotary switch a second, tremulous time in the opposite direction, as Casterbrook backed into his office and slammed the door shut behind him with a crash to find the beginnings of the back bending, knee trembling, moaning relief of pleasure he knew was ever there in the strong, steady pull of his firm right hand on his knob.

A pleasure his mistress of two wonderfully happy, sexually fulfilling years, Barbara Lloyd-Thomas, Dylan's unhappy wife, had, since the 18 June - Waterloo Day, as every true Englishman knows it is, and for no good reason he could discern, denied him was his right. Though he every day begged her she shouldn't. So much did he love her! Adore her! Need her! And every hour of every long day without her; wanted her back! But though he begged and pleaded she refused his every appeal. No matter what he promised. Marriage! Which would be an awful sacrifice of Violet's beautiful house by the river. Hers and hers alone. As his youthful, desperate to be married to a county toff of class and breeding, with a General for a father-in-law, who could keep him safe in the war, he was certain would either kill or maim him before it was done, solicitor witnessed, copperplated, legally binding, signature, would for all time attest. Nothing could or would be his unless she left it to him in her will; a possibility he dared to hope.

And if that wasn't enough to lose, and it really was a god awful lot to lose, after his clog and dirt poor, working class upbringing in that shite hole that was Dudley, then the loss of her considerable monthly income from her late father's estate, which was three times his own salary, no matter he stole all he could get his greedy hands on, would be the end of him. A fortune, like the house, so wrapped up in legal clap-trap and bollocky rigmarole, a divorce would leave him penniless on barely a thousand pounds a year, but even more than the marriage he had promised her, he had rashly promised, and then instantly regretted he did, a permanent position to her growing, too-big-for-his-boots, uppity twat of a cock-sure, two-timing, serial shagger of a husband, he didn't deserve. Despite he was a passably good teacher by all accounts and his HNC in mechanical engineering was going so well he would pass his final exams next summer and want what he thought was his by rights. And an increase in his wages, too, and much more than the fraudulent pittance he paid him and Terry Mack, now. But no matter he did, he had a plan to sack the bastard and his creepy, little friend before the term was done, but only if Barbara gave him time to wriggle free of Violets menacing claw. Which, with his ever-mounting debts and Sydney Plant after his blood like a dog after a rabbit, he really had too, and by next Fridays meet; he had been warned? Would be ruined if he didn't and perhaps ruined if he did!

'Aaaaaaah,' he loudly gasped, as he splashed the polished parquet floor a muscular yard and a half in front of his *Edwards of Manchester,* brown leather brogues – the very best money can buy as every gentleman of quality knows they are, with a primal groan of ecstatic relief the whole school heard with hoots, halloos and a bravo round of applause better even than the ovation the *Tottenham* fans gave the nimble footed Jimmy Greaves – the best footballer England had seen since Stanley Mathews put on his boots and a cinch for the World Cup, when he opened the scoring against *Burnley* at last season's FA Cup Final. An audible groan Miss Paget heard booming down the corridor like a Banshee from hell, but too late by a five long, awkward seconds that instantly saw the three-way rotary switch she thought was off, was now broadcasting live from his office from the microphone he had insisted, Dylan put there. Every primal, deep groaning, asthmatically grunting sound he made heard by everyone in the school, not least Mrs Wiśniewski, who softly cackled she did. Something Dylan Lloyd-Thomas, with his hand fastened on her shapely bum – an intimacy that both shocked and delighted her, she remembered with a blush, had several times warned her would happen if she wasn't careful to switch it off. The second-hand ratchet swivel being loose and an easy mistake to make when first you try.

'Like this Carol,' he crooned into her ear, his breath warm on her neck, his hand holding hers so tight, she knew she could never get away and his taught hard, muscular workman's body pressed so close to hers she almost fainted he might ravish her there and then and with no thought she was a virgin who had never kissed a *real* man, or perhaps because she was, and she would have let him, had he asked. 'The first position is off; no light, easy. Second position is on and broadcasts from, here, your office and the light flashes green; again easy. Third position still on and still flashing green, but now broadcasting from Casterbrook's office. Simple, he whispered into her ear, his lips so close to her neck she thought he would kiss her as he lifted the shoulder length curtain of her jet-black hair in a provocative tease he really might. A caution she hardly heard, nor dared ask him repeat, as she escaped his attentions with an acrobatic pirouette that brought a knowing smile to his face and a deepening crimson blush to hers.

An intimacy he had several times forced on her in the weeks before he installed the *Tannoy*, when he and Madame Doucet, his lover, as everyone knew she was, though she denied she was, had so obviously fallen out. And always with that gently polite, easy on the ears, rather insistent Welsh charm he had, which always made her shiver and blush like no one did; not even Joe, who was always so shy, and she liked him all the more because he was; could make him blush. A handsome, vitally physical man who reminded her of Richard Burton, she always thought, though perhaps not quite as handsome as that fine looking young man, who she remembered with a daft dreamy, starry-eyed smile, she last saw in the film, *Sea Wife,* at the Gaumont, which also starred the gorgeous Joan Collins, whose pictures were always in the newspapers.

A very odd film as she remembered it with him looking so out of place and out of sorts and her dressed as a nun. Such a contrast to her photograph on a recent cover of *Span Magazine,* a cheap and racy, two-shilling rag, her fifteen-year-old, acne blighted, chain smoking, weedy little milkman, Fred, who always ogled her breasts in such a brazen way when she paid him her bill, deliberately left on her front step a few weeks ago. And then had the cheek to ask for it back the very next day and with such a hungry look in his eye she wanted to give him a slap, but pointed him to the dust bin, instead, where she had put it, and he had the nerve to retrieve it.

But handsome or no, Mr Dylan Lloyd-Thomas was a man of growing, if always whispered reputation, with many a shapely, bleached dyed, brazen hussy hanging around his craft and metal work class at the end of school when they had no good business to be there, as she had seen Angela there and Linda Plant and Gerry Walsh, too, who was one of the naughtiest girls she knew and not his sort at all. A man who rather frightened her and frightened her rather a lot!

*

'**M**y apologies! My apologies, school!' She quickly and breathlessly gasped into the now upturned, fiercely crackling microphone, much to the headmaster's perplexed confusion as he slipped his now pliant, deeply grateful appendage back into his trousers with a fondness that made him sigh. 'There is a temporary technical fault with our new *Tannoy* system this morning,' she panicked, 'which to my utter surprise, embarrassment and confusion has been broadcasting a thoroughly distasteful comic revue from the pirate radio station now anchored in Liverpool Bay. *Radio Daffodil,* I think they call themselves. The *Goon Show,* perhaps? Yes, it was the *Goon show,* I remember it now. That episode, do you remember, school? It was that episode when *Neddie*, or was it *Eccles?* I can't quite recall who it was, just for the minute. Yes, I have it now. It was, *Neddie,'* she hopelessly flustered, 'got his fingers caught in *Colonel Bloodnoks* bicycle chain or was it *Blue Bottle's, I* really don't know and groaned so loud he did, I though he must be killed? Aaaaaaaah,' she squealed like a strangled cat, a mimic of the Headmasters sighing groan of satisfaction that fooled no one, not even her, her rather sweet voice trailing to a tittering, slightly maniacal laugh, she thought a clever comic touch, the whole school doubled up to hear and with a hundred echoing sighs, groans, gurgles and gasps to punctuate their unexpected reverie their teachers screamed they must instantly stop; but didn't. 'But have no fear school,' she urged, her voice dropping a semi-octave to resemble the dulcet tones of a reassuringly calm newsreader warning of some important event, Nan Winton or was it Barbara Mandell, she never knew which, was which, BBC or

ITV? Though the whole school heard her as the delightfully eccentric, upper class booby that was ever, Joyce Grenfell, whose police woman, *Ruby Gates* only yesterday afternoon's appeared in the first television screening of *The Belles of St Trinian's*, 'the matter is in hand and will be immediately reported to the police and customs service, who I feel certain, very certain indeed, school,' she intoned with appropriate musical gravity, her voice dropping another half-octave, 'will use the appropriate Parliamentary legislation to close it down. And sooner rather than later, is all I can say. Don't you agree, Mr Mack?' She gasped in horrified surprise as the odd little man burst through the door.

A strange man by any measure whose frayed-at-their-pointed-ends, charcoal-grey shirt collar, loose knotted red tie, armpit hugging, tight fastened to his breastbone, three buttoned, brown tweed jacket, lovat-red, saw-dust flecked, ankle flapping drain-pipe trousers and triple soled, purple sued brothel creepers reminded her of a Teddy Boy or better still, a dishevelled, if not at all funny, Norman Wisdom without his customary flat cap, his smile or his cheerful humour. A sharp-faced, ferret-thin, wiry man of sweaty, swarthy appearance, whose size five tiny feet and thyrotoxic, bulging eyes gave him an ill-deserved comic look and whose thick black oily mane of Elvis Pressley styled, *Brylcream*-slicked, shoulder length, tangled hair added several good inches to his already crepe enhanced five feet three inches of much resented diminutive height. A man who despite his slight appearance carried a threat in his muscular hands and coldly calculating, unfathomable eyes, few of his woodwork class had tested more than once.

A man whose reputation for quick and ready violence had earned him a formidable reputation in the school second only to Cod-Eye, though his was a violence always more bark than bite, but whose want to please his betters, as he imagined everybody was, made a fool of him. A drab Dickensian villain in all his darkly secret parts, a disingenuously ingratiating, humbly toadying, *Uriah Heep,* a maliciously scheming, *Daniel Quilp,* a brutally bad tempered, woman hating, *Bill Sykes* and in his loyal friendship to Dylan Lloyd-Thomas, a veritable, *Mr Pancks.*

'They can hear you, Miss Paget,' he blurted a noisy whisper into her fast-retreating ear, as if she was the privileged confidante to some secret he alone possessed, his breath foul with the fags and beer he loved a second time that awful morning choking her to a horridly sickening gasp.

'I know they can hear me, Mr Mack,' she impatiently answered, her hand shielding her mouth from his bulbous lips, now so close to her own she could almost kiss them; God what a vile thought, worse even than grabbing Casterbrook's knob. A thought so appalling she almost bent herself double to get away, and as she did, almost dropped the brick-like microphone on the floor.

'Switch it off,' he whispered, reaching to grab it from her hands.

'No,' she hissed, tired of being bullied by any man who thought he could and with such an abrupt step backward against her desk, it rocked her colourful bouquet of freshly picked red, purple, pink, white and yellow cyclamen in their *Clarice Cliff, Sunflower* vase to a precarious wobble and tumbled the silver framed photograph of Richard Chamberlain, the impossibly handsome star of *ITV's Dr Kildare,* to a fall beside her typewriter. The only photograph Mr Casterbrook would allow her and then, only because he thought the pretty lad her brother, which she never once said he was, being an orphan without a relative in the world. 'My apologies school for the fit of wheezing you just now heard,' she hurried on, frightened, though she wondered why she was, by the look that for the briefest moment coloured Terry's face an unfathomable threat, 'my asthma is so much worse these cold damp, winter morning, it quite takes my breath away and with a mild bronchitis this last weekend it makes me splutter, gasp and moan like a braying donkey when I forget to take my linctus, which, sadly I did this morning.'

Chapter 3

Monday December 17, 1962
Little Eva: The Locomotion

'Oh yeah, a likely fucking story, Carol,' shouted Judy Dowd, above the raucous giggling noise of the crowded girls changing room, as she dropped her white cotton blouse onto the wooden bench beneath her half-open, olive-green metal locker to reveal the shapely curve of her well-developed, C cups in the firmly swelling balcony bra she wore better than any girl in her class. Better than any girl in the school, she smugly thought and better than Gerry's by a country mile, though they were coming along a treat, and so much better than Ronnie's, whose flat, almost featureless chest simply refused to grow as she daily longed, they would. 'Like we don't know the sound of a wank when we hear one, girls?' She giggled. 'Dirty fucking bastard tried to grope me once, you know, had his hand so far up me skirt in he almost had me cunt between his fingers, quite made me blush, he did,' she shamelessly shrieked, searching the bent stump of half smoked cigarette, Gerry just then passed to her with scissor-like fingers.

'Wank?' Whispered Hilda seated a little way down from her to no one in particular and with a look of impish amusement that said I know what you mean, though you might think I don't.

'Was that really Mr Casterbrook, Judy?' Asked Ronnie, hardly daring to believe it was, as she took half-hearted drag on the cigarette she offered her, before quickly passing it back to Gerry.

'Too fucking right it was,' said Gerry, flicking the lipstick stained, filtered butt through the snow flecked, quarter-open, frosted glass window just above her head and just as, Miss Langford, the perky, newly qualified last summer, and barely old enough to vote, PE teacher hurried through the crowd of rowdy, slow changing girls to find the source of the cigarette smoke she now smelled. But half a second too late to see anything but the shapely forms of the three attractive girls who met her frowning quizzical look with an innocently brazen, defiant stare.

'Miss?' Asked Judy, slowly unhooking her black polka dot, mesh, ruche trimmed bra and dropping it to the bench in an artfully teasing display, Miss Langford, who revelled in her own remarkably trim figure, thought quite improper. Rather wonderful, but quite improper on a day so cold it would freeze her gorgeous, sunset pink nipples to blocks of ice in half a minute. A sight she hardly dared imagine but longed to see; did now see and so close she almost fainted.

'Hurry along girls it really is far too cold to stand about in your underwear,' she briskly commanded, eying the display of colourful lingerie that greeted her eyes that winter morning. Some of it so gorgeous and so utterly feminine on her youthful, oh so pretty, fast growing charges, she audibly sighed she had rarely seen anything like it before, but some so ugly she almost gagged at the sight of the baggy, navy blue knickers, Hilda wore and with a white vest so big on her body it would easily fit a girl twice her size, and what on earth did the girl have on her feet?

'Hilda, my dear,' she winked, 'what are you wearing on your feet, today?' She asked, pointing to her white gusset plimsolls, dyed today, as they never were before, a mottled sky-blue and pink and decorated with a multi-coloured woollen bobble the other girls laughed to see, though not as much as they might, Hilda being an elfin mystery no one properly understood and with a mother so mad in the asylum she would very probably go the same way; and very soon.

'Pumps. I twice dyed them in a bucket yesterday afternoon when I was watching *Mantovani* on the TV and made them each a bobble like I saw Anita West make on *Blue Peter,* the other week. Pretty don't you think?' She brightly answered, returning her conspiratorial wink, as she pointed her toes to display them better in the poor light that filtered through the snow and frost rimed windows and with such a cheerful disregard everyone was laughing and staring at her. Least of all, Persephone, who she pitied, she being queer in her knickers like Judy Dowd, though they both pretended they weren't. She with her jolly-hockey-sticks, breezy zest for life, way of talking; her with her tits-out, outrageous talk of sex, which didn't fool her, not one little bit. Nor anyone else who had the good sense to see what the two of them were up too.

'Hilda you're as mad as a fucking frog on purple hearts, you really are, you retarded little chimpanzee,' remarked Judy, shamelessly mixing her metaphors, still only half dressed and so close to Miss Langford's ear she could feel her warm, smoky breath on her neck and smell the cheap, perfume she wore in such abundance on every fleshy part of her athletic frame, a heady aroma that quite made her blush, much to the scolding look of scorn Hilda gave them both.

'You really think?' Whispered Hilda, caring not a ha'penny what either of them thought, seeing how intimately and effortlessly, Judy moulded her swimmer's athletic body to Miss Langford's, an unconscious synchrony neither saw nor understood, what it meant, but she did.

'That's quite enough, Judy,' scolded Miss Langford, coming to Hilda's rescue and now turned to face her nemesis, her eyes glued to her naked breasts, which rose with every excited breath she took. 'I wish we could all be so cheerfully dainty in our choice of footwear, as Hilda so obviously has been this morning. Really quite lovely, my dear,' she remarked, as she quickly and very self-consciously turned her back on the hard faced, deliciously sexy slut, who now stood behind her with such a smirking, self-satisfied, sniggering pout on her saucy red painted lips. 'I want you all, and I mean all of you,' she cautioned with a finger pointing, brass-whistle-clutching, raised right hand, 'outside on the netball court in two minutes, and that means you, Fay and you, too, Hilda. No dawdling, please, girls,' she scolded the watching pair with a faux concern that was so obviously a Freudian displacement she longed to hold Judy in her arms she almost couldn't breathe her want to touch her. The two of them the easiest of all her many charges and for the simple reason she knew them better than all the rest, except for Greta who watched her, the censure in her harsh smile, a clear warning she trifled too much in things she shouldn't.

*

Clapping her hands in the earnest manner of the Girl Guide leader she so wonderfully and so enthusiastically was, as her *part* insisted, she was, a part she loved to play, she hurried the girls along with breezy scoots and childish giggles that turned her mind to Mrs Scullion, the Commissioner of Guides. Such a dear friend since she began her guiding career, who promoted her above two better candidates, just last year to the post she now held. A reward for winning her Duke of Edinburgh's Gold Award, she was sure, no less than this, her first teaching post. Which she easily persuaded her friend, Violet Casterbrook to give her, though her husband several times said no, and shamelessly said he did, when she first came to Love Street School.

Guiding, she mused in the giddy manner of a woman in love with someone special, was such an uplifting hobby for young girls she wondered so few now joined and with such a smart blue uniform to wear. No, not a hobby, a lifestyle, she corrected herself with a believers slightly idiotic smile that compensated just a little the end of her much missed – oh so very sorely missed, *Kindred of the Kibbo Kift*. The woodland organisation dedicated to fresh air, hiking, camping and woodland craft she once belonged, too, though it was disbanded these last ten years. But if the Guides were not the same as the *Kindred of the Kibbo Kift* - such a pity they got caught up with Mosley's horrible *Black Shirt* fascist thugs in the years before the war, lacking their romantic temperament, Nordic enlightenment and free spirited, naturalistic fervour for all that nature had to offer, it was still an honour to be a member of their company. One that gave her the opportunity to live and play in the open air, as was always her want to do; she was, after all, a creature of the woods no less than Hilda, Fay and Greta, in this time and in all other times. Time being such a mercurial thing and only real to those without wit or imagination.

'Quickly,' she urged, as one by one they changed into their short, navy blue, pleated skirts and white T-shirts. 'And team captains,' she cautioned, pirouetting *á la grande hauteur* to hide her nervousness, Judy still watched her, 'don't forget to bring your team ribbons with you, they are in the box in my office as they always are,' she pointed. Red Corinthians and yellow Thebans, to play the first quarter, Athenians and Spartans the second, do you understand?' A question and an injunction that brought a collective groan of perfect misery from the Athenians and the Spartans, who knew they must wait their turn on the side lines in a December cold, so very cold it would numb them to the bone before they ever threw a ball. But at least they could watch the boys in the gym through the window, which was always a treat, though they were mostly ugly twats, except for, Tinker, who though he was gorgeous, was a retard.

'Miss,' they moaned, as she half turned on pristine white pumps and matching slouch socks to look again at the hard-faced, mocking stares of Judy and her two companions behind her.

'And you three, get changed immediately, I think we've seen quite enough of you for one day. Don't you? We don't want to keep the others waiting, now do we, Ronnie?' She pleaded.

'No miss,' answered Ronnie, wondering why she asked, as she stared into her radiantly healthy face, as if for the first time and with a sudden, startling recognition that knew she had seen her before. Not in school, as she so often had these last few months, though never as close as this, but in one of those saucy glamour magazines her mum's new boyfriend, Ted, was forever leaving around the house for her to find. Like she didn't know why he did. The two timing, dirty fuck had his eye on her, which frightened her more than she could say, would ever say to her mum, and would be waiting for her when she got home after school, as he so often did, now. With chocolate and smutty talk, she didn't want to hear; not from him, or anyone like him.

*

Magazines with ridiculously silly names only men with sex and money on their minds could dream up, names like *Art De Nu, Pin-Up Pix, Revue, Razzle, Span, Reveille, Tit-*

Bits, Fiesta, Showgirl Glamour Revue, Glamour Figure Pin Up she knew them all by heart, so many of them had she seen since her mum brought him home from the *Riverpark Ballroom* last August, where she had gone to see the Beatles, who were an up and coming band from Liverpool. But had fallen hopelessly in love with the out of work, tea-chest-bass, in an outdated skiffle group, who opened the show with a medley of Lonnie Donegan songs from the fifties and said he could stay in their house as long as he wanted, which he did and never seemed likely to go.

Magazines that were full of artistically posed, nudes, or if not completely nude, then clutching soft toys or cushions to their bits, or wearing diaphanous negligees,' that left nothing to the imagination. Or emerging water dripped from a shower or a pool or a forest lake in towels that draped their every curve in a wanton display of sensuous tease, their eyes a brooding invitation to a mischief she longed to know. Or volley balling or sunbathing on some sun-kissed beach in polka-dot, French bikinis, too small to keep their tits in. Or riding Arab stallions in loose tied baggy shirts that showed too much of all they had, or best of all, she so often thought, swathed in expensive couture dresses, so tight about their fabulous breasts they almost popped out.

Yes, it was in one of those magazines she had seen her, she was certain of that, though not in his favourite magazine; hers, too, she had to admit, which for some inexplicable reason he kept hidden in her mother's wardrobe next to the shoe box full of sepia brown pornographic photographs that made her gag with blushing shame men could be so vile and woman so shamelessly rude to allow them to do what they did; a stylishly colourful glossy called, *Playboy*.

A sophisticated American magazine his cousin Albee, who was a cabin steward on *Cunard's, Queen Elizabeth,* brought back from New York every month he made the trip, which had the most amazing pictures in it. Pictures which weren't the least bit tacky, not a bit. Pictures like the impossibly beautiful platinum blonde, Kari Knudsen, who graced the front cover of the February issue and with such a film star ritz she longed to be her; one day would be just like her.

No, Miss Langford's shapely body never graced that fabulous magazine, but she did look out from one of the many others that piled the floor beside their cupboard-like, *Murphy* television set, ten years old and hardly ever working, since one of its doors fell off its hinge three years ago and a valve at the back worked itself loose. Yes, she was in one of them and she would find out which one it was before the day was done, even if Ted did catch her and spank her on her bare bottom like he said he would. Like she would ever let him near her bottom? The creepy twat! Though the thought of it, despite she hated him, the way he was always leering at her, made her feel deliciously warm and moist between her restlessly, aching legs.

'Did you see her look at your tits, Judy?' Whispered, a smirking, Gerry, as she watched Miss Langford jauntily steer her way to her wood and glass panelled office through the crush of girls now crowding the half-open outside door, followed by Hilda, wearing her red balaclava, scarf, and gloves and Fay, who wore the same, but in a very pretty, pale lilac. 'Her eyes nearly jumped out of her fucking head, like they were on stalks, and she blushed too, did you see her blush when she saw your Nips? I never saw anyone blush like that. Do you think she's queer? Oh, I do hope she is I never knew a girl queer before; lesbians they call them; did you know that?'

'Yeah, I did, but you can't blame her for that, who wouldn't,' she smirked, cupping them with her two hands, 'but she's no more a queer than you or me,' she answered with a knowing, brazenly lascivious smile that saw her sneak a last look at her through the poster draped window of her office. A thoughtful, appreciative look she answered with a teasing wink that said, it's *ok,* she understood, she answered with a seductive beam of recognition and delight.

Chapter 4

Monday December 17, 1962
Acker Bilk: Stranger on the Shore

Not that the hurrying boy heard Big Ben repeatedly chime the nine o'clock bell over the static crackling *Tannoy,* or a few minutes later Casterbrook appear to wank himself stupid in his office, or Miss Paget make her feeble excuses, *Radio Daffodil* and the *Goon Show* had hijacked his moment of radio glory, as he rushed into the annex toilet to find the relief he now so desperately needed in the white-tiled, yellow stained urinal that filled the far wall in front of him. His bladder a throbbing swell of pain that regretted the pint of strong, black coffee he had drunk for his breakfast, the only thing he could find in his stepmother's empty cupboard, that now hobbled his legs to a knee splayed, urgently dancing spasm beneath his, knotted, snake-clasped belt.

Which, despite his urgent efforts, he couldn't undo, no matter how hard he tried to loosen it with fingers so numb and cold they didn't work. 'Damnation,' he cursed, his face a grimace of pain that hoped he wouldn't dribble and piss himself before he did, as it now seemed likely he would. 'Aaaaaaaah,' he wailed, jerking his right knee almost to his chin as a sudden, excruciating spasm of pain in his balls and lower belly bent him double. 'What the …?' He bleated, gripping the protruding bend in the green stained, copper down-pipe that washed the toilet from the ancient, black painted cistern above his head in a wonder why they hurt. Had done since yesterday afternoon, but not like this and now so much, he didn't hear the barely stifled grunts and hysterically snorting laughter coming from one of the six, door shut wooden cubicles that lined the adjacent wall, where Hussey and Lomas were watching him through a paper stuffed hole in the door; the lock it once supported, removed by the unpaid workmen last week. Each wanking the other with a whimper of growing more ardent pleasure they rushed to finish.

Abandoning his belt, seriously doubting he would ever undo it, he belatedly began to unbutton his fly, which no less than the knot, resisted his fingers and, as he did, he quarter turned his head and saw with a knowing smile his reflection in one of the age stained, green mottled mirrors that lined the wall above the six, white porcelain sinks to the left of the urinal, their twelve copper flaked chrome taps seeming to leap like dolphins into their water filled basins. His face a swathe of angry pimples and oily blackheads beneath his shorn head, he smiled they were the source of so much mocking contempt and every day wondered how easily people are distracted and deceived by the merest blemish. Who little realise ugliness, no less than beauty, is only of the moment and with no more substance than a breeze? Judy, Gerry and Ronnie most of all who endlessly teased him, though he had known them since he was little and Judy best of all. Who was once his only friend; had almost found him out and now hated him?

His hair cut to his scalp in a vicious crew-cut by his stepmother every Saturday afternoon with a pair of blunt and ferociously tugging, *Browns of Birmingham, 'Swift' No.90B,* manual hair clippers. A woman, who, in her drunken fancy for all things American since the war, not least the American soldiers who made a cheap whore of her at Clooney Barron's easy bidding, thought it gave him the look of a clean cut, American boy. But most especially, the look of Lee Aaker the boy star who played *Rusty* in the hit TV show, *The Adventures of Rin Tin Tin,* which she loved, as only the foolish and the absurdly stupid love a dog or any animal more than a child. But no matter how hard she tried to shape his head to fit the image of the boys she a thousand times loved between her open, urgent thighs; he never did look like the wholesome American boys of her weirdly stunted imagination. Or Norman Rockwell's ingenious pen, who captured their idealised form in a thousand, wistfully nostalgic portraits. Nor ever would whilst she whipped him to a cowering submission and abused him no better than her father abused her, an irony entirely lost on her, as it is on all those deranged thugs who treat children with such wanton, unforgivable cruelty, but one that supported her delusion she sometimes cared for him. The child who came from nowhere into her drink sodden life. And never more so than when Kent

Walton's, not to be missed, wrestling commentary kept her glued to the television just long enough to shave him to the bone. And just before the five o'clock football results spoiled her *Littlewoods* coupon to a crumpled ball of disappointment for another week. A sight Clooney Barron, her pimp and drinking companion of many years, every time laughed to see with the faux good humour that was the cheerful mask for his vulgar sadism.

    Hair, Hilda, Fay and sometimes Greta, who could be difficult, as girls of her *kind* always are, but though she was, was sweet, though Tiro would sullenly disagree, everyday reminded him was once a mass of blonde curls, which were the perfect complement to his almond shaped, azure blue eyes and softly feminine, handsome face. Eyes, which though they were too often sad with bitter tears, did, in moments of joy find a beguiling quality in their hidden depths. An effect made all the more striking by the lustrous shape of his eyebrows, which arched above them in dramatically illuminating, Gothic peaks, Hilda, his dearest friend, said, as only she would, were lovely; not a description he would choose, but was grateful for her compliment. His cheeks, though every day starved and gauntly hollowed by the meals he never ate were high and classically round, his nose, though ill used by those who endlessly took advantage of his tender heart, thin and straight, his lips, too often creased to a worried frown by the wretched life he lived, full and strong and with a hint of laughter along their pretty sweep he longed to share with others, his chin, comically dimpled in the middle to a crescent moon, strong and firm, as was the sharp edge of his jaw, which knew a courage and determination few, if any ever saw.

'Bugger,' he grunted, as he stepped into the piss and paper filled end of the urinal, his battered old shoe leaking to his toe-holed, sock a soggy filth he didn't dare imagine. 'Thank goodness,' he groaned, as his nail-bit-to-the-quick, grubby fingers at last found his knob and pulled it free. Letting fall his sad excuse for PE bag from his bony left shoulder onto the rustic-red, water sloshed, terracotta tiled floor beside the nearest sink, a moth-eaten, choked-at-the-neck, dun coloured, old pillow case, Tom, Donkey Donkin, his year three form master, daily raged was, *a god awful, piss-bloody poor excuse for the ten-bob, neatly badge with the school's coat of arms, plastic-coated, duffle bag he should have and his mother should have bought him,* he tried to piss, but despite he tried and tried it wouldn't come; it just dribbled and mostly down his leg.

'Take your time, Clifford,' he urged he must, looking into the mirror, where he eyed again his horribly pimply face with a bleak resignation that for a moment tried to ignore the painful piss he so desperately needed. 'Mmm,' he sighed, ignoring he did, his fingers finding the biggest pimple he could see. The king of all monster pimples, he laughingly told himself and it truly was. A swollen, shimmeringly tense, double-headed monster of a yellow pointed, red glowing puss bag that sat in the dirt dark corner of his nose, like an unexploded time bomb, he had watched grow over this long weekend to the gargantuan size it now was. Once, twice, three times he gently probed the outer margins of the horrible thing as his flaccid knob dribbled a growing stronger stream of ale brown turgid, smelly piss into the sink, searching, as he expertly did, for the perfect, two finger pincer hold, and when he found it, gave it a careless of the pain, John Wayne gritty, eye watering, wincing squeeze that saw it double pop like a pricked balloon to splash the mirror with a tenacious, clingy blob of yellow matter that clung to it like a mountaineer. 'Mmm,' he sighed again, but this time with triumph and relief he rather enjoyed.

And, though he would never admit it, not even to Hilda, loved, no, liked, squeezing pimples, better even than the black heads he every morning and every night pinched from his face, which to his delight, squirmed from his unwashed pores like worms out of the soil. First their crusty black heads, then their dirty brown bodies and then their pristine, curling, creamy white tails.

For a long moment of growing relief he was tempted to piss the last of his bladder into the already half full, soap bubbled sink on which his flaccid knob had come to rest like a contented cat, but thinking he might be caught by Mrs Wiśniewski or Mr Eldred, or worse still by far, by one of the ever prowling, get-you-into-trouble, fifth form prefects who patrolled the annex building, turned to the urinal and arced a perfect two yard sweeping stream of hot piss against the wall. 'Bloody marvellous,' he sighed, sweeping his knob back and forth like a hosepipe.

*

The attack when it came was both perfectly timed and perfectly executed. Both Hussey and Lomas racing shoulders bent and roaring from the cubicle they hid in like the two, first fifteen, third year prop forwards they were, to knock him headfirst into the urinal with an elbow splash of piss that splashed them both. 'What?' Clifford bawled, in shock, pain and disbelief, as his shoulder jarred against the upright copper pipe and his knob, lost from his grip, squirted a short last fountain in the air until it came to a rest on his fly and dribbled onto his grey shorts a smelly damp. 'Ouch,' he cried again as his head hit the rounded stone step in front of the blocked drain and his reluctant left hand found the mash of piss-soaked paper towels and snot filled handkerchiefs that filled it to the brim. 'Get off me you bastards,' he cried, again and again, as he was viciously kicked and punched to a writhing, squirming ball of pleading, weeping, foetal surrender beneath the seemingly never-ending violent blows that rained down upon him.

But just as quickly as it started, their brutal attack came to an end, when Lomas' realising, they were late for Cod-Eye's, PE class aimed one last kick at the tight closed angle between his buttocks and sent a vicious spike of pain into his arse and tender nuts that made him scream.

Chapter 5

Monday December 17, 1962
The Shadows: Wonderful Land

'What are you doing in here its nearly ten past nine? You should be at your form register by now,' screeched the girl in a rising voice from the half open door of the toilets, her pixie-round, small featured, blemish free, but utterly beautiful face pinched into a disgusted frown by the sight of the shrunken, snivelling boy she saw half turned towards her, who was wringing out the sleeve of his filthy blazer into the already full sink. The front tail of his grubby shirt hanging loose over his piss wet, stained trousers, his socks fallen to his ankles in a wrinkle as deep as the despair he felt, his scuffed and dirty, string tied shoes covered in soggy bits of wet paper.

'Nothing,' he sullenly answered with a pitiful cry of despair, the tears trickling down his cheeks in a torrent of hurt and red-faced shame that couldn't be stopped, no less than the trickle of blood that dribbled from his nose to smear his mouth and chin a streak of crimson red.

'Get yourself to your class this instant you are fucking nasty little shit. Don't you know these toilets are out of bounds; they're dangerous.' She bellowed, taking a tentative, strictly forbidden, step into the toilet to better see him, her gloating, searching, spitefully interested eyes taking in every small detail of his distress. 'Your first period will be started before you get there …'

'Can't,' he interrupted, turning away to wring a second sleeve, never realising he slopped a dollop of water onto his already wet PE bag, as he did, which sat in a puddle between his feet.

'Can't,' she sneered her disbelief, stepping a cautious foot closer to the vile boy, her nose twitching to the putrid smell of fart, shit and piss that hung in the boy's toilet like a blinding smog, her perfectly manicured fingers tentatively pushing open the first of the six toilets that lined the wall beside the piss full urinal with an exhilarated disgust of sadistic pleasure. 'Boys', she hissed, with a revulsion that slapped him in the face, so hard did she now stare at him.

'No,' he whispered, his mood pitched between, defiance and fright. 'Two boys beat me up just before you came in, they punched and kicked me and threw me in the toilet, 'he sobbed, pointing to the urinal where he had fallen in. 'Now I'm all wet and dirty. I can't go anywhere.'

'Did you say, no to me you disgusting, pimple faced little runt? Did you? Answer me, you, grubby little shit before I hit you in the face again.' She heartlessly scolded him, as she carefully pushed open a second and then a third cubicle door, their hinges squeaking as she did. Each one revealing a shit-stained horror so vile she almost choked, but not so vile, it seemed to him, she didn't open a fourth and then a fifth, which, smelling of something she had lately come to know, took a cautious step inside. A smell so intoxicating she sniffed the air to know where it came from, but seeing nothing more than the fat, coiled turd that filled the toilet like a week-old Cumberland sausage turned on the boy, once again. Never realising the answer to that aromatic mystery lay less than a quarter of an inch from the bent fore finger of her left hand.

'Yes,' he answered with a hint of uncharacteristic defiance that wondered why a girl as pretty as she most certainly was, should be so viciously mean to him. A girl he knew by name, but had never spoken, too. And a Corinthian like him. And a prefect, too, by the red badge and navy-blue and gold metal shield she wore on the lapel of her perfectly fitted by the best outfitter in town, Venetian-striped in the fashion of some posh mincing rowing club the headmaster had somewhere seen on his sporting travels, green, navy and white school blazer. A new bought and very expensive *Worsted Barathea* by look of it, not a bit like the shabby, deep-stained-with-God-knows-what, second-hand woollen rag he had these last two years worn. Though every school year, and no less the last, his stepmother had promised to replace it with something better. No, she was every bit as smart as the posh girls who went to the Queens School, but didn't, because she didn't pass her Eleven Plus examination, was a dunce like everyone else.

Her black, square-toed, patent-leather shoes, which had a thick, two-inch heel no junior was allowed, though Judy and Gerry regularly wore theirs an inch higher. Her black, woollen winter stockings, which showed off her slim, nicely shaped, rather long legs to their very best advantage. Her pencil tight, dark-grey skirt, which she wore short almost to her mid-thigh in a perky, self-willed defiance of the very strict school rule, girls must wear their hem an inch below the knees. Her tight fitting, white cotton blouse, which stretched and strained every button it possessed to keep her angrily heaving, though not very large breasts, in place. Her loose knotted tie, which rested on her chest in a fashionable disregard of the half-Windsor it was supposed to be in a blaze of colours, his, had long ago given up to his too often hurried dinner.

'Are you looking at my tits you dirty, shit faced cunt?' She growled, knowing the lustful look he gave her, a compliment from any other boy, but an insult she would not tolerate from him.

'No,' he lied,' cowering a little before the growing angrier blush of her lovely face.

'YES, YOU WERE, YOU STINKING LITTLE PERVERT. YOU SHIT FUCK BASTARD.' She screeched. 'YOU STINKING, ROTTEN LITTLE WORM. YOU WERE LOOKING AT MY TITS. DON'T SAY YOU WEREN'T.' She stamped and stammered her violent indignation, YOU VILE, SNIVELLING SNAKE. YOU WERE LOOKING AT ME. GOD, LOOK AT YOU. YOU FILTHY TWAT. YOU FILTHY TWAT BASTARD. YOU WERE LOOKING AT ME. GOD YOU FILTHY LITTLE CUNT. YOU WERE LOOKING AT ME.'

'No, I wasn't,' he sullenly lied, his staring eyes mesmerised by the top button of her breast heaving blouse, which more than any other promised to burst open and when it did spill her tits clean out. Or so he hoped it would. Prayed it would, if only to shame her. An image that so captivated him he didn't see the crashing fist that sent him elbow deep into the sink. Nor the kick that found his nuts so hard he thought he would cough them up with the gob of bile that found his mouth in a choke that stopped the breath in his chest for half a minute. Time enough for the girl to kick him a dozen times more in an attack that left her trembling with a giddy delight.

Chapter 6

Monday December 17, 1962
Frank Ifield: I Remember You

'You ok, Clifford?' Said the softly spoken boy, finding him collapsed on the floor. The trace of his still pedalling feet making a muddy artwork of the rustic-red tiles beneath the sink he now lay half under, every bit as good as any masterpiece the suddenly popular that year, Andy Warhol or the incomprehensible, but always mesmerizingly amazing, fractalicious, Jackson Pollock, painted and with a better brush and paint than his soggy, old shoes had made of it.

'No, *Tready,*' groaned a dazed and mildly concussed, Clifford, finding his outstretched hand with the happy relief he had come; as he always did, but though he did, saw in his face the sadness and reproach he always felt, when he did. As the boy, who now stood a silent guard beside the outside door, always came. *Himself,* as he called him, who was his *Shade,* the lonely, frightening, void of time and space between him and the boy who now gently pulled him to his feet.

A tall, muscular, athletically handsome boy, whose thick

blonde hair, unlike his own, grew in drapes of languid curls about his ears to touch the collar of his snow-white shirt and Venetian-striped, school blazer in the style of the Greek heroes, Valeria, so loved to talk about, she visibly gushed her admiration. *Achilles,* hero of the Trojan War, *Hector,* son of *King Priam,* who he killed and his brother, *Paris,* flawed in courage, but favourite of the goddess of love and beauty, *Aphrodite.* A boy as courageous as those fabled warriors he had known, since Colin Hussey pushed him off the Jungle Gym at lunchtime on their first day at nursery when he was just four and he banged his head so hard on the concrete playground he saw stars for the rest of that miserable afternoon. A boy, who without him asking, not least because he didn't know him then, hadn't seen him until that moment, knocked Colin flat on his back with single a punch and *Himself* all the time watching, he did, his face a pinch of sorrow it should come to this.

*

A punch that saw them both frog-marched like felons into the Headmistresses' office by the two dinner ladies who said they saw it done and with a testimony of richly fabricated lies, Mrs Edna Scullion, a sour faced, short-sighted harridan believed without the least question. A humourless, mean spirited, chapel proud, Welsh woman, who instantly snatched them up by the scruff of their little necks and threw them face down on the desk in front of her, their arms held tight by their gleeful accusers and thrashed them without mercy until they cried, she must stop.

A punishment she was only too pleased to administer on her two innocent charges, as it later turned out. She is being an unctuous, toadying friend of Colin's mum. A fur-draped-to-her-well-turned-ankles, bottle-dyed, Veronica Lake, look-a-like with a tumble of sleek combed, peek-a-boo hair and bright red lips that could stop the traffic. Something, she very often did, she is being a saucy beauty in those still dismally rationed days of early September 1953.

Who, when she came to collect her son at the end that sunny September afternoon in her fabulously expensive, buttercup yellow, *Jaguar XK, 120 RHD 3.4,* two doors, soft topped in mat black, sports car, introduced herself to him with a winsome smile and a vicious slap across his face? Colin's dad being a well-heeled director of the de Havilland Aircraft factory in Broughton where Mrs Scullion's husband, Eric was an inspector in the *Dove* and *Heron* workshop over at, Two Site. A pair of windswept maintenance hangars a mile slow bus ride from the main gates he was all but forgotten by anyone who mattered. A man forever searching the promotion he richly deserved, but was unlikely to get, if Mr Roylance Hussey, Lance to his frequently adulterous wife, had his way. A wartime reserve, RAF Pilot Officer of dubious merit, but impeccable social connections, he was the cousin and only relative of Violet Casterbrook and the apple of her father's eye, who made sure, he, like her husband, saw no dangerous service.

A handsome debonair man in his youth, by all accounts, with a mop of curly hair and a moustache that gave him the dashing good looks of the popular British film star, Ronald Coleman. A man whose only wartime service as the larcenous Stores Officer at RAF Sealand, was a byword in shagging any woman posted to that windswept airfield and there were hundreds who were and all of them wanting a car ride to the cities favourite *Riverside Ballroom* where all the American serviceman for miles around could be found with their wallets stuffed full of money on a Friday and Saturday night, whilst their comrades died in their thousands overseas.

And never in a million years would he see that clever, conscientious, hardworking little twat promoted no matter his god-awful ugly wife, Edna, begged him he should and with many a half-hearted shag he rather enjoyed - still did, and she did, too, though she would never say she did. Though truth to tell he could hardly find the time now for anyone, but his latest squeeze, the Teutonic Monica. The impossibly energetic German frau who was growing more demanding than he liked his tarts to be, but worse by far, was a worrying drain on both his blistered balls and his near empty wallet. An affair he must very soon stop! Would stop. Had to stop, he a score of times told himself, but couldn't such was the wanton, lecherous hold she had upon him and her husband a gorilla with half a brain who would kill him if he ever found out.

Wouldn't promote him because he was a petty and jealous man of naked, venal ambitions, who possessed in full, the parvenus' visceral hate and contempt for the working classes and all the more because his low born father was nothing more than a second-hand furniture salesman from Rhyl. A rag-and-bone man by any other name, as his father and his grandfather were before him, who married better than he deserved a local socialite of middling good looks. Whose swollen belly was so full of him when they married and because she was. and fearing a scandal it would bring, her dotting, much older brother, then a youthful and very promising career officer in the army and just back from the Great War with a Military Cross on his chest gave them house he now owned in Curzon Park North, to be quickly rid of them. Which he never could, his mother knowing her proper place every bit as much as he did and wanting the same for her only son, a persistence that made a generous uncle of him and a friend of his only daughter, Violet, when no one else cared to know her. A woman whose overly generous size and somewhat bossy manner blinded all who knew her to her thoughtful intelligence, charm, wit and boundless humour; a woman who cared rather more for people than people knew.

But most of all he hated those post war, demobbed, rabble rousing, for ever meddling, socialist twats and union commissars for the moralising, greedy shits they all were. Every last one of them ready to sell their mates down the river for the little advantage it gave them, as Blackjack, his climbed up from the gutter, conscript dodging, bullying fuck of an overpaid factory manager, every day proved they were with his sly temptations to their venal, greedy ambitions. His little promotions, his cost-free gifts and favours, his flattering he gave a shit about them, all too quickly took them from the herd of malcontents they thought to lead. Whose uppity dreams of a brave new dawn and twisted vowels every day threatened his own over privileged, thoroughly undeserved position amongst the bourgeoisie of his narrow minded, bigoted world?

Now more than ever under siege because of his foolish speculations in markets he never understood, or even much cared to understand, notably a very dodgy diamond speculation in Southern Rhodesia that had gone horrible wrong that summer and the purchase of Bolivian Mining and Railway Stocks two years before that had melted to nothing, but fraudulent share certificates fit only for the bonfire he would soon make of them. A sudden and dramatic reversal in his fortune he had yet to explain to his sexually precocious, self-indulgent wife – he knew she had a lover; the latest of many since they married in an indecent hurry in the January of 1950 to give their near bastard son, a son he doubted was his, a son he hated with a passion, a name.

A woman who thought his cheque book her personal possession. Well not any longer, he was fucking broke. Worse than broke, he was fucking bankrupt and broke and without a plan to find a fortune, except perhaps to beg, Violet's help. Which to his happy relief she had rather unexpectedly agreed she would, if he would call on her early next Monday morning, which he most certainly would! Good old fat arsed, Violet, she was a blooming toff and no mistake. A toff who had long made a good friend of his wife, and Edna Scullion, though why she bothered was beyond belief, the two of them being such sullen cows, and now the gorgeous Mrs Daphne Plant, whose violent gangster husband was fast making a fortune from his illegal activities; bookmaking being the larcenous least of them from what very little he had heard of him.

But more even than any of those communist union twats who thought their war time service was an excuse to pull down the social barricades that had kept them in their well-deserved place for a thousand years, he hated bloody rankers like, Flight Lieutenant Eric Scullion, DFC and Bar. Whose seventeen sorties as a pilot with RAF Bomber Command and two years in a German Prison of war camp - *Stalag Luft III,* he bravely three times tried to escape until they stuck him in Colditz for the duration, had earned him a reputation that shamed his own wretched service. But he hated even more Violet's husband, a working-class shit from Dudley who would get all her money when she died; his money by rights, as any fair-minded lawyer would tell you it was; by God! Unless the whispered rumours were true; that he would get the lot?

*

'Who did this to you, Clifford?' Asked Tready, helping him to his feet in the wash of bright sunlight light that suddenly burst through the narrow, ceiling-high, snow dappled, frosted-glass windows above the sinks. A light that so immediately filled the forty-watt gloom of the toilets, he appeared to flicker, like the pages of a fallen open book and when he stood, saw him stare into the mirror at the mask of tragedy or was it comedy, they looked too much the same, he had contrived, and saw it was perhaps, too much. And grimly smiled, it was, as he looked again at the disfiguring pimples and spots, he had squeezed to the painfully swollen red smudge he now gently touched. And when he did, saw his face change by imperceptible degree to something more like the one he knew; not *him,* but someone who better resembled *him.*

'Hussey and Lomas, who else?' He glumly answered, his fingers playing on his face. 'They were hiding in there,' he pointed to the half open toilet, 'and when they'd finished jumping all over me like I was a trampoline that girl, Linda Plant, you know her? Beat me up. Look at my face, Tready.'

'Yes, I know her. A very pretty girl, but not a very nice girl,' he knowingly smiled, as he looked with concern at his bloodied face. 'She's the bookmakers' daughter,' he said, lifting his jacket from the floor, now so thoroughly wet it would never dry in time for class. 'And why did she hit you, Clifford, were you rude to her, she's a prefect you know and expects a little respect?'

'No, I wasn't rude to her! Well, not really. She said I was looking at her,' he sheepishly answered taking his jacket from his hand, which like his face in the mirror, appeared beyond repair.

'Looking at her?' He asked, with a smile that knew exactly what he meant; but why shouldn't he look at her? She was attractive and flirted with all the boys, as girls like her do; so why not him? What right did she have to choose who looked at her, saw in her someone they desired?

'Sort of, but only a bit. I couldn't help it. I didn't mean to stare at her, but she looked at me as if she was about to explode in a volcano of frustrated anger. I just did and she hit me and then kicked me hard in me balls and me belly, which were already painfully sore. Look,' he pointed to his face, smeared in streaks of blood and grime and pockmarked with pimples and spots.

'Do you want me to sort things out? Clifford? Hussey and Lomas I mean? They shouldn't get away with this. You know they shouldn't? I will, if you want me, too? You know I can?'

'Yes, I know they shouldn't,' he shrugged, wringing the sleeve of his jacket into the sink and all the time staring into the mirror and Tready who was standing behind him, his face so close to his.

'Just say the word and I will.'

'No Tready! I mean it! Nor you,' he grinned a reassuring smile at *Himself,* watching them from the door, who had done so many small things to help him since Clooney Barron had taken against him, he every day wondered why he had? And why his step-mum, let him? Still did, despite he had given her every chance to know him as he really was; but she wouldn't. Helping him when no one else could when things got really bad, as they did last week; when they hurt him as they had never hurt him before. A hurt and pain he *deserved,* but a hurt and pain he would not endure a second time! 'Better not! Really!' He almost pleaded, they mustn't. 'They'll know it was me who put you up to it and get me again when you're not around to help me. You know they will and if they don't, Clooney will, those two being so thick with him just now.'

'Are you sure?' He asked, his hand finding his shoulder in a squeeze he found the greatest joy.

'No, best if I just ignore them,' he said, showing the spirited resilience, Tready so much admired in him. 'They're just a pair of wicked, fat bullies, best ignored,' he laughed. 'Who'll soon get tired of pushing me around when they see it don't bother me none and when they do, they'll find somebody else? Tinker, maybe?' He laughed, knowing he was recently one of their friends and well overdue a good punch in the face, though, in truth he always liked him, because he was a simple fool too much under their influence, and his mum was one of Clooney's whores. Had been since before he was born. One of the dozen girls he had working for him in the Highfield Public House, though he pretended he didn't. A nice lady with such sad eyes and a very pretty lady, too, who always remembered him with a smile and a wave when she saw him.

'Maybe they will and maybe they won't. They've been doing this for as long as you and I have known them and Hussey most of all, Clifford, but never as violently as this. Never with such a careless disregard for your safety. Are you sure you don't want me to help you in some way?'

'No,' he winced, straightening himself up to his full height to stand as tall and broad as he was in the mirror, his face, so different from his striking good looks, looking back at him, betraying the misery and pain he felt. But though it did, there was a flattering synchrony between them now, each, in their own inexplicable way, mirroring the other in their facial expressions and in their slight movements, the one seemingly tragic, the other undoubtedly heroic. But though they were were unmistakeably two parts of a whole: contrary, but complimenting. 'It is much worse than it was, but then, you know why? There is a storm coming and they are both in the eye of it, not the cause of it, nor the end of it, but an inevitable part of it and I can do nothing to stop it but await its end. 'But they shan't do this to me again, no matter they think they can, I promise you that Tready and you, too, *Himself,* they will hurt me no more.'

'Sure?'

'Sure.'

'Well, if you say so, Clifford,' said Tready. 'If that's what you want, but don't put up with it more than you must, you have trouble enough with Clooney Barron, your step-mum and now Terry Mack, who has come so suddenly into your life, whose evil designs on you are vile, without those two attacking you every other day of the week and now Linda Plant has you in her sights for no good reason than she is a thoroughly bad girl and one I think you should avoid.'

'No, I won't. I promise,' he answered.

'What are you doing in here?' Asked the perplexed school caretaker, Mr Eldred, coming into the toilet with Mr Pike, the gardener, both carrying six canvass, stacking chairs, Clifford knew were destined for Valeria's store room, who were both a minute listening at the door before they came in expecting to find a couple of loafers hiding from their lessons, but found only Clifford, wringing out his jacket and shirt over one of the sinks, talking to himself in the mirror.

'No one, sir,' said Clifford, quickly hurrying out.

'Damn little fool,' barked Eldred, searching the toilet for the boys he suspected were still there. Knew were there if Robin wasn't a gifted mimic like Danny Kaye, which he was certain he wasn't.

Chapter 7

Monday December 17, 1962
Bobby Darin: Things

'Where have you been?' Barked Cod-Eye Turner from the quarter open door of the gym, watched by his waiting class, his one good eye fixed on Clifford so hard he appeared to visibly tremble under his cold, despairing, hateful stare and tumbled over one of the slatted, wooden benches that lined the green tiled changing rooms on three sides, beneath rows of metal lockers.

'Late sir, sorry sir,' stuttered Clifford, feeling the horrible, smelly wet of his piss sodden PE bag against his trembling knees with a hopeless sense of doom that knew there was no escape from the one eyed monster who now towered above him with such an odious glare; as his class mates saw there wasn't with a mixture of sadness, repugnance and glee, he was such a coward.

'I can see you're late you, half-wit, do you think I'm stupid? Do you?' He screamed without answer. 'No! Well get yourself changed and get yourself into that gym in the next thirty seconds or I'll take the skin off your backside; by God I will. Do you hear me, Robin? Move yourself, now you, execrable little man or I'll *maro you jeldi,* which, if you don't already know, means I'll kill you quickly?' He thundered. *You tum boselica wallah.* And you really don't want to know what that means,' he bellowed, a few of his favourite native Indian words, of vilest disapproval – he was a boy soldier in Meerut before the war in Europe got him. And did so, so loud the girl's playing netball in the snow covered, bitterly cold yard outside the gym heard him with a titter of vulgar delight that knew the delicious trouble Cocky was in and loved he was.

Not least Judy, Gerry and Ronnie who for several minutes, now, had pressed their gorgeous faces, not to say their nipple frozen breasts to the snow and ice rimed, floor to ceiling, sanatorium-like, French windows that lined one side of the gym to watch the boys inside. Who seeing they did, noisily shouted their boisterous, earthy, hormone crazed approval with every lewd gesture known to their pliant hips and madly jerking fists, the three of them laughed to see?

'What the flip are you doing creeping about like that?' Screeched Cod-Eye, seeing Clifford slink into the gym on his blind side, hopeful he wouldn't be seen, which he very nearly wasn't.

'Sorry sir, me step-mum didn't have time wash and to iron me kit last night,' he grovelingly apologised. The smile bright on his stricken face, his spider hands a dancing, nervous fidget, as he pointed to his shabby, two sizes too large, crew neck, canary yellow T-shirt, deep stained, once white, but now decidedly grey, crumpled baggy shorts and dirty, lace knotted plimsolls he wore without socks. Which, despite he had twice wrung them out in the showers, were still so damp with piss they clung to his skew bent, frightened frame like the slime on a slug and every bit as revealing. Much to the concern of *Himself,* who watched him from the darkest corner of the gym with a heartfelt apprehension that longed to help him; would if he could!

'You are vile little man and no mistake, Robin, you really are. And my old Sergeant Major, when I was a boy recruit in Woolwich before the war, no older than you are now, would turn in his grave to see the way you have come to my gym this morning and late without excuse by ten long minutes. God help me, he would!' Shouted Cod-Eye. 'How many times have I told you to wash and iron your own dhobi and not rely on others to do it for you? How many times, Robin?' He screamed, his face a twisted fright of spastic, twitching muscle, but though it was, hinted this was a part he was forced to play against his better judgement, as Cocky knew it was and played his own more dangerous part with a stubborn resolve that was truly *Herculean.* 'Do your own dhobi if your mum won't.' He bellowed with the apparent insensitivity to human distress he was famed for. Much to the frightened, nervously tittering amusement of the boys who cowered behind him in a finger biting, knee trembling, half circle that was glad it was Cocky who was in trouble and not them, though it would be another three quarters of an hour before they would be free of him and find the sanctuary of Madame Doucet's French lesson. The twice weekly high spot of their otherwise miserable school week when they could gaze into her eyes, listen to her deliciously sexy, gorgeously accented Parisian voice and when she wasn't looking, look at her arse and tits, which were better by a mile than Judy's, Gerry's or Angela's.

'Don't know, said, Clifford beneath his threatening, Cyclopean, one-eyed stare, which fixed him so hard he crumbled to his knees and waited the blow he was sure would come. *Don't be afraid Clifford I'm here beside you,* whispered *Himself*, his gentle hands rested on his shrunken, trembling shoulder. 'I'm not frightened,' he whispered back, squeezing his cold hand in his.

'What did you say, Robin you tongue tied, mumbling clown? Speak up?' Exclaimed Cod-Eye.

'Nothing sir, I was just talking to *Himself,*' he answered, his head shrinking into his shoulders.

'Talking to *Himself*? What in blazes are you on about, Robin? Are you mad? *Yourself* you mean? *Yourself*. Not *Himself* you blithering fool. Speak the Queen's English. At least do that for me.'

'Sorry sir. Sorry.'

'Sorry! You will be sorry if you don't up your, game, Robin, do you hear me?' He barked. 'Now, get those filthy rags off your back before I strip you naked myself and whip you black and blue, and I will, believe me I will. Jeldi, jeldi, you, useless little runt! Do you hear me, Robin? Jeldi, jeldi, you little tosser. Get 'em off, now! God damn you before I strangle you with my bare hands and bury you under that, useless, good for nothing, clay heaped duck pond *Torchy the Battery Boy,'* (his pet name for the Headmaster from the children's televisions programme of the same name, as everyone knew it was) 'has dug outside my gym like a bomb crater. Like I ever said we needed a swimming pool in the first place, when we have two of them barely a mile from where I'm standing.' He screamed, the spit and froth of his resentful anger flying from his mouth like foam in a hurricane to drench, Clifford and *Himself* in his jealous wrath.

A jealously born of the social rank and privileges he knew the headmaster's cowards, conscript commission in the safety of the Orkney's had bestowed on him in the years after the war. Whilst he, a man who could boast five years military service in the Indian army fighting Dacoits and Pathan tribesmen on the North West Frontier before the war had even begun and three years active military service in Europe and the Middle East during it, had little more to show for his efforts than a crumbling two-up and two-down terraced house in, St Anne Street the blasted council now wanted to bulldoze for a bypass, no one asked them to build, and certainly not where they intended to build it through the heart of the historic city he so loved, and a job that would never see him promoted higher than he now was. No wonder he hated the twat!

'Here sir?' Wailed a stunned and disbelieving, Clifford, to the mocking, growing more callous, noisy cheers of his growing more raucous classmates, who began to clap and cheer he must.

Don't be afraid, Clifford I'm still here with you, whispered *Himself,* his body a shield against his shame. His outstretched hand pressed hard to Cod-Eye's barrel chest in a restraint he felt with a tingle of trepidation he had gone too far that for the second time that morning left him feeling oddly ill at ease as if a ghost had walked over his grave. The last time not fifteen minutes ago when Madame Doucet stared at him from her second floor, annex window, the look on her face so puzzled and surprised it made him shiver, but not from the Winter cold that blew in Siberian gusts, but from the despair he could not find the words to express himself; but never could. A longing, he had perhaps always felt, he was not the man he had hoped to be but was someone *else*. Someone far better than this; a man tortured by failure. A woman like no other woman he had ever met, whose eyes he could never quite meet without a childish blush, whose friendship he longed to know, whose name he longed to say. A woman he unfathomably longed to protect, as he protected Clifford, but from what? Dylan Lloyd-Thomas, who fancied himself a ladies' man? Was; if all the rumours he had heard about him this last year were only partly true, which he doubted they were. An unfathomably stupid longing that despite himself left him with the most disconcerting feelings of guilt, shame and the strangest foreboding, an anxiety he had never felt before, but why? What had that beautiful French woman to do with him?

'Thank you,' whispered Clifford to *Himself*.

'Get your paw off me Robin,' bellowed, Cod-Eye, pushing him back onto the wall bar with a shove that left him winded.

'Sorry sir

'I'm waiting,' said Cod-Eye, the tingle of restraint now gone, the threat clear in his voice.

'Sorry, sir,' mocked a grinning Hussey and Lomas, who watched his torment from beside the vaulting horse they had, just moments before he came in, carried into the centre of the gym on the wooden shafts they now held like spears at their sides, their sneering, watchful faces, bright red with hate filled pleasure, their appearance a malevolent threat no less than Cod-Eye.

'Shut your face Lomas or I'll kick you into the middle of next week and that means you, too, Hussey, you ginger headed, toe rag,' shouted, Cod-Eye, with all the threat he could muster, and there was more than a hint of threat in his deep scarred by a German grenade at the Battle of Mersa Matruh, twenty years before, red flushed, violently twisted, desperately ugly face for those two squat necked Neanderthals to drop their defiant gaze until he turned his attention on Clifford once again, who stood before him now with a composure that surprised him.

With nowhere to hide and with seventeen boys and a fast gathering crowd of gog-eyed, frost bitten staring girls urging him on in a bawdy, growing ever louder, chanting, taunting giggle of disbelief, that was every day of the week glad it was Clifford and not them getting their lights punched out by Hussey and Lomas, or twice a week bullied by Cod-Eye Turner, when he had a mind, too, Clifford wriggled free of his dirty wet T-shirt and dropped it to the floor.

'And the rest, Robin. Jeldi, you ain't got nothing hide,' he laughed, encouraging his now foot stamping, hand clapping, hollering class to a matey camaraderie that is the way of all bullies the world over, especially those who are bullied themselves by those they despise and there was no one more bullied by Mr Casterbrook in Love Street Secondary Modern School for Girls and Boys than Cod-Eye Turner. Except, perhaps, Miss Paget, who was swooned to a cringing flap by the smell of the aniline dye that filled the small, cupboard-like room across the hall from her office, the Headmaster, with his risible, faux grandeur, fondly called his print room, which stained her fingers the purple she knew it would and sobbed and sobbed to see it had.

Chapter 8

Monday December 17, 1962
Ray Charles: I Can't Stop Loving You

And growing so hysterically loud, Joe Fisher, who was enjoying his only free period of the week, a Monday morning first period that was the cynical gift of his more experienced colleague - who knew better than to accept it, pressed his ear to the tight closed door and listened. His heart filled with the love he had for the most bewitching woman he had ever known and the only one in living memory to show the least interest in his innocently awkward, advances.

Colleagues who were not only content to have him teach more classes than they did - a rite of passage all newly qualified teachers must endure to harden their hearts against the thankless career they had chosen, they ignored Casterbrook had found him a hundred other small things do and all for the pitiful six pounds and ten shilling a week he paid him. A wage far less than they was getting, Casterbrook said was all he could afford until he proved himself worthy of more; but planned to terminate his contract this week with Dylan's and Terry's. Not least of which was organising, with barely a fortnight, notice, and without the least help from anyone, the mayor's reception, prize giving and evening disco, which was to follow the school swimming gala on Friday, which thankfully, he had no part, but the spectator he was told to be.

'Fuck and double fuck,' said Miss Paget, as he leant his ear to the door, though with an anxious, watchful eye fixed on the open door of her office that hoped Casterbrook, who he loathed and feared in equal measure for his hateful bullying of the woman he was now certain he loved, didn't come out and ask him why he was loitering in the corridor with nothing better to do? Even though the print room was only a short walk from the schools surprisingly well stocked by public subscriptions, but little used by anyone, save Mrs Wiśniewski, who appeared to live there, library, where he had just come from and with a book under his arm to prove he had.

A never borrowed since, Friday, May 16, 1924, if the absence of any library stamp after this date was the proof it hadn't, much written upon in red ink by some bygone scholar, copy of John Donne's, *Devotions upon Emergent Occasions*. A volume he had never thought to see within a ten mile radius of that educationally blighted, Sodom and Gomorrah his, thoroughly undeserved, by common consent, Lower Third in English Literature, Dr Leavis, a bitter, passed over for promotion, grown disagreeable old man of eminent reputation, if cruel heart, had thought his thesis, *A Criticism of the English Novel, Notably the Interiority, Realism, Irony and*

Satire of Miss Jane Austin, justly merited, had brought him, too with such misplaced optimism he could scarce believe the fool he had been to think it might have been better than the terror it was.

Which, he had opened and read, under the watchful eye of Mrs Wiśniewski - who he fancied rather liked him, his oft quoted *Meditation*, some would say, his only quotable *Meditation*, his famous, *Meditation XVII.* A meditation he thought to use in a third-year class he would take this afternoon, class 3C, so powerful was its timeless message: *No man is an island, entire of itself, etc., etc.* Which he hoped would spark some interest in this thuggish, frightening class of disruptive psychopaths and wanton girls, who delighted in his embarrassment, not least Judy Dowd, Geraldine Walsh, and though less hurtful, Veronica Morris.

But, better than his *Meditation*, he mused, clasping the brass, beehive door knob in his hand and pressing his ear closer to the mournful sobs within, which so moved him, which after all, were no more than the self-indulgent ramblings of a man who thought himself about to die of some horrible, slimy flux, were his romantic poems. Which though surprisingly mischievous for a High Church minister, spoke to his innocent, romantically chivalrous heart the Christian love he longed to find with a good and virtuous woman; a woman like his mother, who he adored. *The Good Morrow,* perhaps, or the *Break of Day?* Poems so utterly sweet he easily remembered their moving lines, or, perhaps, *The Broken Heart?* Which compares true love, the love he longed to know, to the sufferings of plague and war. 'Oh, *what did become of my heart when I first saw thee? I brought a heart into a room. But from the room I carried none with me,'* he sighed, as he tentatively knocked on the door. A knock so soft, Mr Casterbrook would never hear him, or so he hoped, as the door opened an inch and Miss Paget leaned out to pull him in!

Chapter 9

Monday December 17, 1962
Cliff Richard: Move It

'Off,' chanted Lomas, banging his wooden *spear* on the gym floor. A chant that found an eager, wildly excited, *Bacchanalian* chorus in his now deliriously excited classmates. Who just like William Golding's schoolboys in his *Lord of the Flies,* revealed a primitive savagery that was frightening? Who, though unlike him and Hussey in every conceivable way, now crowded the wall bars in a tightening half circle to watch his humiliation in a thrill of blood thirsty delight that would not let him go until he was done? A humiliation no less than poor *Piggy* endured at the hands of *Jack* and *Roger,* who unfettered by civilisation eventually killed him.

'Off,' echoed Hussey, striding with his banging spear into the middle of the gym with a gawping delight that watched him slowly wriggle his wet pants over his bum. A soggy rag of shit-stained cotton that left a small puddle on the floor, as he clasped it to his knob in a protective hug.

Ignore them Clifford this moment will soon pass, whispered *Himself,* standing beside him.

'Off, off, off,' cried the chorus behind him, finding a growing more sinister voice in his mounting, ever more tearful despair, despite *Himself,* who did his best to calm him; did a little bit.

'Off, off, off,' they cried louder and louder. A cry that became a roar of disbelief when Cod-Eye, seeing Judy and Gerry watching him through the window their breasts pressed to the ice cold, frosted glaze in a saucy, dancers squirm he found torment, suddenly hinted a tumescent so monstrously big they laughed and giggled all the more to see it prod his shorts like a sleepy ferret waking in a sack and blew him saucy, pouting kisses that made it bigger still.

'Fuck me, rigid, why don't you?' Gawped Gerry, seeing his knob bulge in his shorts, 'I heard someone say he was hung like a fucking monster, but I never thought anyone was as big as that? Did you Jude? Quick Ronnie, come and see this, it's Cod-Eye's. He's got a cock like a python,' she called, much to the giggling delight of the girls who now pressed the glass beside her.

'Cor blimey Charlie,' gawped Ronnie in astonished surprise, pushing her way through the jostling, hysterically screaming crowd of red faced, girls, who now filled the window to get a better look. Despite Miss Langford blew her whistle a shrieking dozen times they shouldn't, and with a sudden warm ache between her thighs that made her blush, as she had never had before.

'And who told you that bit of old news, as if it matters

to anyone, Geraldine?' Smirked Judy with a lascivious wink, knowing who it was, but, though she did, hated she was so in love with him.'

'Not telling you,' She answered with a simper of gloating triumph on her pretty lips that knew how jealous she really was. Dylan, the gorgeously hunky, fabulously sexy, Dylan Lloyd-Thomas had chosen her instead of her; despite she was so much prettier. Was secretly meeting her after the swimming practice this afternoon! Not Linda Plant, who was always pestering him, who had warned her off with such a silly bluster of threats, she laughed in her face she thought she was so mean. Nor even that stuck up French tart, Madame Doucet, who Judy said was his lover, though she knew different, Dylan had told her she wasn't; he didn't even like her.

'Get a move on Robin, get those wet shorts off your arse before you chap your scrotum and catch pneumonia,' grunted Cod-Eye, seeing he still held his shorts tight to his waist. 'You ain't got nothing between your legs we haven't seen before except its smaller than my Jack Russell's, dick,' he tittered. Ignoring Miss Langford stared at him with ill-disguised disappointment, despite, she knew he was only doing what he had, to do, but though he was, it was cruel, as everyone knew it was. 'And that's so small I don't think I have ever seen it,' he roared his bawdy tease. Oblivious to the dirt, welts, bruises, scratches and puckered sores that scarred Clifford's naked body from his head to his toes like a threadbare, patchwork quilt. 'Now, now run around the gym until I tell you to stop. do you hear me you, horrible little man? Jeldi.

'Now sir,' cowered Clifford

'Now sir,' yelled Cod-Eye.

'Round sir,' he pleaded, his eyes searching the frosted windows to find Hilda, Fay and Greta, who, blank faced between their grinning companions, watched him with a dark concern that urged him to be brave, as they knew he must be; knew he was. And watched *Himself* lead the way.

'Yes, round.'

'Must I, sir?' He asked, his face begging to be spared the humiliation he must now endure. A humiliation surely too much to bear, despite *Himself,* nearly halfway round the gym. His tear dripped eyes seeing the milling, jostling growing more excited crowd of gawping girls who were staring at him through the glass, despite Hilda cried they shouldn't, and Miss Langford called and whistled them to come away, but wouldn't, so much did they want to see the fun.

'To me Thebans, to me Athenians,' she called without the least hint they would.

'Go on Clifford, you can do it,' called Hilda, her voice a muted bleat of pain and frustration.

'Yeah, go on Clifford, you, sorry little twat,' called Gerry with a spite filled, taunting hate that was a vicious parody of Hilda's tearful concern, 'give us all a fucking laugh you, dozy prick.'

'Wanker,' spat Judy, with a disgust that despised him. Though they had once been friends and despised him all the more because they were. A time she hated no less than she hated her dad, now gone, thank goodness, but leaving her with a mother no better than his; a whore to any man who wanted her. But not one of Cooney Barron's she was thankful for that small mercy.

'Yeah, wanker,' echoed Greta, in a mocking mimic, Judy pretended not to hear, though she was standing next to Ronnie smoking a cigarette, Miss Langford twice called her put out and pretended she did, as she turned and walked away. 'Yeah, wanker,' she said again, as cigarette in mouth she stripped to her bra and knickers - a flat chested, near shapeless ensemble in ivory white it would take another year, or possibly two, to fill. An act of defiant support for Clifford he almost cried to see as he made his first tearful circuit of the gym to the hoots, halloos and bawdy whistles of his heartless class. Not least those of Judy and Gerry, who hammered the windows with their fist as he did, their pretty faces made ugly by the contorted grimaces they pulled.

'Jeldi, you *tum boselica wallah,'* growled Cod-Eye, hating what he did, as Hilda and Fay knew he did, but not Greta, who thought he had gone too far. Had embarrassed Clifford more than was needed and would show him he had, despite she had been warned not to deter or encourage him, as she already had, but must let him do what he must, as he had been told he must.

'Run Cocky, run,' jeered the boys in the gym and the girls at the windows as he ran pell-mell to catch *Himself,* which after half a lap, he did, and when he did, heard their chants rise to a bellowing, clapping crescendo. Hussey, Lomas and Tinker, now running beside him in a canter of exaggerated, horse-like galloping strides, called loudest their hate and derision and would have several times knocked him down, had *Himself* not sent them flying onto their faces.

For the next forty minutes Clifford circled the gym, the arms of his T-shirt, lifted from the floor after dozen laps, now tied to his slim, muscular waist like a Red Indian's breach clout to hide his shame. His bare arse a sniggering spectacle for the girls, who team by coloured team, sneaked a look at him, every bit as much as they did the loose-limbed boys inside. Who sprinted, flipped, vaulted, straddled, balanced, climbed, hung and rolled from every piece of apparatus Cod-Eye could find to torture their youthful bodies to a grunting, wheezing, asthmatic, cramping exhaustion. Which, he did with a relish, until, at long last, he blew his much prized, FA standard, brass whistle and ordered them to the showers in a steaming, sweating relief that had long forgotten Clifford was ever there, or even the girls who begged their attention. Until they saw Greta come out of the driving pelt of snow like a phantom, her hair dressed in a garland of bright summer flowers to press her now completely naked body to the French windows, a second time, a sight that stopped them, thunderstruck, in their tracks as it did Cod-Eye.

Chapter 10

Monday December 17, 1962
Harry Belafonte: There's a Hole in My Bucket

'What are you wearing, Clifford, mon petit chouchou?' Asked Madame Doucet, the beautiful French teacher who had been the talk of the school since her improbable arrival last September. A young woman so glamorous she was unlike any teacher he or his cruel and callous classmates had ever seen before, her deeply accented voice a charm of gushing sympathy every bit as graceful as her lithe and sensual movements, which in four short steps from her cluttered desk found his side. 'Mon chéri, what is the meaning of this? Who has done this to you? She asked, her fingers plucking the hem of the football shirt he wore like a toga to his knees.

'Mr Turner made me, Madame,' croaked Clifford, his face a burning pink embarrassment, as she sank on her four-inch stiletto heels in front of him in a pose a dozen boys stretched to see, her pencil skirt lifted above her knees to show the slim sensual promise of her thighs and so tight around the shapely round of her bottom it might have been a second skin.

'Made you do what, Clifford?' She sweetly purred, her face so close to his he could smell the flowers that perfumed her neck as her fire engine-red painted, perfectly manicured finger nails gently caressed his still damp and wickedly spotty face in a fuss he had never known; though she had always been kind to him; had seen her look at him as he too often looked at her.

'Made me change into this, Madame,' he whispered into her ear, his throat tight with the self-deceiving shame he looked the way he did, like a bald *Dennis the Menace,* his eyes fixed on the sensuous, butterfly pout of her full red lips, which he dared to hope might kiss him. Though he would die of shame if they did, he inwardly cringed, as his fingers found the collar of the dress-like, ruby-red and black hooped, woollen jersey, Cod-Eye had forced him to wear after standing him in a cold shower for ten minutes to get him clean, which it did. *And wanted back,* he had screamed into his face, all fleck and phlegm, *when his clothes were dried in the school kitchen,* where he had just him take them, and Mrs Wiśniewski's, taking one of her many leisurely breaks, kindly said she would wash and iron before he went home that afternoon.

'He pissed himself, *miss,*' jeered Hussey from the back of the room, ignoring, as he always did, she had a hundred times insisted he call her, Madame. 'Dirty little fuck,' he slyly whispered to his neighbour, a titian haired beauty by the name of Angela Dee who wore her long, thick curly hair, like Rita Hayworth, who ignored him with a sniff of her upturned nose he sullenly ignored as he rolled back on his chair to crash against the wall behind him with a deliberately irritating thud, Valeria ignored. 'Pissed himself so much Cod-Eye had to run him naked around the gym to get him dry, should have seen it, miss, it was a real laugh,' he brazenly crowed, to the giggles, cheers and ribald catcalls of 3C. A class of forty, feral-thick, hormone crazed to a lunacy their parents wouldn't believe, pubescent teenagers, eighteen boys, if they all turned up, which they rarely did, and seventeen, netball stiff, freshly showered, preened and pampered girls, many of them wearing a strictly forbidden by Mr Casterbrook, slash of red or pink lipstick only Miss Langford, and the always encouraging, Madame Doucet chose to ignore.

'Yeah, he pissed all over himself in the bog, miss, the useless little fucker, because he couldn't get his *Jack Russell* out of his pants fast enough to have a slash where he should have had it, miss,' laughed Lomas, lampooning the worst excesses of Cod-Eyes vile behaviour in the gym. 'You daft fucking prick, Cocky,' he barked, his foot stretched out to kick him from beneath the front desk beside the door; where Valeria, a week ago, forced him to sit; an insult that every day grated on his nerves. The threat of his eye-popping, nose-dripping, ball-bulging, drug induced, psychotic menace so close to her ear she had to steel her nerves to ignore his hateful presence.

A mindless, bullying vulgarity Valeria had almost become immune, too, in the months she had known him and Lomas that greatly amused the three girls who sat one empty desk away from him in skirts so short their knickers' showed a colourfully saucy bunting of pink, yellow and blue above the constant, itch-like wriggle of their sinewy thighs; the same three girls she had earlier seen walking so brazenly in the snow seemingly without a care in the world. 'God all mighty, he doesn't half whiff, miss,' shouted an exaggeratedly sneering, Judy, poking him in the ribs with her ruler until he backed a foot away in a sulk that wondered why she did.

'Smell him, miss, he stinks like a right tosspot pisser,' laughed, Tinker from the middle of the room, much to the snorting approval of Hussey and Lomas, who since the beginning of term had made a gullible pet of him, when once they only bullied him. Every day encouraging his daft and growing more reckless pursuit of Miss Paget, who he claimed to love, but sillier still, that she loved him; had said she did, as if that was likely? Encouraging him to show her he did with every depravity they could imagine, so crude and so disgustingly inappropriate he never would. But more than this, urging his needy, anxious to please and be liked, stupidity to an ever greater defiance of the authority they both hated and planned to very soon confront in the most hideous way, though he was too much a coward to do more than gently cheek, Valeria, who despite himself, he liked, but never could show he did with Hussey and Lomas to see he did.

A tall, dark and slimly handsome boy who Valeria often thought looked like a youthful Sidney Poitier, in the *Blackboard Jungle,* or perhaps, Harry Belafonte, on the cover of his 1956 single, *Calypso,* who her sister Madeleine adored, who, sadly, was as dim as the now dying light bulb that hung in her cluttered storeroom. Which, to her dismay, she now ogled with such an impatient, distracted desire for Dylan to come, she felt quite ashamed of herself, who promised he would when they met last Thursday night. A reconciliation and unsatisfactory lovemaking that, whilst it wasn't all it could have been, was a resolution of sorts and she was glad of that.

But a boy Angela Dee, who now watched him with a singularly affectionate smile on her full pink lips, adored in that peculiar way attractive girls of her equally dim and vainly superior kind, prefer a pretty face to a clever mind, but far less than men do; for whom a woman's looks are everything. Little realising or caring to realise beauty blinds them to the fools they truly are. That our sensible appreciation of reality is an illusion beyond our grasp, a very small projection of the endless stream of consciousness that might be ours if we cared to know it.

'You tell her Tinker,' Hooted Hussey, urging the rest of the class to a noisy din of mocking sneers and vulgar comments, which came to a stop when Valeria rose to her feet in a challenge he dared not meet. Not least, because she had no fear of him or Lomas, but mostly because the rest of the class liked her, and the boys thought she was hot like no woman they knew.

'Monsieur Taylor,' she said, wondering, as always she did, why he was called, Tinker and not Rick, as the register clearly said he was, and so much better, so hip and modern, her tone resolutely patient, as his voice, the last to be heard in the room by a long ten seconds, trailed to self-conscious silence, 'would you be so good as to sit down in your seat, *vous petit merde.*'

'Miss?' He mumbled, wondering what it was she just called him in a language he would never understand, no matter how hard he tried, but knowing by the smirking look of contempt on little Fay Cottrell's face, now turned upon him from the seat in front of his, it wasn't very nice. And she would know, her mum being a German kraut, her Neanderthal of a dad brought over from his National Service days in Germany, which, as everyone knows is nearly the same thing.

'Sit down, vous petit bâtard. Sit down this instant, Monsieur Taylor.'

'Yes, miss, but ….,' he politely answered, dropping his cowards bum back onto his seat besides, Greta. A stick-thin, flat-chested, cadaverously pale-skinned girl with a tobacco fuelled halitosis. A girl whose short *Betty Boo* hair cut did little to soften her constantly disappointed, ever watchful face. A girl he truly feared, though he hardly knew why he did. A girl with an aura, who now watched him with such a look of malignant scorn in her Dusty Springfield, over blacked, but rather striking, hazel brown, round eyes, he visibly flinched to see she did, and half stood again to avoid her unspoken, yet clearly meant, threat to hurt him in some horrible way.

'But what?' Asked Valeria, amused a girl as slight and physically unremarkable as Greta could be such a fright, not only to him, but everyone else in the class it, would seem? A girl who hardly spoke a word, but whose behaviour was so unfathomably strange no one dared to vex her, not even

Hussey and Lomas, nor even Judy, Gerry and Ronnie, who skulked and wheedled around her like craven dogs. *What was her secret?* She wondered, not for the first time.

*

A question she might have better answered, had she looked more carefully into her freckled face; an understated, beautiful face, so possessed of courage she had no fear of anyone or anything, and Cod-Eye and the boys in her class, not at all. Who, she easily cowered into a pitiful silence when she pressed her slim and shapeless, body against the ice-cold glass of the French windows her arms and legs outstretched like Leonardo de Vinci's, *Vitruvian Man* to melt the ice and snow in a powerfully erotic display none of them could turn their disbelieving eyes away from?

A sight so beguiling Miss Langford could only stand and stare at the strange, elfin creature, who, seeing Cod-Eye stride away in a confounded, deeply troubled silence, stepped from the window and the ice drawn, ghostly shadow she now so perfectly left behind, and utterly indifferent to the spectacle she had caused, or the very strange, sometimes admiring looks her classmates gave her - none more admiring than her own, she picked up her few clothes and walked off into the snow, which seemed to consume her in a haze of shadows and dancing lights.

Her sensuously lean, deliciously naked body holding her and everyone else in a thrall that thrilled to the soft round of her buttocks, that almost cried to see her small breasts, her dark brown nipples and the soft tempting shadow of her virgin's mons and pudendal cleft. A sight even more tempting than Judy, though in a different way, who stared at her with the same lustful, somewhat shocked, inquiring fascination that every minute wondered who she truly was.

Knew, as Valeria didn't, she was a woodland nymph, a Grace full to overflowing with mystery and dangerous caprice. The servant, perhaps of the forever chaste, *Artemis*, the twin sister of the divine *Apollo,* daughter of *Zeus* and *Leto,* who she worshipped for her sacred virginity. Which, like her own, she guarded with her life, and who she so longed to know as only a woman can know another like her; know true love. So often lying naked beneath the sun or the moon on her camps with the now, sadly departed, *Kindred of the Kibbo Kift* or with the *Girl Guides* who had become their near perfect substitute. But never once did. Though she waited for her in the many quiet groves she found on her endless weekend walks in the countryside she so dearly loved hopeful she would come to her, as the goddess *Aphrodite* came to her son, *Aeneas* disguised as a huntress, such a surprise. '*Et vera incessu patuit dea,*' she sighed the lines she knew so well from Virgil's, *Aeneid,* 'and the true goddess was revealed with her step,' the goddess of beauty, love and sexuality; woman personified, but only known to woman.

*

'Nothing, Madame,' bleated Tinker, as his legs gave way beneath him and he slumped back onto his chair a second time all thoughts of feeble jokes and pranks chased from his mind by Valeria's implacable stare, which hurt him more than he dared say; hated she didn't like him.

'Silence. All of you,' said Valeria, her hands lightly resting on her slim and shapely hips, her soft-blue eyes fixed on Hussey and Lomas, who every day she hated more and more for the coarse, loudmouth, bullies they were, and Hussey, a boy from a wealthy, if unhappy home, her voice an exquisite calm, her provocatively, loose-buttoned, tight fitting, dianthus pink, cashmere cardigan a dazzling threat they could not endure, so perfectly did her free-spirited, bra-less breasts mould its soft weave to a daringly display of her ravishingly hard nipples. 'Clifford is not as you wickedly call him a *pisser*, a *shit*, Monsieur Taylor! What vulgar manners you have for one so very young, though better I think than Monsieur Hussey and Lomas, whose intemperance is a byword for stupidity, but is our very own *Léandre*. You have heard the story, n'est-ce pas?' His blank face told he hadn't! 'A beautiful, unhappy boy trapped in a body not yet grown to all it will be; will surely one day be, if time and circumstances are kind to him, as I am sure they will be,' she purred, her much changed version of that ancient French fairy-tale, her long, delicate fingers gently stroking the side of his deep scarred face in a caress, the pink nickered Ronnie, seated barely a foot away from him almost gagged to see; did.

'*Miss,*' she groaned, puckering her very pretty, red lipped, peach powdered face into a disgusted sneer of unbearable contempt for the boy that ignored she knew him almost as well as Hilda and Fay did; better, being a close neighbour of his and once rather liked him, was sorry for him.

'A boy who even now, if you had eyes to see, *mes petite enfants*, begins to throw off *Furibon's* evil spell and when it is gone, you will see how beautiful he truly is,' she teased, her eyes searching, Ronnie's horrified, disbelieving face for the least sign she understood his skin would soon clear of the horribly swollen pimples and black heads that plagued him like a goblin's curse and when it had, and he had grown a half foot taller than he now was, how tall and handsome he would be. Taller and so much more handsome than even, Tinker was, who she had to admit was handsome. Because if truth be told he was a very pretty boy indeed beneath his scars and the weighty troubles he endured with such a pleasant good humour. But she saw nothing in her face, but her silly, unthinking, bitter spite as she crouched down beside him once again. Her impossibly tight skirt, now rising to her black-stockinged, mid-thigh in a sensual, eye watering spectacle no boy in the room could ignore. Except for Hussey and Lomas, who were as queer as dogs without a bark, though no one knew they were, except for Hilda, Fay and Greta who watched their games with a knowing eye and knew what cowards they were.

'*Miss,*' gagged Ronnie a second time, turning as she did to her two best friends in all the world since last September when they so unexpectedly made her the friend she had so longed to be, the magnificently breasted, she was green with envy, raven haired, Judy who looked just like Sophia Loren, in the film *Houseboat,* and the ash blonde, bob-cut-like-a-page-boy, but so fabulously sexy, Gerry, who was Judy's best friend since they were little girls. Who just then stretched her long, shapely leg beneath her desk to kick Cocky in his growing ever sorer, testicles, but missed him by an inch and painfully banged her shin on its sharp edge with a squeal that became a wincing, distracting laugh her two friends giggled and minced to hear?

'Please Miss, can I sit down,' grimaced Clifford, his cringing embarrassment as great as the silence that had fallen so suddenly upon the class. 'Please can I sit down, miss?' He begged.

'Miss?' Whispered Valeria, in a gentle scold, her forehead pressed to his in a fondness every bit as big as her heart. A heart that knew how much he suffered at home and in that awful school, so full of swanking, self-regarding tyrants she could not believe it could be like this, but allowed it was under the mistaken, outdated, truly British belief, it made men and women of children in the fashion it made them; what a stupid medieval race they were; so pompous and so bourgeoisie.

'Sorry Madame.'

'Accepted, now, scoot my petit Léandre, she insisted, as she once again stood to face her misguided class. 'Now, turn your books to chapter six,' she clapped. 'Page forty-eight. Dialogue two: On acheter des vêtements. Repeat, on acheter des vêtements. Shopping for clothes! Lomas you may follow my lead. You will play the part of Mary, a young girl out shopping for clothes. A blouse perhaps, or a short skirt,' she teased, 'in your wonderful *Marks and Spencers,* or *Browns*, which I have come to like so very much since I came to

England. So very like our own, *Le Bon Marché* in the Rue de Sevres, though not as big perhaps, but not I think, the equal of our most famous of French couturiers, those you will find on the Rue du Faubourg Saint-Honoré, the Avenue Montaigne, or the Champs-Élysées. La plus belle avenue du monde,' she wistfully sighed. 'How I miss them! The trees, la cabinet de verdure, the light, the colour, the people, the shops, the cafes; Fouquet's? Oh, Fouquet's, très chic,' she wistfully smiled.

'Très what?' Cursed Gerry, in an irritated slouch that hugged her sore leg tight to her chest in a thoroughly unladylike grimace of pain that flushed her pretty face to a look of such frightening spite, Cocky blanched to see it so vengefully turned on him; but why? He asked himself.

*

'C*hick,'* whispered Judy with a smirk of condescension that knew she said it wrong. Knew exactly how to say it, but didn't care she did, because she *hated* Madame Valeria Doucet in that peculiar and impossibly contradictory way, hate so often expresses the deeply frustrated love we feel for those we most admire; most want to admire us in return; whose desire we desire. And there was no one in the world she admired more than Valeria, except, perhaps, the ravishing, if innocently sweet, Persephone Langford; but would never hint she did, not to anyone.

Her natural, effortless beauty, which instantly reminded her of the French actress, Mylène Demongeot, in the film

Bonjour Tristesse, though she much preferred the stunning Jean Seberg with her boyish short hair, which she and her mum, most unusually for her, went to see at the Odeon on the Town Hall square last year, though her legs were much better than hers, so long and so shapely, she wanted to scream with jealous rage they were. Looked so good in stockings and without. Her makeup, which she wore better than anyone she knew; better even than Colin Hussey's stunning mum, Gloria, who was such a scandalous witch, better even than Barbara Archer, Dylan Lloyd-Thomas's grumpy wife, who was still a looker, despite she was forty and better by far than Carol Paget, who copied every trend in *Honey* magazine, down to the hideous three shades of eye shadow she now wore. But though she did, she did at least try to make something of herself, not like that loony old crackpot, Pauline Fisk, who put her makeup on with a trowel, like so many old women did; didn't they know what fucking idiots they looked like with it plastered on like that. But not Valeria, she smiled, she got it just right.

Her fire engine red lips and neatly manicured, red nails, her smoky black eyeshadow and coal-black lashes and razor liner, which made her blue eyes so much bluer than they truly were, which she turned at the end in the merest hint of the Italian, feline flick, she now copied. So much better than the Loren-like sweeping flash she had previously worn. All of which made her look so sexy, glamorous and understated, not a bit like the acid faced bitch, Gloria Hussey did.

Her blonde hair, which she wore short to her shoulders without fuss, sometimes pinned in girlish plaits, or in chignon, but this morning loosely tied with a thin red ribbon, the tails of which hung to her swan-like neck in dancing wisps as if she meant they should. Her thin gold necklace, which she often played with, her earrings, pearl, emerald, ruby and diamond studs, gold hoops so big they almost touched her chin and a deliciously erotic pair that looked like sabres, which curved halfway down her neck. Her perfume which smelt of summer flowers, which even now, despite the sweaty smell of shower damp boys all around her, softly caressed her nose in an enchanting bouquet she longed to ask its name, but never would, so hard had she set her heart against her. Her clothes, which were always so *chic* and so expensively elegant, yet so young and so irresistibly fashionable; her trademark pencil skirts so tight around her slim bottom and even slimmer waist; her always stylish tops which hugged her breasts in such a daringly natural way, like, the to-die-for, pink, cashmere cardigan she now wore, as if they were made just for her. Her high heeled shoes, the peep toed pair she now had on, which she adored better than any other pair, which she wore with such a cool confidence they seemed to be part of her.

But most of all she admired Valeria's courage. A courage, no less than Greta's that would not be bullied by anyone, least of all Hussey and Lomas, but Casterbrook and Cod-Eye, too, vile and despicable men who both wilted under her steadfast gaze. But hated it was wasted on the likes of Clifford Cocky Robin, who she appeared to like as no one else did, accept Hilda, Fay and that deranged monster, Greta, and made such a pet of him, protecting him in every way she could from the cruel tongues that even now spat their spite at him as she stood to let him go.

'Miss,' wheedled Lomas, trying to distract her in a huff of irritation that hoped she would find someone else to read his part if he loudly banged, fussed and bleated behind the upturned lid of his desk a minute longer than he already had. But time enough, as she knew it was, for Valeria to see Clifford safe to his seat besides, Hilda, before the mocking calls of *Léandre* rose to more than the half-hearted, silly chant they now were. A name she should never have called him, a name that would stick to him like glue, but better than Cocky, which most everyone called him. Though not Hilda, not once, not ever, who smiled to see him find her side.

A girl she resolutely believed was as mad-as–a-hatter, though not frighteningly mad as Greta was, a girl who, she dared not admit, scared her stiff, though she carelessly pretended she didn't, with her hard staring eyes and scary weird ways and no one knowing who she was or where she came from; a loner who went her own way and asked no one's permission she did.

But by comparison Hilda was a childish, dreamy simpleton, whose deaf-to-any-insult, know-best, couldn't-care-less, rather pretty, pointed ears, never seemed to hear anything but her own sweet voice, which once set in dreary motion had the power to dull her mind to a blank. A girl Cocky had known since nursery, as he had known Greta, as he had known *her,* Gerry and Ronnie from mad Mrs Scullion's nursery school and *her,* perhaps better than any of the others back then. Her dad being a friend from the end of the war of his step-mum and that fat pimp of hers, Clooney Barron, until he died. The two of them often visiting his home, sometimes twice a week, her father to noisily shag his step-mum upstairs, a five-shilling whore as everyone knew she was, she to play with Cocky in the overgrown back garden like they didn't know what they were doing and Clooney taking the money in the narrow kitchen where he always sat beside the washing boiler, the gas flame warming his legs and always with that silly grin fixed like wax on his fleshy, red face like it was something to be proud of. And touching her like no one should touch a little girl, if he got half a chance, and Cocky, too, but not in the same way, pinching and punching him to make him cry and smiling with pleasure he did. Had liked him back then; liked him quite a lot, but not anymore. Because he always reminded her of her own wretched life, which, few if any, except, Gerry, knew was every bit as bad as his back then, but could have been so much worse had her mother not left her father when she did.

A drunken, hateful bully, a gambling, no good, chiselling wastrel who too long abused her before, she did, but too late to be forgiven, she didn't leave him so much sooner than she did. No, she hated Cocky for every memory he brought of that awful time, but most of all hated him for the stupid, heart rending looks he sometimes gave her, like she could somehow put things, right? Perhaps hated him more than Hussey and Lomas, did? Who hated him because they were big enough and stupid enough to hate anyone they wanted, too and for the moment they hated him most of all, though Tinker not much less, who was a retard to think they liked him? Hated Cocky because he was vile and repugnant as she would never be. Not now she had grown to be the woman, she was. But a woman better than any man would ever have! Though she saw in their greedy eyes they wanted her; Casterbrook, because he liked anyone in a skirt, as so many men do and Dylan Lloyd Thomas because he thought he could have any woman just for the asking and more fool them for believing the twaddle that gushed from his pretty mouth.

Clooney Barron, she inwardly sighed, as Lomas angrily spluttered the first words of the French text he could barely read, would never be able to read, try as he might, 'Où sont les vêtements pour enfants, s'il vous plait, Madame,' he vainly tried, tripping on every syllable in a flush of embarrassment he couldn't hide. The memory of that awful man sending a cold shiver of fear down her spine far worse than the fierce cold that now frosted the windows behind Valeria in an iridescent sheen made beguiling by the slanted blur of snow that fell in such a strangely hypnotic pelt the world outside was transformed into a ghostly wraith of shimmering light and fleeting shadows, that in the oddest way conspired to trick her eye it was something else; *Narnia* she mused, the smile light on her lips. A place she loved in the series of books by C S Lewis, she adored, imagined herself to be *Susan; Queen Lucy the Gentle,* who loved *Prince Caspian*.

A modern day *Fagin* by any estimation of that callous, *Dickensian* crook, who from his corner eerie in the bar of The Highfield Public House, barely half a mile from where she, Ronnie and Cocky lived, in one direction and Gerry in the other, and never without his saffron yellow cigarette-holder dangling a lighted cigarette from his pugnacious little mouth, or his tan-brown, grease stained, moth nibbled trilby fixed tight on his sweating bald head, or his heavy brown overcoat on his broad back, ran a small, but highly profitable criminal enterprise. Part fence, tout, pimp and bookies runner, it was a place like nowhere Valeria Doucet went inside, but why should she? Men loved her and would protect her as no man loved or protected her. Her mind so full of romantic claptrap her classroom was a shrine to the France she had left behind.

Chapter 11

Monday December 17, 1962
Django Reinhardt: 1946 Jazz Version of La Marseillaise

A classroom pinned, pasted, hung and draped with a clutter of colourful French bric-a-brac, she thought a fitting compliment to her much loved and greatly missed country, a fitting compliment to the children she tried to teach and inspire better than Arno de Roy ever could; ever bothered.

A tricolour flag – two in fact, if you counted the neatly ironed flag that draped the Maplewood bookcase that stood at the back of the classroom between the window and the quarter open door to the storeroom. The other, a majestic thing that hung from a brass coronated, wooden pole beside her chair, its foot planted in a blue bucket of smooth stones she got from the banks of the river she often walked beside; though her mind too often drifted back to another, she far better loved. A photograph of her much loved, General Charles de Gaulle, who she had passionately supported since the 1958 colonial coup d'état forced the end of the

Fourth Republic she so much despised, though her mother, a lifelong communist when it suited her, hated him with a fierce resolve, whose uncompromising face now surveyed the growing fidgety backs of her noisily braying charges with the grand hauteur he reserved for everything British.

A dull black, thoroughly rusted on its every bit of once gleaming chrome, step-through, sit-up-and-beg, 1934, *Humber* ladies bicycle, its fiercely hard, buttock worn by a thousand cheeks, gnarled at the edges, nut brown leather seat, handlebars and bashed and broken wicker basket draped in a cliché of knotted onions she had several times thought to remove, but could never reach, because it was suspended by taut wires from the impossibly high ceiling by her careless, briefly sometime lover of recent weeks, Dylan Lloyd-Thomas. If sex just twice in the last month, or was it even longer than that? She idly wondered, was enough to call him the lover he so obviously thought he was. She had hoped he might have been, if only for the little while she was in England, though perhaps, she smiled, the second time, didn't altogether count, he is being too drunk on beer and truculent self-remorse to do more than grunt and push himself into her. And she, she laughed she had been so wicked, deliberately less ardent than she might have been after the hot, deliciously therapeutic, soapy bath she had too much enjoyed before they met. Where she so *trafficked with herself alone,* as Shakespeare's sensuously explicit sonnet, *Unthrifty loveliness,* (not his best) was wanting to put the sin of Onanism, she had little else to give him, but her body. A vessel for his lovemaking, though he hardly seemed to notice she did, and then only sparingly and with barely a hint of flesh beneath her ballerina, black pleated skirt. A pleasure too much enjoyed by men, but too little encouraged in women who better know how to use their bodies than they can ever know and to such a marvellously erotic transport of the soul it is a wonder they put themselves to the bother of having sex with men at all?

The tall, muscularly strong, roguishly handsome, unquestionably charming when his soft Welsh brogue whispered so deliciously and so rudely in her ear, who was the school's oil grimed beneath his fingernails, metal work teacher. Though in no possible way could Dylan be described as the earnest, downtrodden, though invariably inspiring artisan of either Zola's, Balzac's or Flaubert fond ideal; no, he was a man far to cock sure of himself for anyone like that.

A man who boasted he had been shagging her brains out for a month better than any man she ever had, a delusion that knew nothing of her life, or even how to make a woman happy. A man whose teasing, one sided, exquisitely tormenting, rough and sordid sex, a sex he seemed to so much enjoy, she found a paradox of darkly mysterious dread and deliciously exquisite, all too guilty, pleasure. Because, he was, for the moment still married to the po-faced, but very lovely, if prematurely grey and lustrously pony-tailed in the fashion of a youthful, Brigitte Bardot, in the 1956 film *Doctor at Sea,* Miss Archer. The schools exceptionally gifted, she had been more than once told, Head of History. A diminutive lady – she was barely five feet four inches tall in three-inch heels, but as curvaceous as Bardot in a dress size too small for her ambitious curves and provocatively daring décolletage, he said, was about to divorce him.

*

A Freudian paradox, as she knew it was and of truly nightmarish proportions – and she had lost a lot of sleep thinking about that man's strange behaviour in the last few weeks of their separation, that in the broadest sweep of her clever, ever thoughtful, deeply trusting mind she knew, or perhaps believed she knew, was no more than the libidinous expression of the conflicting emotions she had so darkly felt since her husband, Étienne's tragic death, earlier that year. Felt even before his death, so difficult had their ill-tempered, ill-suited marriage always been.

A death that had brought her back to England, her post war home in a rash and careless hurry she thought both an escape and a refuge from the heartache which had so suddenly and so painfully overtaken her life, despite she left behind a home and friends in Paris she loved, though thankfully not forever, she now realised; AA had convinced her of that. Though he would be surprised to hear her say he had. After all, she still had her little apartment in the Square de la Tour-Maubourg near the Esplanade des Invalides and with a lovely view of the Jardin de l'eglise Evangélique Luthérienne, St Jean from her back bedroom window, which sang with birds in spring and summer and looked so beautiful, as it would now, with the snow heavy on the ground. And, of course, she still had the house in Chartres her aunt had left her when she died, which Madeleine so jealously hated she had. England a country she had not seen since the winter of 1949, not even visited for a holiday though she so often thought she might, a place where she had once been carefree and oh so very happy, as she never was truly happy again!

A death she absurdly thought was her fault; perhaps it was in some wished for way, as her mother harshly hinted it was, as she always did when sibling rivalry made her the easy scapegoat for Madeleine's cruel behaviour, behaviour she all her life found every reason to excuse. Though the policeman who came to her door said he was drunk, as he often was, and driving too fast on roads he didn't know and too late at night to see the sharply turning bend in the road ahead.

A paradox that was no more than her wretched, inner struggle to find a new beginning in her life. A new and better life for herself after the death and betrayal she had too much endured on her own. To find again the happiness she once knew. Had taken for granted was hers by some divine right and in that happiness ease the pain that was now the constant ache in her heart. But more than this, to free herself of the anger, disappointment, guilt and bitter self-reproach that was her constant companion. To know again the pride and joy she once had in herself. The young, talented, self-confident and *pretty* woman she knew she was and not the shame and humiliation that was her bête noire. She was, after all, still only twenty-six and with a life to lead.

And all of this quietly seething emotional turmoil caught up in the maelstrom of petty social pretensions, aggressive back biting and jealousies that characterised the cartoon characters who were her greatly despised colleagues at The Love Street Secondary Modern School for Boys and Girls. But no less surreal and unsettling, was caught up in Dylan's rough and demanding arms, a man who cared for no one, but himself. An idea so preposterous, she smiled it was. A surprisingly petulant, she was shocked and astonished to learn, moody, and hurtful lover, she didn't much care for, as a woman should care for a man she had so willingly and with such a shameless relish, given herself, too. Submitted herself, too with such a desperate, clinging passion it still shocked and surprised her she had, and would again, and very soon, but though she disliked him, desired him in that irrational, almost primordial way that desire imposes itself upon us all, but perhaps more so on a woman who has been hurt by the man she loved. And hurt so terribly she could find no way to forgive him or her sister, his lover.

But it was not the idealised desire of romantic fiction women so adore, that kept her awake at night, that she adored to read, and Carol Paget too much loved, with her head forever stuck in one those soppy, but oddly addictive, *Mills & Boon* novels she every lunchtime read at her ever so tidy desk, with their twee and clichéd, ever so happy endings - and no one wrote better romantic fiction than the English. Who though they do, are a coldly calculating, sexually repressed and unromantic race of bourgeoisie, more so than even their American cousins, who are their cultural slaves, their moody and unforgiving prodigy? But was a desire far, darker than this.

Far, far darker than the romantic love of Jane Austen's,

Regency heroines, her overly pleased with herself, *Elizabeth Bennet,* her childishly controlling, *Emma Woodhouse,* or her self-denying, *Elinor Dashwood.* Darker, too than Charlotte Bronte's rather wonderfully independent, if morally chaste and demanding, *Jane Eyre,* all of them naïve and delightfully preposterous virgins. But it was, perhaps, Flaubert's, *Madame Bovary,* a favourite of hers since she was fifteen, who came closest to what she understood by the absurd desire she felt for Dylan. As did Emily Bronte's, *Catherine Earnshaw,* whose tempestuous love for the monstrous *Heathcliff* was a necessary, if inconsolable torture, someone she could never have, but ached with desire to have. As she could never have, Pascal, her first and only love; a love she all to easily betrayed.

An irrationally destructive, empty and painful desire for him that would never know a happy ending that in the darkest margins of her unconscious mind, knew he was unworthy of her, as she, perhaps, knew she was unworthy of him - though she would never admit she was. A man who hid his troubles beneath the bright veneer of his brash self-confidence, a man no less tormented than she was by a past he had yet to resolve; perhaps never would resolve. In his case, and wasn't it always the case with men, a maze-like Freudian circumlocution of Oedipal complexity, a mother he once loved and adored he now thought a tart for what she had done to survive an imprisonment too awful to imagine; too awful to bear. As many women in war did.

Her mother included, and tens of thousands other French women, she had only recently read, who, like her, too much enjoyed her *horizontal war* with the German

High Command in Saint Germain en Laye to pretend she was anything but the woman she was. A courtesan and an expensive one at that. Though never as indiscreet as the infamous Madame Fabienne Jamet, who boasted she loved the Germans better than she loved the French, and nothing remotely like the unfortunate *femmes tondues* whose *Anées Erotiques* ended in such shame and bitter recrimination. And with guile and sophistication enough to tell her and Madeleine she did it for France, though the meaning of that once and only once, spoken remark was never explained to them.

But then, he was drunk last Thursday night when he opened his heart to her and feeling so bitter and so sorry for himself, he knew no better than to blame his mother for the misfortunes he now felt so deeply, though, perhaps she was unwise to have behaved as she did in that horrible place. So sorry for himself she all too easily forgave him he had been so mean and vile to her during those last few weeks they had been apart and hurt her more than she could say since they first made love and let him love her again as she promised she never would. Each as weak and recklessly tormented as the other in their desire, just as Zola's, *Thérèse Raquin* and her lover, the dissolute and conniving *Laurent* were tormented in theirs. A guilty, empty desire that destroyed them both in the end as desire always does. As it might yet destroy the both of them!

A Lacanian desire - she had yet to realise it was, shot through with ambiguity and dark perplexity that found no hint of meaning in her recent past, as she thought it must. The tragic death of the husband she no longer loved, or cared she ever did, the betrayal of her sister or the selfish stupidity of her mother, nor was it to be found in the conflicting, often irrational emotions those thoughts so easily and so often brought to the surface of her conscious mind or troubled her dreams with their pastiche of frightening images. But rather it was a desire played out in the theatre of her unconscious mind, that dark, unrevealed place of long forgotten memories, that turbulent sea of powerful, unrequited emotion, the players, their features beguilingly familiar, yet masked like actors in a Greek tragedy and with a chorus of background voices, which variously triumphed, mourned or ridiculed her failure to understand the meaning of what they, so puzzlingly said. Desire, which like all desire, compelled her irrationally and dangerously towards the object of her desires; Dylan, it would now seem, though it could have been another just as well, whose hurtful embrace was the answer to the mystery that confounded her. The uncovering of some hurt so long hidden she no longer remembered it in any detail, would never remember it without his help. Because all desire has a hidden meaning that impels us towards the object of our desire. An emotionally charged beginning we have come to repress but must one day remember if we are to resolve the painful secrets it has to tell.

Because the object of desire never satisfies nor ever fulfils, as we think it will - there is never enough cake to eat or wine to drink, or recognition or admiration to receive, or lovers to love us, but ever demands more of the same because it feeds on a longing that is inexpressibly lost. Something symbolised, often perversely so, in the object of our desire.

A loss that can only be found — if found it can be? In the deepest recesses of our unconscious minds, minds, which are the well spring of all we are and ever will be our happiness and our unhappiness. A bottomless, seemingly impenetrable space that is as old as time and as big as the universe we inhabit — is truly the entirety of the universe we inhabit, which speaks to us, not of this, our present life, but of the many past lives we have lived and might yet live again; where all the pain and pleasure we feel has its roots in memories that are, but a fleeting dream; a wisp of recollection.

A desire which had twice hurried her into the sumptuous back of his 1954, beautifully maintained - as only a dedicated and talented mechanic like him could maintain a car in its factory new perfection, exorbitantly roomy, always gleaming, white-walled — as all Americans apparently like their tyres, *Vauxhall Velox,* motor car. Though the second time, a sympathy fuck was really no more satisfying than the first; do the Chinese really fuck like that, as he fucked her then barely taking her knickers off? She wondered, doubting they did and thinking she must ask, AA, who must surely know, though how she would slip that tantalising question into one of their many delightful conversations she hardly dared imagine, as she remembered again the deliciously erotic tale Dylan had told her of the beautiful Chinese woman in the red bikini who had seduced him on a secluded beach on the island of Cheung Chau, barely an hour's ferry boat ride from Hong Kong, where he was stationed, to the sound of the crashing surf behind them. The same island, coincidentally — and it was the most extraordinary coincidence, AA bought his twelve original Chinese *GongBi* painting she so admired. A lie she was sure, but so erotic it still made her blush and why not, if that's all it was?

An impossibly exotic image, which instantly brought to mind the sight of Deborah Kerr and Burt Lancaster in that memorably iconic love scene they played so effortlessly well together in the 1953 film, *From Here to Eternity*. Though she much preferred Frank Sinatra's private *Angelo Maggio* and *Montgomery Clift's, Prewitt,* to Lancaster's bullying *Sergeant Warden*. But no sooner had she conjured that perfect image than she saw another, this time the beautiful, Jennifer Hughes in the 1955 film, *Love is a Many-Splendored Thing* with the gorgeous William Holden playing the part of her lover, which like Dylan's story of conquest was set-in postwar Hong Kong. Holden so handsome, so debonair and so troubled by their adultery and Hughes so ravishingly exotic in the colourful, silk Cheongsam dresses she wore, her lustrous black hair draped to her shoulders in gentle twists. Then, by the same ingenious elision she remembered she first saw her playing *Madame Bovary* in the 1949 film adaptation of the novel of the same name, and so perfectly chosen for the part she dreamed she might be her.

Was that she wondered? Why she so easily agreed to have sex with him that second time, because she imagined herself to be, *Emma Bovary* and agreed without the demure to his entrez par derrière, as he quietly insisted he must, though not, as he had tried before; a painful sodomy she had fiercely resisted, but almost surrendered, too, so much had she wanted him that time? Some mental acrobatics that thought *she* was *her* and *he* was *Rodolphe,* or perhaps Louis Jourdan, who so looked like, Étienne, who never wanted her that way, nor any other man before him? A submission she detested and would never agree again. An empty, hollow thing, no matter how it is done, for any woman to endure, the Homeric Greeks, long ago named for what it is; *parthenos adamatos,* the virgin (taken, but not) conquered. The taking of a woman, though she does so out of fear, or *dutifully* submits as a lover or a wife without care for her pleasure, without care for her, and because she is, is not taken at all, but is a figment of his imagination.

Something that excited Dylan, as much as it left her cold, though she was certain he could be taught a better way, taught to know how to love a woman better than he clearly so little did. Today she hoped, if he would allow himself the woman's instruction he so needed and who better to teach him than her, she smiled at her reckless vanity, and why not? he owed her a *treat*. And a *treat* she would have! Something Barbara, his surprisingly three times married wife had so far failed to tutor him in their loveless and apparently soon to ended, unhappy marriage, if she had her way. Yes, she would show him everything he must know to love and fulfil a woman as he should, as any woman would want him, too, if he would only let her.

A giddy, irresponsible idea, as she knew it was, that instantly took her now utterly distracted eye to the far corner of her class and the store room door, which now stood two inches ajar on its white painted, heavy wooden jam, so pointlessly large and so utterly strong, as all the doors in her classroom were, it would admit no one without a key. Its sharp edged, aperture of black hinting the pleasure she so wanted and would soon find in its cluttered space. Her mind conjuring the image of Caraglio's, *Herse* lying naked on the end of a bed, her sister, *Aglaulos* forced beneath the dark slash of her satiated vagina by her lover, *Mercury* to see she was.

A Freudian imagining, as she once again preposterously knew it was, as so many of her thoughts and dreams of her sister were, of her jealously humbled beneath her, as she longed it one day would be, she coyly smiled, as her eyes danced over her still shower wet, red faced, watching class to where Lomas waited her reply, his face a hollow smile. A class so tedious she longed for it to end, so uncaring were they of everything she had done to make their lessons a treat. Making a picture postcard of her classroom, a place so unlike any other place in that horrid, parochial school! That horrid, empty annex, she wondered why she bothered so little did they.

A smile that instinctively found Clifford, now safe in his seat besides, Hilda, but looking at her in that oddly knowing, intuitive way, he often did, as if he could read her deepest thoughts, a sympathy she found difficult to comprehend as if his heart knew what she longed to say!

'Oui, madame,' she cooed, back at him, her voice a mischief, 'alors, nous avons des anoraks de toutes les tailles et de toutes les couleurs, est-ce que la fillette préfère un anorak bleu, rouge ou vert?' Her eyes turned from his dark eyes to her classroom, which gave her so much joy.

Chapter 12

Monday December 17, 1962
Françoise Hardy: Oh, Oh Chéri

A picture postcard, which had as its centre piece the battered, but still intact front bumper and grill of her once much loved, but now two months gone to the scrap yard on Bumpers Lane, red, 1957 *Citroën 2 CV,* which had carried her around the streets of Paris since her graduation and on a hundred holiday weekends since then, which sat beneath her chalkboard like Marcel Duchamp's, *Fountain* to provoke, tease and frustrate anyone who saw it. And no one was provoked, teased and frustrated by her surrealist sculpture more than Arno, Casterbrook and Mr Eldred, who individually and collectively hated it and daily planned its removal.

Which was the result of an accidental shunt on one of those impossibly stupid roundabouts the British so love and yet always drive around like bat-blind, bloody idiots, it's a wonder there are not more accidents like hers. An accident that wasn't her fault, no matter the frowning policeman said it was and with a magistrates summons through the post last month that cost her five pounds and eight shillings in fines and costs, she hated she had to pay; thought she might appeal to some higher court but hadn't. Which shrine-like to its fond memory pointed its two upright chevrons to a lesson in French grammar only last Friday done and now entirely forgotten by those who did it. So utterly defeated were the children she taught in this god-awful school the *Fates* in their infinite wisdom had sent her too, she wondered what they planned for her next, some of them so socially, morally and intellectually retarded they cared nothing for the language she loved and taught so well; cared for nothing but their fun and games.

Endlessly trying to distract her with their mischief, sometimes playful, but mostly sly, vulgar and often painfully offensive, as Hussey and Lomas always were, who watched her now with their menacing, hard staring eyes. Other times just prankish, silly and so stupidly immature their constant attention seeking interruptions and their endless talk of last week's episode of *Maigret,* a boring, growing tedious irritation, and in an exaggerated, sometimes quite funny mimic of her French accent she found herself laughing, despite it was their cue to taunt her all the more.

The *Fates,* she smiled, determined to make the best of the next forty-five minutes, despite, Hussey hawked his throat like a pig behind her back as she walked to the window and spat, she was almost certain. he did, his filth into his desk, and Lomas, nervously smirked and giggled his reply. *Clotho,* the spinner of life's thread, *Lachesis* who measures its length and *Atropos* who cuts it. Who since she first read of them in Plato's *Republic* during that first, rather lonely term she spent at the Sorbonne in 1954 she had come to accept with a conviction that was unshakeable? Believing her life was Fated, as all lives are, despite she might wish it otherwise, as even Sartre came to believe his was. Confessing to Simone de Beauvoir he was, *not mere dust, but expected in the world,* something, AA chuckled to hear. And why not it was an extraordinary thing for him say, a man whose trademark, existential, steadfast communist beliefs asserted the distinctly atheist doctrine, *there is no essence before existence,* that we pre-exist any label or story others may attach to us; that, *we are left alone [in the world], without excuse.*

That our lives have a purpose of sorts, no matter how futile they may appear to be, we must accept and try to understand. A purpose that is not a reward or a punishment, as religion would have us believe, as she was told they were, but chosen by each of us before we are born, perhaps as a challenge we commit ourselves too, never knowing how and when it will end as end it will?

A simple belief in metaphysical otherworldliness, and she knew it was, and was often teased it was, that had its tentative first beginning when she read Robert Graves, *The White Goddess* in 1947. A Christmas present from her mother when they lived in London just after the war; did until 1949, she carelessly chose for its evocative, perhaps sensuous title, thinking it a fairy tale for her clumsy, still childishly naïve, eleven-year-old daughter, rather than the complex poetic work it was; which mostly confused her! But though it did, it contained the germ of an idea, one so new and liberating to her in the harsh tedium of those post war years she wondered she had never thought of it before: God is Woman! Or, more precisely, God was Woman, until the God of Judaeo-Christian belief replaced her with the man it insisted, *He* must be.

And if God is woman, the essence of all that is good, then man is evil! And with this startling realisation came an even more remarkable idea, one she artfully, if pretentiously called the wisdom of the White Goddess: Woman is the Soul of Creation, Man the Flesh of *Her* Corruption!

A wisdom that so violently clashed with her relatively strict Catholic upbringing, she felt giddy with excitement for weeks afterwards. A giddiness that didn't go unnoticed by Madeleine or her form mistress at her very English school, which then, as now, enfeebled, infantilised and stigmatised women to believe they were inherently inferior to men; but worse, bad by some measure of their own crass stupidity. Bad, she rightly supposed, because they are a temptation too much for them to resist, as resist they must if they are to keep faith with their patriarchal God. But it was an idea that resonated with her dreadful experience of the recent war in France, a war of men! A war conceived by men and fought by men with the most violently obscene brutality imaginable: a self-deceiving vanity careless of the good of others that was truly evil. A brutality no woman would ever knowingly inflict on another woman, no less a man.

But more than this, it was the book that first introduced her to the myths, legends and folklore she now so loved to read, as Robert Graves, perhaps hoped it would, if not the Celtic stories of his poetic imagination. Stories of gods and heroes, demons and monsters, the sacred and the profane, of love thwarted and love triumphed, of elfin and fairy folk, of witches, seers, hags and harlots, of sacred stones and sacred places, of tabooed things now turned to oppressive law, of nature's healing magic, of minstrels, poets, bards and balladeers and times and people so long gone they are now nearly forgotten. But more than just forgotten, derided for their beliefs, customs and understanding of the world as it was known to them, then. Their inspired truths, wisdom, poetry and magic recast as immature, rural foolishness we are better off without.

When it is so much more! The echoes of a truth that lie beyond the rational and the empirical science asserts is the only way to know the world we live in, that can only be grasped by the imaginative and the intuitive part of our unconscious minds. The ineffable, as the English writer, C S Lewis, a contemporary of Robert Graves, came to realise it was, as his friend J R R Tolkien knew it was, for something suggested rather than known, and though it is, is glimpsed in art, literature, poetry and beauty. A longing for longing, he called it – desire by any other name we experience as nostalgia we are not all we think we are as others assert, we are, but something so much more. But though we are, are stranded, wandering as if lost in the life we live.

Stories that opened her mind to the idea the world was never before as it was then. Thought, believed or behaved as it did then, as few of us realise or care to know it didn't.

A time before global religions, global political economies, science, industry, mass media, mass culture and the vast urban colonies of people we have now become. A world we can only imagine.

And in the grumpy, melancholic, horribly rationed gloom of that cynically broken, post war Britain, when she never ate a meal she liked or ate enough of, or wore a dress or coat that fitted her fast growing body, that didn't make her look like the refugee she and her family had become, there were a thousand other places in the world she would rather have been than in the echoing hollow of their shabby rooms in Stanhope Gardens; and often dreamed the day away, she was.

Though it was dreams of the *Famous Five*, which captivated her imagination most back then, not *The White Goddess,* though *she* quietly weaved her magic spell on her, as did Tolkien's, *The Hobbit,* which she adored*,* a fantasy so different from Enid Blyton's jolly adventures, and so cleverly written, she really did come to believe there was a time between the *Dawn of Færie* and the *Dominion of Men.* That Tolkien knew there was in that intuitive way some of us do and others, most others, think an infantile *phantasy.* A book she bought for one shilling and six pence from a market stall on the Portobello Road one Saturday afternoon when her mother was gone away for the weekend. As she so often did with a handsome man who had a petrol ration to carry her off to some country place where she could be wined, dined and fucked to her heart's content and no woman liked to be fucked better than her. And with so little concern for how she and Madeleine would cope on their own and with so little care for their safety, which she just assumed they would be! And Hans Christian Anderson, of course, *The Snow Queen, The Little Mermaid* or best of all his, *Ugly Duckling,* which now so reminded her of Clifford, hoped it would be like that for him. Or the collected fairy tales of the brothers Grimm, which she knew Carol Paget adored in that immature way she did as if they were *real.* But why not, they were enchanting in every way a children's story should be, particularly, their retelling of *Cinderella,* a story as old as time of unjust oppression triumphing over evil, as is their, *Snow White?*

But not as enchanting as *The Arabian Nights*, which she read in French by J C Mardrus, because her mother insisted, she must, because she was becoming, too English. And because she was, and she didn't want to be, *too English,* whatever that meant? As if a French girl could; would want to be? She read again the stories of her early childhood, *The Story of Blondine, Bonne-Riche and Beau-Minon, The Little Grey Mouse, Princess Rosette, The Lost Children, The Little Prince* and many others besides, though they were far too young for her by then, though like Carol she never tired of them. Not least *Le Prince Lutin* by Marie Catherine d'Aulnoy, the story of the handsome *Léandre,* a tender-hearted boy turned into an imp and the evil *Furibon* who was the cause of it, though she much preferred her own version. Which like the *Ugly Duckling,* had the most perfect ending, as all fairy stories should, she smiled? Her eyes instinctively finding Clifford's, who returned her gentle look with a blushing, tender smile of his own, a smile that would come in all its sad innocence to haunt her in the coming days of fear and pain.

Perhaps all children think the same when they are very young? Believe in magic, fairies, witches, goblins, Hobbits, pixies, elves and, of course, talking animals? She asked herself, knowing they did, her eyes turned to the shaft of bright sun light that fell on the river to her right and the trio of swans it found. One, its long, sinuous, muscular neck arched to its full height, its angry, outstretched wings flapping a warning to a rival, she supposed, who had strayed too close to his mate, who circled them as if wanting them to fight. An oddly captivating sight in the swirl of snow and haze of purple shadows that caught them, that brought to mind the seduction of *Leda* by *Zeus,* who came to her disguised as a swan, and the birth of *Helen of Troy,* their daughter, who dominates Greek mythology, as perhaps no other woman does. A beauty without equal brought to ruin by the guile and faithless cruelty of men, not least *Zeus,* her father. Both she and *Paris* utterly deceived by the shallow sensual desire that consumed them both.

An explicitly sexual, if highly clichéd erotic symbol in art that not only spoke to her of her irrational want for Dylan, who longed to make a whore of her, but reminded her, too of the paintings of Correggio's famous depiction of that classical scene, though both Bos and Rubens did it better, *Leda's* surrender to the *Zeus* so complete there is little room to doubt their meaning.

A favourite device, too, of the symbolist poets her husband Étienne tried so hard to emulate, but never succeeded, Mallarmé's tragic, *Le Cygne,* being the measure of all he ever wanted to be. Obscure to the point of obfuscation, though she never said it was. The symbolist poets, though they tried, never achieving in words what art and music can so easily and so exquisitely express.

But the idea of otherworldliness most children leave behind with their dolls and toys, grew and grew in her mind, not from any particular story she read, or any lonely hurt she felt her mother neglected both her and Madeleine, doing work of national importance she never explained, never tired of telling them, but insisted was work that would very soon take them home to France. Nor was it because Madeleine, now a beautiful young woman of almost sixteen was growing so recklessly wild and so thoughtless, she worried her so, but because it felt so very natural to her. And all the more when she read James Frazer's, *The Golden Bough,* and Thomas Bulfinch's, *Mythology,* perhaps the most vividly exciting book she had ever read back then. A book she kept in her bookcase at home. A book every child should read and then read again.

Bullfinch bringing to life in the most compelling way the beguiling myths of ancient Greece, of King Arthur and of Charlemagne, but most of all the myths, stories and legends of the Hellenes, which gave her such a pleasure and instinctive knowing to read, but never more so when she was newly returned to Paris and taken so very ill during the autumn and winter of 1950 and 1951, when she and everyone else thought she would die; and die she very nearly did.

Stories she knew did so much to make her well again. Perhaps the only thing that did. Despite her mother's care, so begrudgingly given she was everyday sorry, even in her drowsy sleep, she bothered, and Madeleine's sullen moods, which were so dark and overpowering she thought she had, in some unknown way, deeply hurt her, when it was, she, who had hurt her with her behaviour at the summer jazz festival at Juan-les-Pins. So much so, she thought of little else, but gods and goddesses, heroes and villains and the strange creatures that came to life in her dreams and imagination, and was glad she did, because they were even now a comfort.

A time when she first read Homer's *Iliad* and fell helplessly in love with the handsome *Paris,* the flawed son of king *Priam,* who risked so much for the love of the beautiful *Helen,* not least the wrath of her husband, *Menelaus.* Something her own sweet love, Pascal had failed to do, who left her so alone when she was most in need of him; had so hurt her as she knew she had hurt him.

Devouring every book, she could read on the subject with an insatiable, all-consuming hunger. A hunger that by degrees astonished, alarmed and then irritated her mother, who because she was so sick in bed with pneumonia complicated by rheumatic fever, was every day forced to scour the book shops and libraries in Saint Germain en Laye and with forays into the heart of Paris, ten miles away to find her something new to read, which she always did.

But her belief in metaphysical otherworldliness persisted beyond that unhappy time of illness, a time when her youthful innocence, her youthful *joie de vivre,* her youthful optimism fell under the shadow of the ghost that haunts her still, into university; the Sorbonne, the heart of French learning, three years later. A belief that was always more visceral than it was intellectual, though the intellectual was nurtured by the pre-Socratic philosophers she came to know in the final years of her Lycée and the preparation for her baccalauréat she passed with ease, Heraclitus, Pythagoras and Parmenides, who with others of their extraordinary kind, were the first men in Western philosophy to question the nature of reality; to question the very nature of being in the world. Questions which to this day remain unanswered and perhaps will never be answered, not by philosophy or the empirical sciences. As the inimitable, Socrates and Plato, later nurtured it! Who to her way of thinking have no equal, though she would be the first to admit she had read too little after them, and Aristotle hardly at all, until the twentieth century loomed its head, though with so little else to say, everything was a foot note to those two great men?

Socrates, even though he thought mythology, *a vulgar cleverness,* an *absurdity,* because he said at his trial, *the unexamined life is not worth living* and died for his belief, but more than this, that *all learning was remembering,* a reincarnation of the past into the present she knew to be true. But a reincarnation of the soul not the body we temporarily and so often uncomfortably possess, as so many of us feel we do. Though there are fragments of mind, the intimate of body – memories inevitably, which return to haunt us all. A body no less strange to us than the lives we live, a life we perhaps little want to live, but must know any sort of peace.

Plato, because he said so much and said it so wonderfully well, it has never been bettered, not even by Molière or

Voltaire, who she adored, who all the French adore for their irony, wit and sometimes farcical humour, or Shakespeare, who she had lately come to read saying much that she knew to be true: *no human thing is of serious importance; ignorance is the root and stem of every evil* and *for a man to conquer himself is the first and noblest of all victories,*

But it was a gut belief, too often gushingly expressed that made her student friends laugh, that made Étienne laugh, she was so *naïve* when she was everywhere surrounded in the Sorbonne by French existentialism then at its precocious height. A belief that was in such stark contrast to the work of Sartre, Lacan, Simone de Beauvoir, Merleau-Ponty and Camus, whose writings she came to admire, if not always agree, not least Sartre, an influence, but never a sage and Camus, who was a man who captured her heart more than he ever did her head. A handsome, heroic man, who died when he was so young his reputation soared beyond its worth. Writers who inspired her to explore and know herself as she never had before, to live as Socrates and Plato encouraged her to live, to be learned and inquiring, but most of all, to be authentic.

To be herself and not the fiction she had become; we all inevitably become! The fiction of our parents, who have first call upon our empty heads and because they do, bequeath us every pain and prejudice they ever knew and a little bit more to help us on our way; as her mother did.

Pain and prejudice that grows with the endless stories we tell ourselves, that everywhere imprison us in their steadfast, clinging maul. Our hollow gender identities, our class pretensions, our national identities, our politics, our religions and now, as never before, our obsession with popular culture – and she was the first to admit she adored the glamour and excitement, she so easily found in films and the new fad of television. Which had become such a part of all our lives, exerting by far the greatest influence on who we pretend to be; making us want to be, if only in some small way, what we never can be, part of the fantasy reality of meaningless symbols.

Symbols without truth, poor, Étienne tried to capture in his aimlessly silly, truly awful poetry. Invoking gods of this new world order on our wishful, often unhappy lives. Celebrities of every imaginable type; pop stars, film stars, vacuous, haute couture models dazzled by their own good looks who think themselves an ornament to our lives – Toby Jugs who think themselves special because they dazzle, and worst of all, heroes who are good at mostly trivial games, and silly games at that; golf, tennis, cricket and football, men have turned into tribal war.

But though she had yet to master all these contemporary thinkers had to say and Beauvoir most of all, whose life and work she so admired, and perhaps never would, inspired her as a teacher she had become, wanted to become on her graduation in 1957. But not of French, which she now taught for the first time in her life and taught rather well, she thought, certainly better than Arno, but of psychology and philosophy, which she loved and so missed to teach.

But always from a metaphysical viewpoint that from those desperate months of fever and nightmare believed human life and human suffering are but a temporary state of *being* in the world. That death is not the end of *being,* but a return to the unconscious from which we come.

That believed in soul as few of her friends now did, were too sophisticated to think like her, since the war robbed them of their innocence, a war that even now, seventeen years later, still had the power to frighten her; as little else could. Though something else did! Something, no matter how hard she tried, she could not remember, but came closest to knowing when transported by the erotic desires she often felt, not least when in the arms of a man. But not the erotic desire of modern misunderstanding, but the erotic as it was conceived by Plato, an irrational, vital force within us all, which strives to remembers what we have forgotten; the divine! To articulate, as Lacan would say we must, what our desire lacks and in that lacking, constantly searches. When for the briefest, cruellest moment her soul reached out to another place, a place almost beyond her imagining; beyond words; the sublime that is both the end and the completion of all things; where music, art, poetry, literature, wine, drugs and love can also take us.

Soul the incorporeal essence of our *being* in the world, but emphatically not, she had a hundred times argued in some café or bar - Les Deux Magots in the Place Saint-Germain-des Prés, the last time she remembered she did, smoking *Gauloises Bleue,* her favourite cigarette and drinking far more red wine than she should, to be confused with mind or mental states. Minds with free will! Minds controlling our actions as the driver of a car might control the way it moves this way or that through a complex of mental states and processes: perceptions, thinking, introspection, information processing, attitudes, emotions, volitions, creativity, beliefs and imagination. Most definitely not! Mind and body are one and the same thing, as the English philosopher, Gilbert Ryle eloquently said they are as most philosophers now agree they are.

Minds with pre-determined capacities and limitations, no less than the bodies they are a mutually engaged part, which are made better or worse, good or bad, happy or sad, rational or irrational by the 'stories' we are told as children, some so singularly prejudiced they short circuit our capacity to perceive the world as it is known to others and might be known to us. But equally important diminishes our capacity to imagine other than we know through our sense perceptions: the unconscious. As plants and animals can only know the world; know it only as biological automatons. Which, though intrinsically a part of our mind experience lies beneath our conscious awareness of it and too such a degree it is a landscape that only hints its presence and so obliquely it leaves us frustrated, confused and disbelieving of what it has to say.

And say it most emphatically does, but not just to us, but others, whose understanding may be more certain than our own, particularly when it is expressed in literature, poetry, art and music, showing us what we have overlooked, and they have glimpsed of that world beyond our dreams.

But to talk of soul is to talk of something quite different. Something that stands in reflective contemplation of not only our physical and mental states, but the universe we inhabit. Empathic (or divine) self-consciousness by any other name, though names in this context are nebulous to say the least! But divine self-consciousness should not be confused with self-consciousness per se, condemnation or celebration and every feeling in between, mirrored in the gaze of others, but in the illuminated self-consciousness mirrored in the divine gaze of the White Goddess, the font of all that is good in the world. Though her friends laughed she was guilty of substituting one tantalisingly meaningless concept for another, but though she did, and knew she did, it came closest to what she believed. And who in 1962 knew any better, or would know any better in some future time, given the confounding nature of this idea, which defied definition?

But for her divine self-consciousness wasn't a product, process or part of body and mind, but a moral relationship towards them, an idea better understood, she liked to think, if body and mind is thought of as a glove puppet, which though animated from within, lacks the moral perspective to control or guide its own behaviour, save what is conditioned by reflex and reward.

Puppets like the French *Guignol,* she loved so much as a little girl or the British TV stars, *Sooty* and *Sweep,* both so head strong and naughty they are almost beyond the control of Mr Corbett, the puppeteer, who despite his best efforts is endlessly frustrated by their mischievous behaviour, the essence of the slapstick humour of this popular children's show. Both of them absurdly resistant to his constantly restraining voice, a voice, which describes the moral space in which they should live their lives! The incorruptible voice of the Goddess they may choose to hear or not. But if they do, experience a self-conscious awakening that is profound and must of necessity address the good in others, rejecting or accepting them on the basis of some perceived moral value, truth or understanding mutually shared in the good of others.

For people like Hussey and Lomas, damaged and self-absorbed by their limited sadly intellects, their warped ideas, their vilely prejudiced beliefs, their dispositional attitudes to behave in the vicious way they did and their infantile emotions, which produce a conditioned, reflex stupidity in every social situation they find themselves, the good in others is beyond their grasp.

Boys fit only for the whip and the plough, as AA once so uncharitably remarked they were harsh, if unpalatably true. As it is so often beyond the grasp of those who are blessed with the physical, intellectual, social or material advantages they never had, who believes their superiority is gifted to them by God and because it is, warrants their indifference to lesser beings.

Divine self-consciousness: soul, is the tiniest illumination of the vast unconscious the mind with all its power of thought can only partially and imprecisely know; cannot know without it! Simply stated, as soul grows in mutually satisfying, morally principled, reciprocal interactions so imagination grows; cannot fail to grow. But crucially the reverse holds true, if minds are careless of the good of others, careless of what they have to say, the soul is diminished. As

Plato and Socrates knew it was, speaking of something they called *psychagogia,* the growth, or more precisely, the leading of soul in conversations between people holding different points of view to a common understanding. And leading them, she would insist, though her friends scoffed she did, to the wisdom of the White Goddess; the divine.

And though they would scoff at her, she was convinced mind/body was *masculine,* a cruel *machine* bent on nothing more than the avoidance of pain, the pursuit of pleasure and the survival of the organism, whilst the soul was *feminine* speaking to us of truth, beauty and goodness. And because it was, it was the role of women, the disciples of the Goddess to show men the truth they too often ignore, the world is a temporary place and the unconscious our home.

The unconscious she had now long believed was not some ethereal, Freudian place, but the source of the material reality we everyday perceive is empirically and palpably *out* there. That the universe in which we play out *our* lives like actors on a stage, is merely a projection of this unconscious we are all a part. An unconscious she truly believed is able to conjure realities other than the *one* we now experience; the low crackle of the *Tannoy,* the noisy voices of the children impatient for her to continue, not least, Lomas, red faced and seething she had for too long ignored him and the world outside her window grown so beautiful in the snow that had so utterly changed it. But not imaginary realities invented by fanciful or deluded minds to justify their ideas and emotions, but the realities which shaped the lives of our ancestors for thousands upon thousands of years, and might do so again?

And looking at the sullen faces of her class that cold and gloomy morning she wished it would as just a while ago she glimpsed it had.

A counterintuitive idea because we are programmed to believe the universe is a place we physically inhabit; that pre-existed our being here. To ever look forward in contemplation of what it appears to be and never beyond its illusion, as Plato saw it was in his famous *Allegory of the Cave.* Thinking the ever-dancing *shadows* we see in front of us are real, when they are not. Something AA, the arch rational empiricist, had smiled, though never laughed, to hear her say.

But not only is soul the smallest illumination of this vast unconscious, it is the moral lens in the membrane of the compacted particles the human body is, that is all anything is solids, liquids and gases. That is, if her recent, if rather hesitant understanding of particle physics is to be believed – it was a work in progress she would readily admit that had yet to make any sense of Schrödinger or his little cat, but whether it was or not, it was a metaphor that suited her purpose. A lens through which the universe we imagine it to be, is made real to us.

A hologram conjured by our collective unconsciousness, she smiled, rolling that delicious new word across her tongue like a tasty morsel – a *Fry's Turkish Delight,* a perfumed confection without equal, she was now addicted, too, but no less than she was addicted to good red wine and French cigarettes. And thought about it all the more as she stared through the snow flaked window. The crisp snow now falling less hard than it did an hour ago, but still carpeting the school and the city beyond its spiked walls in a thick and yet unspoiled white as far as the eye could see; the low hills in the distance, too, she supposed, though they were now lost in the grey clouds that covered them. And with the same feeling of a short while ago the world is a fiction that might easily disappear, pulled by some unseen hand to reveal the emptiness beyond it. As Lomas would never understand, she thought, as he stared at her with ill-disguised hate, 'Est-ce que la fillette préfère un anorak bleu, rouge ou vert, Mary?' She firmly asked him.

'Pour elle, un anorak rouge, je crois, Madame, Doucet,' he spluttered, his head and shoulders bobbing with the effort, as he read his reply, much to the amusement of Ronnie, Judy and Gerry, who with brash unconcern he was twice their size, half turned in a sexy slouch to look at him and with smiles so broad on their mischievous faces he blushed and snorted they did.

'Poor Ellie her anoraks so fucking rude she doesn't want to put it on, not for you or anyone,' mocked Gerry, sitting closest to him, but with an empty desk to protect her, in fits of giggles that danced her shapely legs beneath her desk, her suspender belt, visible beneath her skirt.

'Repeat and then translate, if you would be so kind, both the question and the answer, Mademoiselle, Gerry, I'm sure everyone would like to know what it is you find so funny about Monsieur Lomas' rather splendid attempt at this difficult French pronunciation and so well-articulated he would easily convince my beloved General de Gaul he was a son of France? Frowned Valeria, her eyes lifted to the photograph of the General hanging on the wall in front of her.

'What? Groaned Gerry, her face a spiteful, sullen amusement that little cared what she asked.

'Rapidement, Mon chéri, we all wait on bated breath to hear what you have to say, do we not Monsieur Lomas?' Said Valeria, her face a mischievous, inviting smile of encouragement that ignored she looked at her with such a gleam of malice in her cold eyes. A beautiful, effortlessly sexy young woman at the height of her allure that strangely entrancing morning of near blinding white, shifting, purple shadows and lights that everywhere dappled the town in a wash of pastel colours, she would forever remember her that way, as if she was suddenly caught between two worlds; the world that was here and now and the world soon to come.

Her smoky, darkly made-up eyes so expertly done and with sleekly daring, Italian, feline flicks at each corner that were better than her own, bright and full of mischief, her lips firm and bright with red lipstick and anticipation, her blouse and skirt so tight about her perfect body she could not be mistaken for other than she was, a sensual woman! The swelling, firm round of her ample breasts a pleasure to every male eye that looked at them, her shapely legs crossed one over the other beneath her short skirt to reveal their perfect form; sinuously long and inviting. But a demon child as *Nabokov's* comic paedophile - if there could ever be such a thing, and she felt absolutely sure there never could be, despite his charming tale, *Humbert Humbert,* would have instantly recognised she was *un enfant charmante et fourbe.* But so stupid and so wicked in her careless disregard, she would never truly feel sorry for her. The second murder victim found that day, but not the last, but raped and brutally battered like the third!

'What the fuck?' She blurted in a brooding drawl, as Valeria turned on her heels, little interested in anything she had to say, her mind once again returned to her thoughts of just a moment ago.

'Holograms,' she whispered.

'Hologram's,' repeated a quizzical, Greta, from beneath her watchful, darkly hooded brows.

Chapter 13

Monday December 17, 1962
Helen Shapiro: Tell Me What He Said

A concept still novel to science she had earlier this year read about in the *National Geographic* or was it something Jacques Spitz or perhaps, René Barjavel had written in one of their marvellous sci-fi books, she so much enjoyed? Books as implausible as any *Mills and Boon* novel, but every bit as enjoyable. The extraordinary notion we humans, no less than any other biological organism, and like all matter in the universe, be they solids, liquids or gases, are composed of billions upon billions of electrically charged, sub-atomic particles called protons, neutrons and electrons suspended, no matter how tightly they are compacted – and solids are the most compacted, in a mind boggling immensity of sub-atomic space and time no less vast than the vastness of space and time that separates the stars and planets in the universe which *appears* to encompasses us. But, in truth, does not encompass us, as we perceive it does – is out there, so to speak, but is an intimate, inseparable part of our sub-atomic existence and we must, in consequence, interact with it in ways we little understand, but no less understand our *being* in the universe, is understood. Particles coalesced by some unknown energy - a sort of quantum glue, she had read, that is all we really are, be we beautiful, ugly, tall, short, fat, thin and every variation in between. Particles which presumably fall to an infinitely small nothingness when we physically cease to exist, but perhaps could be made whole again in an artificially constructed hologram. As Spitz and Barjavel posited we could, as the future may show we can. We are quite simply, objects in the universe no less than any other, even the hardest stone, but possessed of a consciousness, a sense of being perhaps unique to us; an idea she found captivating and utterly convincing explaining much of what she understood by reality.

An illusion, call it what you will, shaped by our collective understanding/consciousness of the unconsciousness it is but a tiny, fractional part, an unconsciousness that *is* surely the quantum space in which we exist in our sub-particle state, which intimately connects with the furthest reaches of the universe. The furthest reaches of our, imagination. But, which, from time to time, and often when we least expect it, admits our barely grasped, often ignored and too often mistaken, intuitions of a far greater reality. Intuitions which speak to us of worlds beyond the temporary bubble of our own tightly bound quantum reality, which by tacit consent is all there is: heaven perhaps or something like it, she supposed, little knowing what it could be.

Intuitions barely glimpsed in the distorting prism of our

primitive sense perceptions, but grasped more fully, if never completely, in the art, poetry, literature and music she loved. And in the wisp-like emotions and ideas that came to her in her dreams, her meditation, her reflections, her passions and her pains and far more dangerously, came to her in the mind-altering drugs she had sometimes used. Which her husband Étienne and Madeleine, too much used and Pauline Fisk to her surprise, now smoked incessantly in that silly pipe of hers, though she urged her not too and with vivid hallucinations that would be comic if they were not so tragic.

That saw Dylan and Terry, she said, changed into horned and hairy Satyrs their muscles and penises grown to a monstrous size, a terrifying erotic image that came straight from the Eleusinian Mysteries of ancient Greece that wondered if she, too, drank the sacred juice of the flycap toadstool, as the *Maenads,* did? But sadly, a vision that bore no relation to the truth, because Dylan was rather disappointingly small in that area of his otherwise slim and solidly muscular form; adequate to the task, as most men are, but really quite modest after all he pretended to be.

What on earth was she thinking? Or perhaps, more accurately, what was she dreaming? She asked herself, knowing how much *she* liked Dylan and how much she hated Terry, as she herself hated that horrid little man, her eyes turned to find Fay, Hilda and Greta looking at her, who, in Pauline's waking nightmare, she was now everywhere followed by goblins, had assumed the role of fairies. And, as she did, saw them look at her with a strange, beguiling look in all their eyes, a look she had an hour before seen in

Hilda's, as she stood on the steps of the gym, a mixture of understanding, warmth, charm and approval that knew how much she liked, Clifford.

Intuitions, Jung, once Freud's good friend and faithful apostle, but now long fallen from grace and favour, thought an *irrational function* of mind, but never-the-less saw how important they were to his concept of the collective unconsciousness, his *unus mundus,* his belief in an underpinning reality that binds us all. The connectedness of all minds and all things through archetypal ideas and repeated assertions of truth, myth, fable and storytelling, which reveal a parallelism and synchronicity in human thought none of us can escape, but few of us truly appreciate.

Not least her husband, who she doubted truly understood the symbolist poetry he professed to love and wrote with such an indifferent art he never sold a word, nor ever really tried. An artistic affectation that never quite grasped the meaning of the invisible that is a part of us all, that Baudelaire, Mallarmé and Rimbaud so elegantly and so persuasively wrote about and tried to reveal in their poetry, though with less success than Picasso, Monet, Renoir or Matisse, did in their captivating art. That despite the empirically rational logic of our minds - our centre of being, there is a tantalisingly ephemeral, barely grasped reality beyond our crushingly immediate and always persuasive sense perceptions, though they are the most fragile part of our knowing anything, seeing only a trillionth part of the colour spectrum and hearing little more. An invisible made even more densely opaque by the warped realities of Modernity with its socio-cultural attitudes, norms and practices – not least our obsession with posturing celebrity figures of little worth, our vanity, our limited capacity for rational thought, our unstable and all too often distorting emotions, the imprecise meanings of the words we use and the stories we tell ourselves of the world we live in that so thoroughly forgets the world our ancestors once inhabited. A reality that is conceivably our spiritual beginning, our home! A home we will perhaps return, too, when our cycle of life and death is done, each life a test *we* choose to undertake in the hope we will better succeed in life than we previously did, she thought. Her face turned in quiet reflection to the collection of Parisian street signs she had so carefully cut in cardboard rectangles, each boasting the familiar white lettering and azure blue backgrounds of the *1938 Paris Ordinance,* which softened the sharp lines and bleak, gooseberry green walls of her classroom, blistered by heat, damp, cold and neglect in a score of ugly scars. Evidence the annex was in dire need of repair and Casterbrook a fool to halt the work that would put it right.

The Avenue des Champs Elysees, the Rue de Rivoli, the Rue des Rennes, the Boulevard des Capucines, the Boulevard Haussmann, the Boulevard Saint-Germain and of course, her own chic and private cul-de-sac, God bless her dear aunt the large sum of money she left her, La Tour-Maubourg, a daily reminder of the sophisticated world she had left behind and so missed. One of which, the aptly named Rue de Petites Ecuries, was pinned on the back wall just above Hussey's bullet-like, shorn-to-the-bone, ginger head. An amusing epithet that perfectly described the dunce's corner she had only last week sent him, too for the constant cheek he and Lomas gave her from the two, front row desks they thought they owned; but now bayed and seethed they didn't.

Both of them vulgar louts, who hated Clifford in that irrational way people hate those who are different. Who have no choice, but to be different? A visceral, cankerous hatred that cannot be assuaged by any appeal reason or appeal their better nature; they had none and would think it a triumph if she asked. A gentle, unassuming boy who she had always instinctively liked, who reminded her in some unfathomable way of every hurt she had known. Boys whose moods were becoming more dangerously sulky and unpredictably with the cocktail of drugs, Ronnie said they took, when they spoke together last Thursday as everyone knew they did. The alcohol Hussey stole from his self-absorbed, evermore neglectful parents in measures too much to enjoy, the purple hearts and black bombers, she heard them called, they easily bought, which quickened their wits to dizzying highs or slowed them to a silly, babbling lows of mild confusion. The heroin they smoked which gave them such a terrific rush but left them wanting more and the cannabis that better than all the rest put a sharp edge to the paranoia they both displayed in the wild staring set of their blood shot eyes and the snake-like, dribbling purse of their lips.

A paranoia, Ronnie also told her, not only daily threatened Clifford's safety, but hers for being the woman they could not easily bully, as they easily bullied Pauline Fisk, Miss Roberts the Domestic Science teacher, whose jam layered sponge cakes were a dream and Joe Fisher, who they thought as weak as any woman and weaker still for being a fool, but most of all because she liked him and did what little she could to save him from their evil maul. But sadly, she had to admit, could no more save him than she could save her from her mother's boyfriend, Ted, who she tearfully confessed she feared would one-day rape her, as he often hinted, he would and couldn't tell her mother who was in love with him and had no proof he would.

Could do so little to save any child briefly in her charge, whatever that meant? When Casterbrook cared so little about them and when she knew in her heart, she must soon return to the city she loved and never should have left. The sights of which everywhere charmed her classroom walls. Posters of the Eiffel Tower, the Arc De Triomphe, the Musée Rodin, the Musée du Louvre, the Sacré Coeur, the Jardin du Luxembourg, near the Sorbonne, where she often ate her lunchtime sandwiches in summer and winter, the Cathedral of Notre-Dame, the Château and Parks of Versailles, from every side speaking to her in a montage of picturesque colour. Prints of Monet's, *Bathers at La Grenouillère,* his *Lily Pond at Giverny,* his, *On the Banks of the Seine, Bennecourt,* and his, *Waterlilies* and, rather shocking, so Casterbrook once remarked with a leering grin that so unnerved her she blushed, a print of Pierre Bonnard's, *The Red Suspenders,* taking pride of place on the wall above her desk, which pressed to the outside windows, was as far away from Hussey and Lomas as she could ever hope to be in the same room.

Lithographs of Leonardo da Vinci's, *Mona Lisa* and

Toulouse-Lautrec's, *L'anglais Warener au Moulin Rouge* were hung in wooden frames on the two stout, pillared walls that separated the three, metal framed windows that overlooked the back courtyard and of course, she sighed, she had to every day look at it, the Headmaster's long time sporting obsession, if not success. His five years in the digging, through concrete, dirt and broken drains - he was proud to tell anyone who asked, ice cold in summer and winter alike, four feet deep, finished last May, but not yet covered in anything, but ice and snow, six lanes, marine blue swimming pool.

On every side Somme-like mound of brick, clay, broken pipes and twisted metal rose out of the ankle-deep snow to taunt the pitifully shivering class of blue lipped, first year boys and girls, who to her amazement, swam, splashed, walked, or near drowned their way up and down its twenty-five yards. Much to Cod-Eyes apparently cruel delight, now changed, she was glad to see, from the Greek warrior of an hour ago – was she losing her mind? As Pauline had so obviously lost hers, she wondered, who screamed his Indian army insults the should; jeldi, jeldi.

On the opposite side of the room, on the two pillared walls that framed the three frosted glass windows that overlooked the corridor in a myopic squint that only saw the ghostly shadows of the few people who now passed – Mr Eldred being a frequent visitor to her store room, who she had three times seen that morning with Mr Pike, two more posters were taped to the flaking paint; each a yard high. One, the nearest to the door beside, Lomas, a bright red map of France divided into its twenty-one mainland regions and on the other, a yard in front of Hussey's now oddly bobbing head, a bile-yellow map of Brittany's mysterious Quiberon Peninsula – one of her favourite holiday haunts, and a place of magic and mystery she longed to return, too. Would return too and very soon! Staying, as she always did near the forest of Le Petit Ménec and the megalithic stones she so loved to wander through; to sit and dream beneath a world now gone.

Lastly, and taped only that morning, a timetable of the Paris Metro, with stations signs showing Balard, Créteil, Les Halles, Bologne, Gare d'Austerlitz, Châtillon-Montrouge, Saint-Denis and Les Courtilles, so familiar to her she knew their every start and finish, covered the frosted, half-glass window of the storeroom door. A door, which to her half blushing delight eagerly awaited Dylan's arrival, and wherein, at coffee-time that morning, and not ten yards from his growing more suspicious, ever watchful wife, and his not to be trusted friend, Terry Mack, he had whispered a promise *to fuck her 'til she ached with pleasure*! He hadn't forgotten her.

A rude way of talking that gave him a crude thrill of intimacy beyond their love making she didn't share. That too much reminded her of *Mellor's* earthy familiarity with the sexually awakened *Constance* in D H Lawrence's charmless love story, *Lady Chatterley's Lover.* A book so full of maudlin social philosophy, social conflict, dismally silly class pretension and faux rustic sex, she almost didn't finish it, but finish it she did. But it was a talk that suited the mood of self-reproach and debilitating ennui that had so engulfed her life since her husband's death.

But not so much she would much long endure its

proprietary implication she was a *thing* owned by him and only him. A *thing* to be used by him; a *thing* that might be talked about by him. As she knew he did? So, knowing had Terry Mack looked at her as she left the staff room. A look, though she knew she was surely mistaken, that hinted an intimacy he, too wanted to share with her. A thought so awful she visibly shivered he might dare to think such a thing could happen!

Chapter 14

Monday December 17, 1962
Connie Francis: Don't Break the Heart That Loves You

With her chin rested on the palm of her upturned hand, her sleepy eyes dreamily watching, Madame Doucet, as she shivered and stared out of the window, her beautiful face a troubled frown of distraction that steadfastly ignored, Gerry's half-hearted attempts to read what Lomas very obviously could not. Hilda recalled the first day at nursery school, all those years ago, when she, Fay and Greta *met* Clifford 'Cocky' Robin - that curious name he was now called; so, unlike his own. Knew him before then, of course, and knew why he had come here and what he was doing, but didn't know him to speak to, as they knew Tiro and Persephone, who came first and would remain long after they had gone; would live he life they had chosen.

How, with shrieks of alarm that wondered if he had been killed, they had rushed to pick him up from the wet playground when, Colin Hussey, showing the first signs of the sadistically violent psychopath he now was, pushed him off the Jungle Gym climbing frame without the least care he nearly knocked him senseless. Did knock him senseless. And when they did, saw a dizzy and barely able to stand, Clifford punch him so hard in his face, he broke his nose to the bent out of shape it now was and heard Colin tell the two dinner ladies, who patrolled the yard like sheep dogs in their wrap-around floral pinnies, cheap perms and Do-rag knotted scarves, he did for no reason. An outrageous lie, as they both knew it was, Clifford being a tiny boy, a head and shoulders shorter than he was, even then. But though they did they took a perverse delight in straightway reporting him to Mrs Scullion for the bloody nose that soaked his jumper to his khaki shorts. His mum being a woman of substantial means and spiteful temper.

But despite they rescued him and did their best to save him from the irrationally savage beating, Mrs Scullion, a few minutes later delightedly gave him, beating him so hard with the sharp edge of her eighteen inch, wooden ruler as he lay stretched over her desk like a white faced corpse, he almost wet himself, she never knew him as a friend, until a few months later; though all three kept a close eye on him. When one cold and wet June day in 1953 they found themselves abandoned to the care of Mrs Scullion, who against her best wishes was obliged to keep the nursery open on the afternoon of the coronation day parade for those waifs and strays who had absolutely nowhere else to go, leaving them to play as they never had before. A magical time that even now brought back such warm memories of those hours they spent together.

A day much trumpeted by Mrs Scullion and her colleagues in the weeks before the event, who was an ardent royalist of that constantly curtsying, deludedly loyal, murderously bigoted, social climbing type, but even more by the local press. Who daily wrote of its fabulous coming, so everyone might enjoy this craftily conceived, historic pageant on their new bought, television sets, though few had one, before they sat down to the street party, they all would have? Which no one of her limited acquaintance did, except, Colin, who didn't count because his family were so rich, they had most everything they wanted. Even a *Bendix*, front loading, automatic washing machine, he daily boasted his parents had been renting for years; like she cared.

An abandonment with distinctly republican overtones that further embittered, Mrs Scullion towards, Clifford, who railed she knew his stepmother was a slut from before the war and, worse by far, was a friend of that Irish crook, Clooney Barron. She being a regular chapel going woman of the strictest moral virtues, or so she pretended she was to those who hadn't seen her swoon like a giddy schoolgirl on the rare occasions, Colin's lecherous dad came to collect him from school and twice, to her certain knowledge, took her into the cleaners closet by the stairs.

'Are you sleeping, Hilda?' Whispered Clifford, gently nudging her, as her eye lids flickered shut, her round, bespectacled face, a smile of pleasure that ignored, Gerry's mocking French.

'No, Clifford, I was thinking about us.'

'Really?' He smiled.

'Yes, that first day we played together, just you and me. Do you remember?'

'Yes, coronation day. Why would I forget? But where were Fay and Greta, I don't remember?'

'This has never been for them as it is for you and me, so they had no reason to stay,' she answered.

'Why did you?'

'Why did you?' She smiled, ignoring his question and Valeria saw she did. The same smile she saw on her face when she stood between Miss Langford and Cod-Eye on the steps of the gymnasium.

'Atonement,' he answered, the smile slipped from his face, as looked at Valeria, now turned to look at Gerry.

'Pour elle, un anorak rouge, je crois,' whimpered Gerry, strangling every vowel, but with an accent so breathlessly sensual she instantly reminded, Valeria of the stunning Jeanne Moreau, in the 1958 film, *Ascenseur Pour L'échafaud*. A thriller made all the better by the music of Miles Davis, she could hear it now, and with that same look of frightened innocence she captured. Which she saw one summer night with a girl friend at the famous *Cinema Le Champo* on the corner of the Rue des Ecoles, her favourite cinema in Paris and so close to the Sorbonne, she and every other student a hundred times went there, and to the basement nightclub below. Though that was now gone and with it so many hours of pleasure she had enjoyed.

'Et pour le garcon?' Answered Valeria, brightly, her arms folded across her chest as she stared at the clock tower, the time dragging so slowly she thought her ordeal would never end.

'Pour lui, un anorak bleu. Oui, c'est ça,' groaned Gerry, through gritted teeth.

'Voilà madame. C'est la taille exacte pour lui et pour elle, je crois. Vous aimez ça?' Said Valeria, turning on her heels to look directly at her, her face a sweet smile of encouragement, Hilda, Fay and Greta adored to see, so much were they enjoying Gerry's humiliation.

Oui, treś bien,' said Gerry, her growing more frustrated reading now silently echoed by the class behind her, who tittered and laughed and smirked to see her squirm like a snake on a hot tin roof, under, Valeria's watchful, if warmly encouraging eye. A squirm so intensely sensuous, Tinker, quiet in his seat beside Greta since she insulted him barely ten minutes ago - as he knew she had, found his eyes were glued to every subtle move she made, as if in a trance. The flare of her brows, the bright concentration of her eyes, the provocative brush of her hair against her face, the crease and pout of her red lips, which held such a promise he hardly dared look at them, the soft caress of her wet, pink tongue on her snow-white, perfect teeth, the dance of her red painted finger nails on the top of her open book, the stretch of her tight blouse over her ample breasts, the slide of her skirt over her long legs, now pulled so high on her thighs, he easily saw the deep cleft in her knickers and the electric tension of her body, which was so strained by what she was trying to say, she glowed. A sight so hypnotic the thought of seeing Carol Paget later that morning left him as stiff and as painfully hard as a poker.

And he so loved Carol Paget he would do anything to be with her. To have her, if only for a moment. The most beautiful, the most perfectly wonderful woman he had ever known, who liked him, as he liked her, who teased him she might let him kiss her one day and he so longed to kiss he, so longed to hold her tight in his arms, as he knew she wanted him to hold her.

A stirring that didn't long go unnoticed by Angela Dee, sitting a yard behind him, who watched him with a doe-eyed fascination that wondered anyone, could be so handsome. But nor did it go unnoticed by Hussey and Lomas, who in an exchange of sour glances marvelled anyone could like an easy tart like, Gerry. A girl so long overdue a kicking they wondered they hadn't bothered, but soon would, they would wipe the silly smirk clean of her gobby, self-important, laughing face. Like no one knew she was hot for that sad twat, Dylan Lloyd-Thomas, but would get more than, Thomas between her legs, if he ever got his hands on her; would get Terry Mack. The pair of them so thick together they shared the same women. Though he liked boys, too as they knew he did. A man who frightened them both more than Cooney and Cod-Eye.

'C'est tout, Madame?'

'Miss?' Groaned, Gerry.

'C'est tout, Madame?' Said Madam Doucet, her accent so entrancing, Judy longed to speak like her.

'C'est tout pour eux. Mon Mari cherche un pullover, 'answered Gerry, her face a tearful fury.

'Les pullovers sont au rayon ....'

'Miss. Miss. Miss,' interrupted Gerry, with a pleading, almost feeble squeal, which implored she really couldn't go on. 'I can't do this. Please, Miss. You know I can't. Let somebody else try. You know I'm not very good at this sort of thing. Really, I'm not,' she wheedled, in a seductive, misplaced pout and so like a silly, petulant child, Valeria almost laughed at her. The Nabokov nymphet she tried so hard to be revealed in that instant to be an artful sham that hid the naïve and immature child she really was. A child in a woman's body, but a child no less and her rape, mutilation and murder later that day all the worse because she was.

'Perhaps a little more care, Mademoiselle Gerry before you criticise others and you will become the young woman you so very much want to be and not the silly little girl you are, n'est-ce pas.'

'You think. Well at least I tried, didn't I, miss? Didn't I Judy? What about that silly gawp?' She sneered, pointing a vindictive finger at, Hilda, who appeared to be sleeping on her upturned hand, her pretty face a blissful contentment bathed in the shaft of light that just then pierced the snow frosted window. 'You never ask her to do anything, just all the time picking on me.'

*

But she wasn't sleeping, as Clifford and Valeria knew she wasn't, but was dreaming. Her hand beneath her desk holding tight the small posy of fresh flowers she had just a moment before picked. A red anemone, a purple withy, a pink and white asphodel and a yellow narcissus, so new and sweet smelling the dew that bathed their petals shone with summer sunshine, as the grass and flower filled meadow that stretched out before her, did. A place she had known in every season's colour and knew by heart every mountain peak and path she, Fay and Greta had a hundred times walked upon and every glade and grove they had played in and every stream and crystal pool they had bathed in. Knew she was safe there from the hurt and pain that every day and everywhere surrounded her. Had, since she had come into this strange world!

Chapter 15

Monday December 17, 1962
Billy Fury: Letter Full of Tears

'I'm going to have that fucking French tart and that smart arse, know it fucking all, twat, Gerry, you see if I don't,' hissed Lomas, over the electric, whine, whistle and crack of the *Tannoy* announcement, Carol Paget was just then trying to make, as he and Hussey pushed and shoved their way through the now crowded classroom door to the empty corridor beyond. Which politely ordered all swimmers in Friday's meet to assemble inside the front gate in five minutes. Not outside, where they might be run over on the road, she anxiously intoned her worst fear they would, the gasp in her voice plain to hear, but inside where they would be safe. A caution that all too well remembered the many dangers to be found in busy city traffic for the unwary, or playfully inattentive child and Love Street was always so very busy, but so much worse on that Monday morning with the hazards of snow and ice making driving so very, very difficult.

Dangers she long ago learned from the *Tufty Club* – she

still had her little red squirrel badge pinned to her cherry pink anorak; she knew every one of them by heart. Dangers which gripped her nervous chest so tight her sweetly pleasant, breathy-falsetto voice dropped an unconscious *octave* below her normal modal register to sound a warning very much like the friendly warnings *Policeman Badger* often gave *Tufty, Willie* and *Minnie* when they got themselves into some naughty scrape. 'No, definitely not outside the gate children, please.' She begged, suddenly and very clearly remembering a particularly harrowing incident when *Minnie Mole* and *Willy Weasel* were almost squashed under the headlong rushing front wheels of a London *Routemaster,* red bus driven by a charming, West Indian gentleman on a visit to Piccadilly Circus. Gosh what an awful fright that was. 'But inside by year and by House. Please. And Team Captains you must take the register of all your team members, noting any absence, which must be reported immediately to Mr Turner or Miss Langford before you set off against the lists, I have this morning typed and copied for you with the help of Mr Fisher. Who has been such a dear help to me I doubt I could have finished them without him,' she wistfully sighed? Hardly daring to believe he really was coming to her office to share a lunchtime sandwich with her. *Frey Bentos*, Corned Beef, with a liberal splash of *HP Brown Sauce,* he said were his. Not her favourite, she had to admit, but she would certainly try one, if he asked, which she dearly hoped he would, so much did she want to share her own with him. Boiled egg and cress sandwiches with a hint of homemade mayonnaise, she was certain he would enjoy them. Would know what a good *cook* she was. 'Yes, I hardly know how to thank him, but I do thank him most sincerely for his kind assistance. 'And lastly, and this is most important. Team captains you must also take the register before you return to school from the baths at 3.30pm this afternoon.'

'Mmm,' she sighed as she carefully turned the microphone switch to off and wondered again where Mr Casterbrook had gone in such a pell-mell dash, twenty minutes ago. At twenty minutes to eleven by her watch, which was most unlike him, and said he wouldn't be back until late that afternoon when the practice meet was finished. His mood made so much worse than it already was, and he had been in a thoroughly disagreeable mood all that morning, by the telephone call he had received from his wife, Violet. A charming, rather genteel lady who always asked how she was and always by her first name, which was always so nice she remembered.

But no matter where he'd gone, perhaps it was to see the builders he had so annoyed they wouldn't come back to work no matter how much he begged and pleaded, and no matter what he promised them. Or Mr Plant, his *accountant,* Linda's dad. All of them daily badgering him for the money he owed and threatening him, too, though he didn't know she knew they did, and would be very angry if he did. But no matter where he was, she was glad he was gone, and she could be alone with Joe as she never had been before. Joe, who she liked. Liked so very much, who said he might come a little earlier than they planned, now that Casterbrook was out.

'Too fucking right, I am,' spat Lomas, careless he might

be heard as he cast a flint-hard, sly last look at Valeria, now seated cross legged at her desk gently tapping her lips with a rubber tipped pencil in a thoughtful silence that watched, Hilda and Clifford gather up their things. Hilda, a simple, delightfully kind soul whose character was surely the embodiment of Flaubert's, *Simple Heart, Félicité,* whose ill-used, sadly unloved and impoverished life was poor reward for the virtuous, uncomplaining love she gave to all those she so willingly helped. Her mistress, *Madame Aubain* and even the vagrant, *Colmiche,* who was rumoured to have committed many terrible atrocities in '93, who died alone in a pigsty, an end no better than hers.

A wistful distraction that loved they liked each other that didn't see Lomas's wicked stare of hate and contempt as he pushed Hussey and Tinker out of the door in a barely suppressed rage that tripped Fay into the corridor where she fell flat on her face with a squeal. A squeal that produced a shriek of cruel delight from Judy and Gerry waiting at the door for Ronnie; the last time she saw Gerry, she would tomorrow tell, AA's friend, Chief Inspector Tomon Hughes.

'Yeah, we'll do her on Friday after the swim, like we planned we would. Fix her once and for fucking all, the smart arse, fucking whore, but we'll have, Gerry first, cheeky fucking cunt,' answered Hussey. 'I'll have my knob so far down that Frog's fucking throat she'll choke on it.'

'Yeah, you and me both, Colin,' smirked Tinker, nervously, the delicious thrill of their vile talk sending a spasm of tingling excitement down his spine, better even than the sight of Gerry's crotch a few minutes ago, an excitement that longed to see, Carol Paget, even if he had to miss the meet and the chance to see Judy, Gerry and Ronnie in their skin tight swimming costumes.

'And while she's chewing on that fat bastard, Colin,' he smirked, winking he knew just how thick and hard it was, 'I'll have her up that tight little arse of hers she won't never shit again without thinking of me inside her,' laughed Lomas. 'Best she's ever had, hey, Tinker? And I bet there's been more than one hard cock been up that tight little arse of hers,' he cruelly laughed again. But this time so loudly, Valeria turned in her chair to look at him and saw such a strange, unfathomable look in his dark eyes it sent a cold shiver down her spine, no less than it did, Ronnie's, who heard their every word he said with a fright and disgust that knew he meant it.

Chapter 16

Monday December 17, 1962
Elvis Presley: Blue Moon of Kentucky

With his right ear pressed to the brass keyhole in the door of Carol's office, Tinker listened to the seemingly empty silence within, his mood a mixture of excitement and pensive trepidation she might not want to see him; that he had somehow got it all wrong in his head as his mum everyday said he did, just like his useless twat of a father, always did. Had hidden from Cod-Eye in the upstairs annex toilets for the last ten minutes for no better reason than the vicious beating he would give him when he discovered he wasn't at the baths to swim the hundred yards' crawl, butterfly, breaststroke and relay as he had these many weeks practiced, he would. An excitement Hussey and Lomas had stoked to an irrational bravado before they left.

'Just, do it, Tink,' said Lomas. 'You know the silly cow wants it. She's been giving you the come-on for weeks, everyone knows it. Ain't that right, Colin? More even than Angela who's suddenly got the hots for you, though why she, or anyone else for that matter, would want a fuck-brained, stupid wank like you, even if you do look like, Cliff Richard is any one's guess?'

'Yeah, Casterbrook's gone out and won't be back 'til late, well, that's what I heard Cod-Eye tell, Langford a couple of minute ago and both of them fuming he was, said Hussey, his nose dribbling in the cold wind more than it normally did, as they stood in Indian file by the front gate. The snow underfoot churned to an icy mush by the hundreds of feet now gathered there.

'So, he ain't there to see you, Tink. So, as soon as the coast's clear, leg it down to her office and plant one on her, and if she likes it, put your hand up her skirt and give her cunt a squeeze. You never know, this might be your extra special lucky day; the day you lose your cherry.

Could be? He dared to hope, feeling his tumescence rise in his trousers like it never had before; like it was about to explode. *But was she in there?* He wondered, thinking he heard a muffled moan come from, Casterbrook's office, where she sometimes ate her lunch when he was out, which was most every day. Sitting in his comfortable leather armchair with her feet on the low radiator reading a magazine and with a view out of the large sash window behind his desk down the sharply curving front drive that just saw the near corner of the wrought iron, front gates, but just enough to quickly warn her of his return to one of the two reserved parking spaces beside the stepped front entrance he insisted, were his and his alone. Though Cod-Eye said one belonged to him and had since the war brought him home a wounded, near broken man and parked his always gleaming, 1951, *BSA, B31, 350cc,* blue motor bike and open topped, steel-grey and blue combination on the opposite side of the steps to his immaculately polished 1957, grey, with silver trim, *Wolseley, 15/50 saloon,* despite he a hundred times told him not, too.

The only noise he could hear in the school as he cautiously retraced his steps to stand beneath the elegantly domed and colonnaded vestibule entrance, his man-sized, dirty black shoes planted on the rim of the neatly crafted, circle of mosaic tiles, which so grandly announced the schools misplaced by any stretch of the Headmaster's lofty imagination, raison d'être, where he hid behind one of its two feet wide, fluted columns. A draughty, rather sombre, church-like space of bright colours and elegant words that formed the imposing centre to the T junction of empty corridors he now cautiously searched. The one in front running a straight sixty yards or so from the iron studded, wind rattled, Gothic front doors behind him to the back of the school, where it opened onto the girl's playground. The one to his left, shorter by thirty yards, passing the headmasters office and print room. The one to his right, passing the staff only staircase to the second-floor staff common room, the library and the school hall that was its far end.

'Mmm,' he groaned, his fingers instinctively finding the warm shaft of his swollen knob in his neatly pressed trouser pocket as he searched the three corridors for any sign he had been seen; might yet be seen. Not least by the few teachers who were left behind to patrol and guard the school. Or worse still, by one of the prefects who prowled the corridors in search of someone to torment and terrorise with their inflated, viciously bullying authority; Linda Plant, the Headmaster's favourite, being the worst of all. A girl every bit as beautiful as Angela, Judy, Gerry and Ronnie, but a loner like, Greta. Who was a nutter as everyone knew she was? The two of them a law unto themselves and just as frightening, though he doubted Linda could scare Cod-Eye the way Greta did in the Gym earlier that morning and stripped herself naked to do it. A sight both terrifying and wonderful at the same time and her as slim and shapeless as a boy, but though she was, so weirdly sexy he couldn't imagine why she was; why he liked her like that.

But search though he did he saw nothing, not even Mrs Wiśniewski, who having seen his, tip-toeing, deeply suspicious arrival outside Casterbrook's office a few minute ago, now watched him from behind the wooden jam of the half open library door, not thirty feet away, and with wicked gleam in her rheumy old eyes that wondered what business he had with, Miss Paget? Who that nice young man, Mr Fisher had rescued from the print room just a short while ago and with such a kind attention to her hysterically sobbing distress; she had twice seen him hold her tight in his arms and twice seen him gently kiss her on both her tear smudged cheeks? And when he had, wiped her clean of the ink that stained her hands and arms to her elbows with the rag and white spirit he had borrowed with every courtesy a woman might expect from a well-mannered young man, from her well-stocked, but little used, cupboard, she hardly knew how to thank him. Save to invite him for the lunch he had come early, too, barely five minutes ago. Some lunch, she thought, knowing what a passionate, emotional creature Carol was beneath her barely controlled reserve, though she was doubtful the timid, Joe Fisher was the man for her!

And who, despite she never said, nor ever hinted she did, but teased and frightened her because she was such a silly, immature young woman to put up with Casterbrook's lecherously obscene behaviour, she liked. As she liked, Valeria, whose misplaced love affair with, Dylan Lloyd-Thomas was fast becoming a scandal. But since their falling out three weeks ago – oh yes, she knew all about that, was now an open secret every day fuelled by the wink-wink, childishly silly rumours, Mr Terry Mack was spreading about her. Much to the relish of his stuffy male colleagues, who, though they hated him for the creepy little shit he was, appeared to hate her even more. As so many men hate beautiful, bold and independent women and all the more when they are in every possible way cleverer than they are, as Madame Doucet certainly was.

'Mmm,' groaned, Tinker, his eyes lifted to the picture that decorated the inside of the domed roof above his head, which he knew, because everyone did, was copy of Titian's famous, *Bacchus and Ariadne,* spoiled though it certainly was by the ugly window that opened the vestibule to the snow framed leaden sky above. A picture so oddly and disquietingly out of place on that cold winter morning he wondered what on earth he was doing, and half thought to run to the baths as fast as his long legs would carry him with some pitiful excuse, Cod-Eye would accept as half true and only half beat him because it was. But though it seemed the safer option, sheepishly tip-toed back to Carol's office, where he slowly, ever so slowly turned the elegantly forged, but never once polished by Mrs Wiśniewski's bony hands, brass forged, beehive doorknob and pushed the door ajar. And saw to his relief her little office was empty, as it often was at that time of day, save for the faint hint of perfume, which now filled the air as it never had before. A perfume he later learned was an unexpected, but much appreciated gift to his longed-for *lover,* from, Madame Doucet for the small favour she had done her some days before.

A very expensive French perfume called, *Chanel No 5,* Carol at first refused. Saying, in that nervous, blushing stammer of hers, he had so often heard - he could hear it now, it was too expensive. Which, of course it was! But Madame Doucet insisted she must have it, saying she much preferred another by *Rigaud of Paris,* called *Féerie*. A perfume with an exquisite floral bouquet she had for many years purchased in the Rue François, near the corner of the Rue Lincoln. A perfume, she said, reminded her of Paris, as *Chanel,* never did. Which was a lie. Knew it was wonderful in every way. So, chic and so sophisticated and so utterly French everyone wore it but gave it to her and said she must wear it, if only to please her. Though she never had until now, keeping it safe for a very special occasion – and this was a very special occasion.

Its heady, short lived, but exquisitely sensual top-notes of ylang-ylang and neroli plant oils catching his nose as he silently tip-toed to her desk and bent to look at its famous, clear glass bottle beside the photograph of her *brother,* Richard, he remembered it was and her little bouquet flowers; roses he thought they were, but very small roses, though they might have been daffs.

Lifting the glass stopper of the reassuringly heavy, rectangular bottle, he dabbed a little of its precious contents onto his left wrist as he had so often seen his mother do, when she prowled the makeup counter in *Boots* or *Browns* and smelt, as she would never allow him to do, the scores of pretty coloured bottles, pots, jars and plastic containers she always found there.

None of which ever caught her the husband she so desperately wanted, had achingly longed for since her post war GI lover of several happy weeks of violent, sometimes back breaking sex in the uncomfortable back seat of his canvass topped, *Ford CJ-3A, Jeep,* got her pregnant the very first time they did, it. The ever so handsome, muscularly fit and athletic, but backwoods, thick-as-a-racoon, Rick, who took himself home to Little Rock, Arkansas in the August of 1949 and so very quick he never said a proper goodbye to her. Nor knew she had a son.

Though she everyday telephoned his Colonel at Burtonwood he did from the kiosk up the road from where she and her mother lived near the army camp on Gorse Hill, though she hardly knew which button to press on the telephone, had never used a phone before. Was it A or B, it was such a confusion, and she was cut off nearly every time? And when she wasn't, he said he never knew a boy called, Rick or anyone like him, and every time harsher than the

203

last, until she called no more. But went instead to meet his adjutant in a pub in Warrington, a tall, handsome boy with short blonde hair and smoky grey eyes, called George, who said he came from a place called Glens Falls in New York State, who very kindly brought her home in his little *Austin A40, Dorset,* two doors, saloon and shagged her better than Rick ever did on the front step.

Rick being so big and rough and never caring she was only just turned fourteen and still quite little, when he told her she must, or find someone else to give her the good time she so desperately wanted, and never even caring she never *knew* a boy like that before. That he was the first boy she ever loved in that special way, nor even caring how much he hurt her when he turned her this way and that like she was a rag doll. A PX slut, he boasted, he could have any night of the week for a packet of *Luckies* - which she didn't smoke, until he gave her one and now, she couldn't stop smoking the things, or a stick of chewing gum, or a *Hershey Chocolate Bar.*

And her mother listening to *A Case for Sexton Blake* on the old wireless behind the curtains no more than two feet away from where she and George did it and did it so nice, she almost died with pleasure. And *Tinker, Sexton's* sidekick, *come quick, guv'nor, come quick,* just as they both did, him faster than her, but he did wait until she finished, which Rick never did.

But then he hurried off with barely a kiss on her cheek to say how nice she was and with her best knickers in his pocket she found on the grass verge by the road the next morning, all wet and dirty as she hurried to catch the school bus by the railway station. And knew he must have thrown them out of his car as he drove off. A hurt no less than the hurt, Rick had brought into her life that made her cry all the way. And cry and cry so much Mr Casterbrook took her into his office and stroked her leg all the way to the top until she stopped and said how very pretty, she was, which she knew she was. And because he did, let him shag her there and then on the hard floor of his office because he was so kind to her, as he had been so many times since then, he being a friend of Clooney's, who said she must and gave her half a crown every time she did. And she so wanted men to be kind to her and when they shagged her, they were, for a while.

Which is why she called her little Rick, Tinker, as everyone else now did. But not after Sexton Blake's intrepid partner, as he once supposed she did, but because her maiden name was Taylor and Tinker Taylor reminded her of nursery rhyme she sang when she was just a *little* girl; the one which promised to tell the name of the boy she would one day marry. Every day wishing it was George who had got her pregnant and not, Rick, but never doubting for a minute the little brown *Golliwog* who popped out of her belly one dark and lonely night was his.

But fearing he would never know his own dad wrote to him at the address, George gave her the last time they did it in his little car and with a kiss when they were finished that made her cry, so sweet and tender was it on her trembling, tear wet lips. Better than the sex, which wasn't half as good as the first time they did it, him turning her upside down in a doggy squat just like Rick did and hurting her just the same, pushing his knob into her arse hole so very hard it hurt. Saying her fanny would still be sore so soon after Tink's birth the week before, which it was. But George, like every man she ever knew and Clooney Barron most of all, had lied to get his way and no letter she wrote or photograph she sent of little Tink ever found his dad.

But even if he had seen her letters and photographs, England was now long forgotten, by that lazy, work-shy, sleep-late, drink-hard, couldn't-give-a-damn, fat-balled, womanising, Ouachita Mountain boy. A boy who never learned to read or write, save to spell and say his name and never cared he didn't, until the day died in a drunken brawl. Stabbed through the heart in a late night bar and grill on 12th Street in the late August of 1954 to the sound of Elvis Presley's, *Blue Moon of Kentucky* playing on a 1948, *Seeburg Trashcan Jukebox,* His last ten cents had just turned on to the irritation of a beer soaked, red neck rough with a crew of bad arse boys to back him up, who said he didn't much like, Elvis. Him being a Mississippi boy who liked the nigger music better than his own, which was a terrible sin back then; still was in '62.

'Mmm,' moaned Tinker, with an oddly girlish pleasure of delight, as he smelt the perfumes heady mid-notes of May rose and jasmine. A ravishing combination so perfectly blended with the faint, but now growing more discernible base-notes of sandalwood, vetiver and vanilla, he couldn't help but try a little more on his upturned wrist, but in his absent-minded hurry spilled its precious drops down the front of his jacket and trousers. A mishap that so distracted him he was a minute too slow to hear the urgent low moans and sharp gasps of blissful, sighing delight that were now coming from behind the headmaster's inch wide open door.

Chapter 17

Monday December 17, 1962
Elvis Presley: She's Not You

A sound once fixed in the slow turning cogs of his sadly retarded mind he instantly recognised, as one he only too well knew. A soft, throaty noise he had heard a thousand times before through the cardboard thin walls of the post war, Jerry-built, two bedroomed, *Mark III,* corrugated asbestos and cement prefab he and his mother shared not half a mile from his Nan's. When with a careless disregard for his feelings – not to say his adolescent hormone raged desires, she let every man who walked her home from the Highfield pub, shag her until she screamed aloud, they shouldn't stop. Though they always did! She being too drunk on the whiskey, Clooney Barron every night gave her to ever find the rapture of bliss she longed to have.

And sometimes, if it was a quickie on the doorstep, her foot wedged so deep in the letter box to give her the height on her toes she needed, it once got stuck and wouldn't come out until he pulled her free. Her ten-bob lover, a spot faced, twat of a lanky milkman called, Fred, laughing fit to burst he hadn't paid her as hurried off up the road as she lay on the step in a giggle.

'My love, my love, my darling, love' he heard, Carol moan, as he pressed his ear to the door. Words, which like poisoned barbs, stung his heart a pain too much to bear to know she loved another; not him. 'My darling, my darling, Joe, I never knew? You never said?' She murmured.

'Nor you my love,' he answered, 'I have so longed to hold you like this. To kiss you like this. To touch you like this. But I never thought, I truly never thought, I ever would. Though I dared to hope you might one day be mine. My true, my only love, the love I have so often dreamed.'

'Really?' She gushed, so thoroughly taken aback by his sweet, romantic words she could hardly believe her ears. He loved her. He really did and after so short a time together as this.

'Yes, my love. *Though shalt not love by wayes so dangerous. Temper, O fair love, loves impetuous rage, Be my true Mistress still, not my feigned Page,*' he gently urged, quoting a favourite line from Donne's, *Elegy.* His, *XVI. On His Mistris.* A warning he hoped she would understand. A warning he lived his Quaker life by. As he once again breathlessly grasped the soft, delicious swell of her naked breasts, which to his startled surprise, she had bared without his asking. A sight, which, like the fast swelling of his now painful knob, left him dazed and confused.

'How lovely, Joe no one has ever said anything like that to me before, words so lovely you make me want to cry; look, I am crying,' she swooned, kissing him hard on his lips and so effortlessly she wondered why she had never kissed anyone like that before and how foolish she had been to want to practice on, Tinker; a boy! Though in her growing more reckless passion she didn't understand a word he said, but knew as any girl, would, it was poetry that spoke to her bursting, adoring, starry-eyed heart, better than any other words he might have conjured.

An unfortunate mistake on her part because she wanted him a lot more than he wanted her, just then; didn't. A principled, growing more nervous, utterly naïve young man, who had never kissed a girl before, let alone seen one half naked in his arms. She, a girl whose, every romantic thought of love was a consuming, sexual passion that ached to be conquered by a man.

'What the fuck?' Groaned Tinker, the whispered sounds of the two of them so close behind the door he thought he could reach through the wood and touch them with his hands. *Would touch them,* he silently screamed his impotent anger. His hurt and frustration to be so deceived by her; by him. *Would strangle the fucking bitch with his bare hands if she was shagging that useless twat of a four-eyed, newly qualified, useless fucking English teacher, Joe Fisher. With his long curly fucking hair, bum-boys soppy talk of romantic love, Romeo and fucking Juliet and other such twatting rubbish that fell from his fat, clever lips in a gush of half remembered prose. Donne, Byron, Wordsworth, Keats and Shelley, to name but few of his fucking favourites, no one gave a shitting toss about, or ever listened for more than half a fucking second, least ways Hussey and Lomas.*

Who regularly took the piss out of him, as Judy and Gerry, did? All of them, except him and Clifford. He listened, didn't he? He cared to listen and understand! And all the time the treacherous fucking twat was shagging her; the girl he adored! Stunned to a trembling, almost ashen despair he slumped against the white painted door jamb and fell sobbing to his knees as listened, though he didn't want too, to their lover's talk.

Joe's voice, polished by the Cambridge degree he every day boasted he had - wished he had, cautiously restraining a passion he could hardly endure, but must endure if he was to survive this all too thrilling encounter as chaste as he had begun as he knew they had both begun.

Carol shy, hesitant and seemingly unsure, but in some indistinct way he had yet to fully grasp – an odd catch in her breathless, sometimes gasping, often garbled, unfamiliar voice, cleverly calculating, urging, shaping, moving and controlling his awkwardly unwilling love making.

'What?' He hesitantly asked, the shock on his face and panic in his voice all too clear to see and hear, as she effortlessly undid her belt with her thumb and unzipped her skirt at the back.

'It's ok, Joe, really it is.' She gently responded, surer of herself now than she had ever been in her life before, her right index finger reaching out to touch his troubled, trembling lips.

'I'm ….,' he choked, as she wriggled her skirt from her waist gathering as she did her primrose yellow knickers and tights in the hook of her two thumbs, as she slowly pulled them down. 'Please, Carol. We must…. We must be careful.

We might be seen,' he panicked as her naked right leg snaked about his hip. 'Mr Casterbrook ...., anyone might come in, really,' he begged.

'It's ok, Joe, he left almost an hour ago and won't be back until late this afternoon,' she gently cooed, her hand once again reached to his, lips as his jaw fell slack at the naked sight of her.

Her ebony black, riotously dishevelled pubic hair beneath her thrown open blouse, so perfectly crowning her swollen, moist, slightly open, deliciously kinked, scarlet-pink vagina, he almost fainted at the sight of it and longed to comb his fingers through its lustrous curls, to gently touch her *lips* as he never thought he would. A sight that reminded him, though he hardly dared remember he had seen anything like it before, of the shockingly erotic symmetry of Gustave Courbet's masterful painting of a nude woman in silent, surely, post coital repose; *L'origine du Monde.* A glossy lithograph a close Cambridge friend of his had shown him in a drunken revelry he had never repeated. Though the image of that magnificent work and others like it he had seen that night was a terrible torment to his soul. Images that every night haunted him to a shame he could not bear; his mother said was a sin as much as any. A sin that was now visited upon him like a test he must overcome; would overcome as, Donne had surely urged he must.

'No. It's not,' he answered, his voice a trembling whisper. No, he would not make this beautiful woman the servant of his lust but would make her the mistress of his true and loving heart. But how? He asked, as he looked at the soft white of her naked body in a hypnotic fascination that never knew it's like before, not in art or poetry and touched again her breasts so perfectly formed they were all he imagined they would be better than he ever imagined they would be.

Her eyes a devilish, almost mocking glint, her lips a teasing invitation, her nipples dark and swollen - darker and more swollen now than they were a moment ago, her softly heaving chest, her flat, hard belly seeming to quiver with the thrill of her artfully crafted, squirming invitation. Her pliant, open thighs, the slashing gape of her vagina, her dark mons risen to meet him and so like Courbet's model of his dreams he fell upon her, his hands forcing her legs apart in a violent paroxysm of blind, uncontrollable lust, his tongue searching her like a snake in the dark of her lust.

'Aaaaaaaah,' she screamed, as his hard tongue found the swollen hard of her clitoris as nothing ever had before, a fierce, truly unexpected delight that was so overpowering she almost fainted.

'What the fuck?' Gasped Tinker, wondering what they were doing, *now,* but knowing they were doing something they shouldn't be when she screamed a second, then a third and then a fourth time, each time longer and more urgent than the last time. And he, the pig, grunted his slavering delight in her moist flesh, now arched in an uncontrollable spasm to meet his gorging mouth in an ecstasy she couldn't bear or delay a moment longer, her spasming, blissful, rapturous coming rising from deep within her like a wave, each ripple a growing swell upon the last.

'Holy Mother of god, Joe,' she cried, holding tight

his hair and wrapping her legs so tight about his neck he couldn't break free the frenzied, urgent, rhythmic thrusts of her wanton hips in his face. 'Don't stop, please, my darling, don't stop now, please?' She mewed as the bliss of her climax rose to its end. But too soon, she suddenly realised and not like this sham sex.

'Did I hurt you?' He gasped, as she roughly pulled his head from between her legs by the thick of his hair, his breathless, blush red, wet dribbled, astonished face lifted to hers in an anguish he had.

'No, you didn't hurt me,' she growled, her wild eyes a dance of mischief, her lips a wicked grin as she drew herself back in a wriggle from him and hungrily raised her knees and parted her legs.

'What?' He asked.

'Like this, Joe,' she breathlessly urged him, the tip of her tongue clamped between her teeth, her fingers opening the cleft of her vagina to a silky gape. 'Fuck me. Fuck me hard, Joe. With your knob. Put it in me, now, Joe. Quickly,' the words a vulgar joy to her maiden's ears, every bit as much as they were a violent shock to his. No. He wouldn't. As she must know he wouldn't.

'What? Of course, you hurt her you flop eared fucking twat of a useless, dozy cunt, Fisher. What are you doing in there?' Groaned Tinker, now pressing so hard against the door it silently, ever so silently opened to a room that at first sight appeared to be entirely empty of anyone.

Until, he saw a sight so shocking, so utterly depraved he could barely suppress the scream of desperate rage that came so quickly to his throat he almost choked on his hand, but stared instead at the two of them hidden, or so they thought they were, in the small, carpeted alcove on the far side of the Headmasters desk. Which though it perfectly hid them both from the now open door, reflected their every lewd behaviour in the very expensive, Edwardian, mahogany, cheval dressing mirror that stood at its front end. Which half turned towards him on its four brass castors and with the flooding light of the frost rimed window opposite so perfectly angled upon its polished surface, saw them better than if he had stood above them. Better because the mirror had a five times magnification in its glass to assist a gentleman's dress.

'No,' he reproached her. No, we mustn't, Carol,' his two hands rested on her thighs, now curled about his waist, the smell of her womanly musk so overpowering he physically trembled.

'No,' she teased, the wicked dare they really must unmistakeably clear in her husky voice as she quickly opened his blue denim shirt and loosened his chocolate brown, knitted tie at the neck.

A tie, Tinker, now crawled as close as he dared to the mirror without being seen and with a view far better than it was from the door, had often admired. 'But why not, Joe, you love me don't you?' She sweetly purred, as she effortlessly brought his lips to her naked breasts. Breasts more perfect and more beautifully round than either he, or Joe, had ever imagined they could be and where he saw him gorge a greedy feast on her nipples for several long seconds, before, as if caught like a ravenous boy, he sheepishly lifted his head to look into her smiling face.

'Joe,' she moaned, as he rose bare to his slim waist like a Baroque nude between her legs - a muscular, *David*, perhaps, or a tormented, *Saint John the Baptist,* under the gentle push of her firm hands.

'What?' He asked, a hint of deep concern creeping into his faltering voice as she sat up and with a kiss so deep and so languorous on his salty lips opened the thin brown belt and zip of his baggy corduroy trousers and with a wanton, lascivious greed found the shaft of his swollen knob.

A sight that so transfixed, Tinker, his chin fell to his chest in a gawping stun of disbelief that watched her brutally wank him to a hypnotic stupor in less than half a minute. His bestial, dog-like groans so loud he was beyond caring anyone might hear him in the corridor outside; as Mrs Wiśniewski most certainly did. Keeping watch, no, one would come to spoil their pleasure, but with an idle wonder that asked where that fool of a boy, Tinker was gone, too.

'Fucking bastard,' whispered Tinker into his tightly clenched, bitten fist as he watched the two of them in the mirror, every subtle movement they made exaggerated in the glass, like he was watching television, but so close it hurt his eyes to see the dearest, most precious love of his life, the sweetest, most innocent, most attractive woman he had ever known, who since last summer had in so many ways, and with so many hinted words and unspoken gestures promised herself to him, behave no better than his mum; no better than one of Clooney Barron's whores.

Saw her roughly pull his trousers from his hips and kick

them from his legs, as if he were a child and when she had, spread herself in the vilest and most recklessly squirming, lascivious way on the small rectangle of burgundy-red carpet that covered the six-foot patch of floor beneath them. Her head fallen between the headmaster's box shaped for sturdy comfort, brown leather, gentleman's armchair and smoking stand, replete, he now saw, with a collection of pipes standing in a row like soldiers on parade, he never once saw him smoke. Gifts, like the carpet, the mirror, the bookcase, the hat stand in the corner beside the door and the antique desk he had now fallen upon from his father-in-law. Gifts he stole when the bad-tempered old skinflint died leaving his wife rich beyond belief and him forever penniless in her debt. Her blouse, now the only semblance of clothing she wore, hanging loose about her shoulders to reveal her red ravished breasts, which rose and fell in the heat of her now growing frantic passion. 'Fuck me, Joe,' she begged, her legs stretched-to-an-impossible-open on the heels of her feet to greet him, the scarlet pink of her moist vagina an aching torment to his anguished soul.

'Carol, my love we mustn't, we really mustn't,' he begged, with an ever-faltering resolve.

'Please, she begged him just as hard, pulling him closer.

'No,' he hoarsely, barely answered, trapped in the thrall of his Quaker piety. A piety that now struggled to be free of the lust that must soon overwhelm his growing frail want to run away.

'Please, don't leave me like this, Joe. Please I know you want me just as much as I want you,' she teased him, through the twist of hair she held in her mouth, like she was Jane Russel in the film, *The Outlaw,* her left hand holding tight his still his iron-hard knob in a craving that urged him to fill her with its muscular strength. 'Fuck me, Joe. Fuck me like I know you want, too.'

'Carol,' he sighed

'Joe,' she moaned, her ankles now loosely draped around his bare hips.

'My love,' he answered in a swoon.

'Joe,' she moaned. 'Joe my dearest, sweetest love, please, now.' She begged and saw in his face something of the handsome Jack Buetel, Jane's cowboy lover, 'I want you,' she cried, as he rose up between her legs. 'Joe, what is it my darling?' She cooed, fearing the slightly mad, growing more helpless look in his eyes, no less than the weakening of his knob in her hand.

'Can't.' He mumbled, his eyes inexplicably drawn to Donne's fallen open book, which lay beside the radiator, which like some horrible rebuke called to him in words he knew so well, he knew them by heart. *No man is an island entire of itself; every man is a piece of the continent; a part of the main. If a clod be washed away by the sea, Europe is the less, as well as if a promontory were, as well as if a manor of thy friends or of thine own were any man's death diminishes me, because I am involved with mankind. And therefore never send to know for whom the bell tolls; The bell, it tolls for thee.* 'It tolls for me, it tolls for me,' he sadly groaned.

'What?' She asked.

'I can't.' he bleakly answered, the booming noise of

the bells in his ears now so loud he clasped his hands to his head to shut them out, his face a rictus of aching pain and growing despair.

'Can't?' Whispered Tinker, whose own massive erection - the best thing his dad ever left him, his mother often said, had long spilled from his trousers in a warm, hurting throb. 'Well, if you can't, you, silly fuck, I can,' he giggled, the madness in his eyes so clear it was frightening.

'Please, you can my love,' she begged him again.

'No,' he firmly answered.

'No?' She asked, her voice a soothing balm that watched in hopeless disbelief his desperate inner turmoil, her hand violently urging the shrinking shank of his knob to stay a little longer.

'No. I'm sorry. I shouldn't have let things get this far and in the headmaster's office, too. I feel so wicked. So utterly and completely depraved. It is unforgiveable. I have treated you so very badly. I am so ashamed. Carol, please forgive me, I never meant, too, we must wait.'

'Wait? Wait for what?' She almost screamed her aching disappointment.

'Yes. Wait you, useless fucking twat,' laughed Tinker, wanking himself stupid as he watched him force her rigid hand free of his now rapidly shrinking little knob, her face a picture of despair and regret as he rose to his knees and searched beside her restless hips for his shirt and tie. Her naked body so white and so pure he gasped his disbelief anyone, his Carol, could be so beautiful. It was as if she was sculpted from marble by some ancient hand, her every curve, her every sensuous, sinuous line, her every secret place, a perfect copy of the perfect woman.

'Wait until we are married,' he answered, the sound of Tinker's energetic wank and sniggering laughter, which like the bells in his head he still heard, taunted him he could be so weak.

'No,' she begged, her voice a plaintive scream.

'Yes, we must,' he sternly answered.

'Please, I want you, Joe,' she murmured, her right leg arched at the knee, her foot balanced on his smooth hip in a caress that shivered his spine, her right hand rested on his shoulder so lightly he hoped she would never let him go. But must let him go, he almost cried she must. As her left hand found his knob and stroked it to a hard, again. A hard so blissfully hard he felt his head swoon and the breath run from his body in a dying gasp as she cupped his chin with her hands and kissed him with such a deep and longing passion, she devoured his soul.

'No,' he groaned, pulling himself free of her choking embrace. 'We can't. We must wait. Please Carol, I beg you. Help me I'm in agony. I'm in torment my love why is you doing this?'

'Because I love you, Joe and I know this hurts. But I'm going to make it all better I promise I will. But you must trust me,' she cooed, as she slowly turned him on his back and with a strength he didn't try to resist, so weak and helpless had he now, become. 'It's ok, Joe, really,' she shushed his meagre protest and so in control was she now she easily tore his slim fitting, long white underpants from his left ankle and with a delighted giggle threw them on top of Casterbrook's desk and sent his microphone spinning in a blasphemy that knew she would never fear him, or any man again. Not even Dylan Lloyd-Thomas, who thought himself such a handsome lady's, man he could touch her whenever he liked. A touch, she had always recoiled from; but never again. No, if Dylan wanted her, she might let him try. Would let him have her before the week was out! Friday would be best when all the school would be at the meet. Yes, Friday!

And when she had, and with a smile so utterly bold, so utterly lascivious and so completely changed from the frightened girl she had been just a moment before, she climbed on top of him. Her hand guiding his knob to the moist squat of her vagina, the swell of his glans so hard against her clitoris, she groaned aloud her deepening pleasure, which rose again like a distant wave to consume her in its flood. 'Are you sure you wouldn't like to fuck me, Joe?' She asked, knowing all his protests were ended, now, as she teased him with the perfect joy she felt.

'I don't know,' he feebly answered, as he tried to push his knob into the melt of her flesh.

'It's not too late, Joe, we can still be good,' she teased, letting him slip a little deeper into her. An inch or two, but no more. But a sweeter, more dangerous pleasure she had never known, he answered with a sudden thrust she had to lift her hips to escape. 'Not so quick, Joe, you might hurt me,' she laughed, as she slowly, ever so slowly, once again let him slip a little deeper inside her, and when he had, and his eyes begged for more, let him find the very deep of her.

A thrill so overwhelming she gasped aloud and threw her head back in a bliss so liberating she felt herself exquisitely reborn. A heady, truly emancipating moment of pain and joy that reminded her in that way some things do, of *Ensign Nellie Forbush,* the gorgeous, Mitzi Gaynor, washing the soap out of her hair in the 1958 film, *South Pacific,* which she adored and saw three times at the Odeon, or was it the Regal, she couldn't remember, which one it was? But it wasn't soap she was washing out of her hair, as she shagged Ban-the-Bomb, been to Cambridge, duffle-coat Joe, but all the inhibitions and fears her dull and lonely life had heaped upon her.

'Aaaaaaaah,' he groaned, his voice rising to a crescendo as she effortlessly rose above him in a rhythm that was hers and hers alone. Her perfect, naked body appearing like one of Ivo Saliger's, Aryan Nudes, Hitler so admired, her parted, usually neat fashioned hair fallen over her face in a damp curtain, her eyes languorous, drowsed by the opium of her sublime happiness, her lips parted to show the white of her perfect teeth and the searching tip of her tremulous tongue, her jaw slack, her neck arched, her spine gently twisting to better find the exquisite pleasure that rose within her with an ever quickening, unstoppable pace. The pert round of her buttocks pressed to his hips so tightly he could hardly move to help her find the climax now so close upon her he could sense it's coming in every keening move she made. Her breasts pressed so close to his face he longed to kiss them, to take her as he now knew he could.

'You like, Joe?' She suddenly asked, the brazen pleasure she now felt inside her vagina so vast and so timeless it had no measure in this life but spoke of another life; a better life than this.

'I like. I like it very much, Carol my love,' he breathlessly, haltingly answered, as his knob pushed into the silky depths of her vagina in a pulse he arched and pressed his hips to better find. 'Oh my god, Carol, don't ever stop, please don't ever stop fucking me,' he yelled, his one hand cruelly pulling her hair as he found her lips in a kiss that tried to suck the life from her, his other finger clawing at her anus she found the most excruciating, but no less, blissful pain.

'I won't ever stop fucking, Joe. Not ever,' she answered. *Though maybe not you, my sweet,* she mused, tasting again the salty sweet of her vagina on his lips and wanting a man who knew how to use her better than he would ever know how. A man who would fuck her without asking permission. A man who would know how to give her the pleasure she wanted. Not the pleasure he wanted from her. She was a woman now. Not a silly little girl. A *Cinderella? A Snow White* or a *Sleeping Beauty?* Waiting for her handsome prince charming to wake her from her misery, but a woman whose lonely spell of despair was now broken and gone forever.

'And I won't ever stop fucking you, Carol,' he boldly answered, missing the barbed point of her cruel sarcasm. The look on her face more beautiful and more serene than he had ever seen in the face of a woman before, an erotic, ethereal look, a transcendental veil that held her lightly parted red lips in a spasm that knew her orgasm was near, a look that suffused her face in a radiant glow. A bliss so rapturous she was transformed into an empty void of wanton pleasure, a pleasure that knew no end until she fell exhausted and silent on his spent and aching body.

'Carol that was wonderful,' he gushed, his arms wrapped tight around her limp and dreamy body.

'Wasn't it,' she sighed, their bodies entwined like a Japanese, *Netsuke* carving as she kissed his lips and stroked his brow and he, in turn, traced the outline of her nipples with the tip of his delicate fingers. A distraction they both enjoyed that was so complete they didn't hear, Tinker bent to his knees tiptoe from the room, his heart so irretrievably broken it would never mend.

Stopping a moment to close the door behind them he looked one last time at Carol's beautiful, but strangely changed face in the mirror, the ruin of his life, so happy in the arms of Joe Fisher, whose ankle length, well-tied, thick soled, brown walking boots looked so incongruously stupid on the ends of his otherwise, naked, hairy legs. What could she see in that silly, useless twat, he didn't have? Certainly not his pencil thin knob, which was half the size of his, and barely as thick as his middle finger? 'Fuck all.' He answered himself, as he passed her desk and saw again the bottle of *Chanel No 5,* he so admired. A beautiful smell, he painfully realised, she had worn for him. A sight that brought a flood of warms tears to his eyes and in that instant came to symbolise all he had endured from the women he had loved, who had never loved him.

A betrayal he would avenge, he promised himself he would, as he left her office and quickly made his escape, never seeing Mrs Wiśniewski was watching him and with a hags toothless, beaming smile on her face that wondered what he had been up too with, Miss Paget and Joe Fisher.

Following him to the vestibule she watched him run headlong up the empty corridor, its high, curved ceiling, glazed red and yellow brick walls and near windowless gloom giving his flight a sombre, almost sinister melancholy. Watched as he stopped a moment at the crossroad that marked the entrance to the Girls Laundry & Cookery Department and the Boys Manual Instruction Department, inscriptions so deeply carved into the stone lintels above his head there could be no mistaking the limited aspirations the school had for him and every child in its charge.

'Fuck you, fuck everyone,' he loudly called, turning to see her standing there, the threat in his voice resonating up and down the corridor as he ran, as she guessed he would, into the Boys Manual Instruction Department. 'And fuck you, Wiśniewski, you, mad old woman, I hate you all.'

'And fuck you,' she whispered back, but though she did, feared for him.

*

A moment later he opened the door into the warm, but welcoming heat of Mr Dylan Lloyd-Thomas's metalwork room and to his astonished surprise found a girl sitting on one of the twelve, heavy wooden work benches that filled the room from one end to the other, smoking a cigarette.

'What the fuck are you doing here, Taylor?' She softly asked, as she tossed her half-finished cigarette into the smouldering, Blacksmith's forge she sat beside with such an elegant and provocative ease, her skirt drawn seductively high over her neatly crossed legs, her blouse beneath her blazer open to reveal the pretty white trim of her bra and the firm swell of her breasts.

'Nothing. None of your fucking business, anyway,' he raged. 'So why don't you just fuck off and leave me alone before I fucking hit you with that fucking hammer you stuck up fucking twat.'

'Oh, I don't think so, Tinker! I really, don't. Tinker, Tailor, Soldier, Sailor, Rich Man, Poor Man, Beggar Man, Thief, Doctor, Lawyer, Indian Chief,' she softly sang with a deliberate sarcasm that knew him by reputation. A strikingly attractive boy, but a moron as everyone knew he was. That had no idea his mother had sung that same rhyme to him a hundred times when he was little and with a deliberate emphasis on Indian Chief, once so sweet and endearing to his infant ear, but now a hurtful tease he hated. That knew the coffee brown of his skin marked him for the nigger he was. 'Oh, and what is that smell I smell on you, Tink?' She asked, her voice a lascivious purr, as she slipped to the red painted floor beside him, careless of the heavy ball-peen hammer he now held so tightly in his hand, his knuckles blanched with the effort, her skirt momentarily snagging on the metal edge of the bench to reveal a long and shapely leg.

'Perfume,' he gulped, his violently contorted face now pressed to hers in a threat she ignored with such a brazen, self-assured confidence he felt powerless to do anything but stare into her eyes.

'Come.' She countered, with deliberate vulgarity, the perfectly manicured, pink painted fingernail of her right index finger pressed to his lips in a gentle hush. 'You've been wanking, Tink, when you should have been up the baths swimming,' she whispered. Now tell me the truth and tell me every detail of what you have been up, too.' She demanded, slipping her arm into his as she turned him towards the door. 'Because I can see from your face you have been a very naughty boy, indeed. Mmm, but you do smell nice. Come and perfume. Come and very expensive perfume,' she guessed pressing her nose into his neck. Oh my, you haven't been wanking over that French slut have you, Tink? Madame Doucet, who thinks she's such a dream?

Chapter 18

Monday December 17, 1962
Anton Karas: The Third Man Theme

The bludgeoned body of Mrs Violet Casterbrook was found in the music room of her delightfully appointed, two storied, Corbel turreted villa beside the river at twenty minutes past two that afternoon by her maid, Ruby. A thin, cheerfully dotty, middle-aged woman, who was a constant reminder to Violet, in life, of *Ethel Hugget,* though without the working-class charm and cheerful good humour that made her such an endearing character in those delightful post war films she loved. Found her after her late return from the lunch time chore Violet had sent her on and barely five minutes before the arrival of her regular, Monday afternoon, Bridge party.

Mrs Edna Scullion, a friend from church for so many years she couldn't remember a time when she wasn't. Mrs Gloria Hussey, the wife of her cousin, Roylance, a fashionably elegant, Veronica Lake lookalike of disreputable reputation whose racy talk was always a delicious treat and

Mrs Daphne Plant, a friend of just a year, who was her very able partner for that afternoon's much anticipated game. Who, despite Mr Casterbrook's protests he didn't approve of her or her husband, a bookmaker who looked like the film actor Humphrey Bogart, had made the perfect fourth for their contented circle and with such a sunny disposition she adored her?

Her lifeless body left draped like a shot dead hippopotamus across the white wooden door sill of the French window that opened the *strings*-end of that graciously elegant room – as Violet was want to call it with a grandeur entirely in keeping with her elevated social position, to the garden terrace. One of two generously proportioned Rennie Mackintosh inspired, stained-glass windows and doors that flooded that south-west facing, rectangular room with the very best of the mid-morning and afternoon sunshine. The other, but firmly closed, at the concert grand piano end, but without the latter's sobriquet her guests found both affected and amusing. And opened, as did the other, though not for several weeks now, onto the gravelled terrace that overlooked her steep-lawned and neatly terraced in the Italian style, formally planted, back garden. And with such a panoramic view of the slow turning bend in the river and meadows to the village church and spire beyond, she never tired of it. Nor the small colony of swans that endlessly swam there, as they did now in graceful circles, though they had fearfully argued that morning; had even come to flapping blows. Her *Toni*-permed only last Friday morning battered head and outstretched upper body covered in a thick carpet of snow so deep not a trace of blood could be seen outside to suggest a terrible murder had been done.

A carpet of snow which gave the singular impression she was cut in half at the waist or had squirmed beneath its upturned, oddly crumpled edge, as if escaping from this world into the next. As Ruby would forever say she was. A deeply superstitious woman of dark imagination who in those days of terrible murder to come would endlessly tell what she had seen that afternoon in that dreadful house of horrors. The second murder that house had known since it was built, but not for a hundred years and once gain it was a woman who was brutally killed. An impression made all the more powerful by the drawn up, faintly ridiculous, posture of her left leg, which even now seemed to be in a rush to escape her attacker, but not into the world beyond the door, a world stilled by frosted mist and unblemished snow, but somewhere else.

A pristine white snow that blanketed the terrace she lay so pitiably dead upon like a duvet, as it did the Wisteria-snaked for sixty years, hip-high, grey-stone balustrade that surrounded it on three sides and the four, green-stained, Tibetan cremation urns that stood on their solid square plinths at the top and bottom of the wide steps that for the last fifty one years of her sheltered, rather indulged and mostly protected life, had carried her into the tranquil retreat of that delightfully private garden. Her own *secret garden,* she liked to say. A garden Gloria Hussey loved every bit as much, as she did, and a hundred times said she did. A garden inspired by the book of the same name and she the lonely girl who brought it to new life after so many years of sad neglect. As *Mary Lennox* brought the garden at *Misselthwaite Manor* back to life in Frances Hodgson Burnett's enchanting book, an inspiring book she had many times told her husband every little boy and girl should read. A book her mother gave her for a present on her eighth birthday in 1919; the year she died of the awful influenza, which killed so many.

A lovingly tended garden that boasted a stock of mature trees and artfully shaped bushes that were the envy of her neighbours up and down the gently curving, hillside lane her villa stood so magnificently upon, near the top. Apple, pear, cherry, damson, peach and Victoria plum, whose sweet, fleshy fruit she so adored, fir, beech, oak, cedar, Japanese maple, silver birch and a magnificent pair of weeping willows with a trunk so broad she could hardly get her arms about them, now. A favourite place for the swans to nest she every spring encouraged, who even now gathered beneath their draping branches, as if knowing something ghastly had happened.

But her favourites were the two Californian red wood sequoias that soared into the sky just where the garden's, carefully stepped and manicured fall to the river neared its bottom and so perfectly planted by the platoon of soldiers her father sent to dig them in, all those many years ago they hid nothing of the view from her bedroom window, just above where she now lay. But framed it with their majestic, unbending forms as if it was a painted picture. As she often thought it was, particularly when she saw it in the sun dappled early morning mist or in the moon-kissed late evening when the world appeared to be so unreal, as if it was just born or about to die. A bright and spacious corner room that had been hers since she was a little girl she chose for the fairy-tale, Corbel turret, one of two that dominated the front entrance, as they did the back at the corners, which gave her such a perfect view across the city almost to the bridge.

But sadly, hers alone since her husband left her bed and never came back. A day she remembered as if it was only yesterday, so horrible was the abandonment and hurt she felt he had found someone else to take her place. One of many women who came and went over the years he quickly tired of. Pauline Fisk his on-off lover for so many years, though never anything special, but with a theatrical love of life and art, she rather admired her from afar, but now replaced by that silly little creature, Barbara Archer. A teacher, like Pauline, at his school she had several times met, whose husband was the handsome lothario, she had come to hate and longed to leave. Wanted to leave him to be with her husband, as he so much wanted to be with her, but couldn't and never could because he too much liked the house and money her marriage gave him.

But a second favourite in the garden were the three palm trees that had grown beyond all measure of their expectation, she, and her much loved and everyday sadly missed father had bought on a whim in Torquay in the early summer of 1946 when he was returned from Paris. That in a closely planted, fan display beside the red lacquer painted, elegantly tall, Japanese pagoda that stood on the small promontory, marked the northern end of the garden's seventy yard, long riverside bank. As the thicket of red, blue, white and yellow flowered rhododendrons beside the boat house marked the other, a display of early colour she always longed to see but would see no more.

A glorious idyll made all the more amazing by the criss-cross of cinder paths and flagged steps that meandered through the dense grown Hosta's, ferns, bushes, shrubs, and tall, feathered grasses her mother had planted with such a loving care before the Great War. Junipers, azaleas, Acers, Forsythias, Camélias, Clematis and Magnolias, to name but a few of her huge collection. A collection that brought such an astonishing show of vibrant light, shadow, colour, figure and form to that peaceful place and all the more wonderful now it was cloaked in winter snow and with a raw, wraith-like fog of mist rising from the river behind it in an icy chill.

Snow that draped every leaf, stem, spine, prickle and branch of that hidden garden in an eerie glaze so startling in its sudden, untouched, delicate newness; in its quiet, serene isolation it bewitched and deceived the eye to think it was never more beautiful than this; perhaps it never was.

Even the eight feet high, ivy clad, grey-stone walls that enclosed both its northern uphill and southern downhill boundaries in an ambling stepwise fall, managed to look more perfect than they ever did before. As did the long, brick and wood, greenhouses, sturdy sheds and forty gallons, wood barrel, water butts that stood beneath them, their wood silvered by age to a sheen. The summerhouse she often read in, the arbours, the arches, the pergolas and the red cedar, gable roofed boathouse, the upturned boat and oars beside it, the white and green painted Dove Cote that marked the gardens middle. And the score of statues, Greek, Roman, Byzantine, Syrian, Nabataean, Ethiopian, Tibetan, Chinese and Japanese that gave that expansive two acre plot an exotic grace and haunting beauty her father had brought from every overseas posting he ever had. But nothing more so than the ten-foot-tall, standing stone he had stolen and shipped from Carnac forty years before, which sat in a circle of twelve smaller stones on a secluded terrace.

*

'A bad business,' said Chief Inspector, Tomon Hughes, rising from the body with ill-disguised anger and disgust. A veteran of twenty-seven years in the city force and a man who had seen more than his fair share of violent death and murder, but never one so seemingly out of place as this one, so jarring was the sight of her corpse in that tastefully decorated room. A man whose six feet two inches of broad shouldered, well-muscled flesh, curt manner, grim expression and sometimes harsh tongue, hid a kindly heart from those who knew him. And kindlier grown, they would be surprised to learn, since the death of his much-loved wife of twenty-five years, just a year ago from the cancer that had stalked her for the last five years. And with two teenage daughters he loved, who exasperated him more than he could say; dare ever say.

'Yes sir,' answered Sergeant Brian Fasthead, his brisk agreement, who was standing half a yard behind him fingering the black shiny peak of his flat, uniform hat in a distraction that hoped the sickly shock he now felt was not too much noticed by his superior. A man he envied, feared, disliked and generally avoided because he had twice in the last two years - the last time just four months ago, refused his well-earned application to become a detective. Whose good opinion he also needed if the promotion to acting Inspector he was half promised by their Chief Superintendent, and he so much wanted with a fourth baby due next January, was to be had.

A steady, reliable, if flawed man in the opinion of the man who now watched him from beneath his jaunty, though sadly worn by many years of constant wear and tear, finger bent, two and a quarter inch wide, snap brimmed, brown felt hat, with sphinx-like, though far from dissatisfied eyes. Who with his companion, Constable John Williams were the first to arrive at the scene in their black four doors 1959, *Morris Minor, 1000?* A toadying twat of a buck-toothed grinning, nineteen-year-old, ex-police cadet with barely ten months' regular service under his slim waisted belt. Who now stood an impressively smart, can-you-see-me, can-you, sort of guardsman's sentry beneath his flat hat beside the hallway door, directly in front of the body?

Were called to the scene, Williams was the first to inform him, by the strikingly attractive, bottle-blonde, Gloria Hussey, whose elegant haute couture, shapely, yet provocatively slim beauty, high class, snooty manner and surprisingly calm composure at the impressively pillared and porticoed front door had done so much to disarm them both to the horror within. Which, now seemed so much worse than it was when they first arrived at precisely 14.44pm, their journey from the City Road, *Mackenzie Trench* call box taking them less than eight and a half minutes in the icy slush and snow that had slowed the traffic in front of them to a crawl? Called them on the house telephone that sat on the Tiger Oak stand beneath the magnificent sweep of the Italian marble and oak spindled stairs. An old, but serviceable, 1947, black, *Bakelite, King Pyramid, 232, GPO* rotary dial telephone, Tomon could easily see over his left shoulder. A call that was routed to the City Road box from the police headquarters on Foregate Street, a call that was logged at 14.31pm, six, long minutes after Mrs Hussey saw the body.

Was it the bitter cold breeze from the open French door that made him shiver or was it the sight of Violet's body lying in that singularly odd pose, one that even Alfred Hitchcock would find difficult to credibly pull off? Sergeant Fasthead wondered. A cold that had done so little to rid the room of the horrible smell of piss and blood, though there was little of it to be seen, except for the slight splash he could see on the carpet beside her left leg. Or was it death's finality that made him tremble and cloyed at his nose, as his eyes once again swept the room for the clue, he hoped would make his reputation. A bravura moment of *modus ponens* or was it *modus tollens*, he could never remember, which, his detective instructor at the District Police Training Centre at Bruche, a year ago, had said was so vitally important when building a sound evidential case. Though his recently passed - though only just, Inspectors exam, said he must. A triumph that would earn the Chief Inspector's admiration, as he so much wanted the admiration of that reticent, hard-faced man. But if clue there was and he was sure something else was twitching his nose, it clearly wasn't for him to find, he felt certain of that, though in his bones he knew there was something not right, something he had overlooked before Tomon came in.

'How much longer?' Snapped, a waspish Gloria Hussey with dagger-like irritation as she smoked a third cigarette and slow walked a path between Constable Williams and the polished to an impossible shine, 1911, black satinwood, *Steinway & Sons,* art case, grand piano and matching, pink cushioned, duet stool that did so much to dominate that far quarter of the room behind him. Where a second door, the twin of the one Williams stood beside in his unflagging sentry duty, opened a second, if never used exit into the russet brown, cream and blue, geometrically tiled hallway that pierced the house from front to back in an arrow straight line.

A doorway, which elegantly framed the George II, *Chippendale card table* that stood in front of it and the 1910, *Edison Amberola phonograph* and silk flower filled, *Wedgwood,* cobalt blue vase that sat on top of it. A piece of furniture he and his ambitious wife would never own on his still modest salary, which had a rectangular top, cut with squared candle recesses over a shallow case with a small, brass handled drawer at the front of it that was supported by two deeply carved acanthus knee, cabriole legs, which ended in a ball and claw foot at the front and two slightly cabriole legs on padded feet at the back. A stylish table finished to perfection with a gadroon apron carved with a shell pendant beneath the drawer. A snip at £1500 that was looted by the crafty old General during the German revolution of 1919 when he commanded a small detachment of soldiers in the West Berlin suburb of Charlottenburg and liberated it with several other portable pieces from a well-appointed, four bedroomed, apartment on Sophie-Charlotten Strasse. Though the owners, a Prussian military officer and his stuck-up wife said he mustn't and with such a fierce resistance he had to shoot them both dead in the face. But then the wily old bastard hated every foreigner he ever met and none more than the fucking Hun.

Both doors white painted with a stained glass, half window which matched the design of the French windows they both stood opposite and each one, set in matching, Ovolo architraves that did so much to emphasise the generous height of the ceiling and draw the eye to the ten-branch, silver and glass chandeliers that hung in front of them. Their light twinkling above the Stannard's, the Drummond's and the John Yeend King's that hung on every wall. Pastoral, rustic and marine scenes his wife would adore, even if they were cheap prints from *Woolworths.*

Doors with a fist sized, reeded, brass handles, roses and escutcheons that would make a fine finish to the three bedroomed, end terraced house he was busily renovating in Saughall, just now. A thankful escape, two months ago from the god awful police house he had lived in, in Hatton Road for the last eight years, which had the county police coat of arms above the front door that invited every kind of nuisance neighbour and troublemaker to knock on it whenever they liked, which was usually about three o'clock in the morning when he was long asleep.

Not so calm now, he thought, casting an appreciative look at Mrs Hussey. A woman Tomon would be surprised, and perhaps a little shocked to learn, he knew if only by sight. Had several times seen before, the last time, and every time before that, in the lounge bar of Greyhound Public House, his latest, late night watering hole. A coincidence, and he was always wary of coincidences, thinking them more than mere chance, as most people do, but spooky, improbable things that set his teeth on edge and always connected, as life often is, without we know it is. Like everything in the world is linked in some mysterious way. Past, present and future just one and the same thing, if we could only see it was! See what was staring us right in the face!

But a coincidence made spookier still when he remembered the nightmare hallucination that assailed his eyes the last time he did. Last Thursday evening, the thirteenth, to be precise, the coldest night of that growing ever colder winter, when he saw a man in the bar, turn into a horned Satyr right in front of him and a dozen others in the room turn into ghouls in a sun bright meadow. Had, just before that, seen him kissing a gorgeous blonde woman in a black beret and equally stylish black ensemble, who looked like a *Vogue* model and because he saw he did, and with an appreciative, perhaps even jealous look in his eye, came over to him all prick and balls and tried to pick a fight. A posturing bully who backed away when he solidly stood his ground, as men like him do. A story he didn't dare tell anyone; never would, realising it was a symptom of the stress he had been under these past few weeks. A stress that was about to get worse, that imperceptible paled and flattened his face into a look of faintly troubled concern.

A look Gloria Hussey was quick to notice and quick to ignore with a snigger, despite he was a handsome fellow with the tall, dark, sharp featured, good looks she so admired in a man and with that glint in his eye that knew him for the ladies' man he was or would like to be.

But snigger though she did, she was worried and no mistake, as he and Tomon saw she was, but was still far more composed than her two companions, the quietly sobbing into her handkerchief, Mrs Edna Scullion and the sickly pale, but now fast recovering, Mrs Plant, whose own understated, well rounded good looks had not gone unnoticed by him or Tomon, who watched them.

Both of them sitting in the one of the two, deep cushioned, red chintz settees behind the second French window that boxed the well-lit to a roaring flame, Neo classical, white marble fireplace that dominated that end of the room. The eighteen inch high, pierced Edwardian brass and red leather cushioned fender, the matching swan bellied, coal filled scuttle, the set of barley twisted brass fire irons, the flower painted, plum green, smoked glass and brass fire screen, the decorative fire dogs and heavy grate casting a dance of sparkling light and shadow onto the frieze of finely traced egg and dart moldings that clung to the underside of the dimpled white ceiling above the soft pink, Regency styled, two tone striped wallpaper that covered the walls on every side. But no less impressively than the enormous, well stocked mahogany bookcase, *Giuseppe Rocca,* cello, bow and music stand that filled the other end. And where a three-fold, mahogany framed, linen screen, decoupaged with English country flowers stood to the right of Constable Williams and two, three feet high, fat bellied Chinese blue and gold enamelled vases painted with ugly fish, added to the refined display of wealth and taste that filled ever corner of that room. A wealth he instinctively knew was the reason, Violet Casterbrook had been murdered.

'A little longer, ladies, if you don't mind,' answered the Chief Inspector, with a hard worked bonhomie that ignored Gloria Hussey was still pacing a hole in the carpet and hid the seething irritation her companions, were still sitting where Sergeant Fasthead had found them when he arrived. Had refused his polite request they should leave, not once, but several times, content, it would now appear to tearfully ogle Violet's body, their friend of many years, he wondered they could stand the sight of her. A sight that made him blanch with shock and disgust anyone could do a thing like that. Kill a defenceless, old woman without the least compunction. An act of unmitigated evil that could never be assuaged or forgiven by the blandishments of a barrister but try they would. As he knew to his cost they would and often succeeded.

'Really. That long,' answered Gloria Hussey, spitting her impatient irritation back into his seemingly placid face, as she fixed him with a sullen stare that hated she was so confined by a man who ignored her, as few men did. A handsome man like his sergeant, but in a very different way, who reminded her of Trevor Howard's, *Major Calloway* in the 1949 film noire, *The Third Man* and just as annoyingly self-satisfied and comfortable in his old hat and coat as he was in his. A man who had never once looked at her with anything more than a cynically disparaging, almost accusing eye, who even now, stared at her like she had something to hide; she did.

A film she had seen when she was pregnant with Colin, the son she had never truly liked, not as a mother should and grown to dislike and distrust even more since he had taken up with that unbearable lout, Lomas, who stared at her with such a sneer she hated to be in the same room as him. A horrible time of pain and anxiety that even now, thirteen years later, was instantly brought to mind by that awful zither music that played throughout the film and still did. Music she couldn't bear to listen, too, that mocked her misfortune she ever met her husband and was pregnant by him at barely sixteen, mocked her as nothing else could, who even now thought Colin wasn't his. Though Lomas came close to it, shagging her Colin like he was an arse-up, gagging for it little queer and all the while knowing she knew he did; and laughing she did; the twat. She didn't mind queers, as men do, but she didn't want one of her own with a lover like that. Not in the least feminine, sweet or artistic, as so many of them were, but a dirty thug.

'Have you called, Dr Marcus, Sergeant?' Asked the Chief Inspector, ignoring her with a calm he knew would infuriate her every bit as much as his refusal to acknowledge she was anything more important to him or his investigation than the witness she was, since first they met.

'Yes sir,' answered Sergeant Fasthead, knowing he knew full well he had. Had very clearly said he had, in the first, brief report he gave to him the minute he stepped out of the back door of the 1958, *Series II, special edition 6/90, black Wolseley* police car, his bagman of many years everywhere drove him and at speeds that were never safe, sane or legal, despite the noisy, two tone blare of the roof mounted, air sirens and flashing blue lights that cleared his way.

And a second time said he had, at the end of the extended report he was then asked to give and with instructions from the doctor that were as particular as they were rude. 'Leave nothing out,' he said, as he knelt on one knee beside the body, his hand touching the back of Violet's leg. 'First impressions to last, sergeant, I don't care how insignificant they may appear to be, now, they may offer a clue of sorts. Anything. Anything at all that struck you as out of place, or the least bit odd, or noteworthy when you first came in. You'd be surprised what the mind will all too quickly forget when you see a thing like this. Just walk me through the scene. The ambient temperature, the smell, the feel of the place, everything you saw or heard when you first stepped through that door,' he had said. 'Just walk me through it.' And he did just that not ten minutes ago and he knew he hadn't forgotten but was surely playing some sort of clever mind game.

Chapter 19

Monday December 17, 1962
Frank Sinatra: I Gotta Right to Sing the Blues

'*Well.*' He had tentatively begun, really not wanting to say any more than he already had and fearing a trap that would bury his career forever in the mire it appeared to have fallen into these last three years. Though why it should have, he couldn't imagine, given his twelve months, twice mentioned in despatches, National Service in Korea and near record breaking promotion to Sergeant in just six, faultless years of tireless effort. Something he had not done in the ten minutes he had sole charge of the crime scene, which would further earn his disapproval, for he was certain the Chief Inspector disapproved of him and rather a lot; but why?

A fear made all the more palpable by his bagman, a baleful, physically powerful, shorn to the scalp, bully of a passed over sergeant, whose impressive forty-four years' service was almost a record in the force. A crony of the Chief Constable from the First World War, it was rumoured, who looked at him with such a curious, dare-you sort of thin smile on his flint-hard, red flushed, smirking face, he felt like a worm on the end of a very large hook; and he knew he did.

*

'*As you can see, sir the property is a substantial, six bedroomed house in one of the most sought after residential areas in the city,*' he continued, sounding, though he had yet to realise he did, like his own, deeply mistrusted, estate agent, '*and with neighbours to the front and sides in houses just as imposing as this one, though none more so than this is, which is a real peach, whichever way you look at it.*' He Smiled. '*Upstairs there is a broad, carpeted landing at the top of the stairs you see behind Constable Williams, which overlooks the front drive and leads, of course, to the bedrooms, two dressing rooms and four upstairs bathrooms and toilets. All of them empty and undisturbed when we looked in, though Ruby said, she thought Mrs Casterbrook's room has been searched, though we could see nothing untoward to confirm it was. There's an attic above, they use as a storeroom, which is accessed by a narrow stairway on this front side of the house and a second back stairs, which comes up from the kitchen. Mr and Mrs Casterbrook appear to occupy two different bedrooms and use two different bathrooms, both of them substantial, as you might imagine. Hers above this,*' he pointed with his finger to the ceiling above their head. '*His on the same side overlooking the garden and river, where else, at the far end and with easy access to the back stairs, which may or may not be significant,*' he pointed again with his finger, his face clearly suggesting it wasn't. *'The door to the attic was open when we arrived, but by the look of it, it is little used by anyone except, perhaps the maid, Ruby, who said she sometimes goes up there, but hasn't for a long time. Usual junk, but not so much you can hide and not so much you can't comfortably walk from one end to the other and with good light from both the two working fluorescent lights and the two skylights, which I doubt have been opened since Adam was a lad. Downstairs there are four or five reception rooms, depending on your point of view and all of them as beautifully decorated and furnished as this one is. Which is as good as any I have seen,'* he again smiled. *'And that includes the upstairs bedrooms. Down the corridor that way,'* he again pointed with his finger, *'and adjacent to this room, is a morning room which has been set with a folding, green baize Bridge table and chairs, which like this one and the formal dining room beyond that, opens through French windows onto the terrace. Opposite is a study/library, a breakfast room and a large kitchen with a walk-in pantry, utility/washroom. The back door into the yard and garden was also locked when we arrived, and Ruby said it had been all morning and the key hanging on a hook on the pantry wall where it always does and no way in or out without it. Mrs Casterbrook allowing her to use the front door when Mr Casterbrook was out, as he was, him being a stickler for that sort of Upstairs-Downstairs sort of master and servant, Edwardian thing. Beneath the stairs, just behind you, is a substantial basement come coal house, which Constable Williams made a quick search of before you arrived, but like everywhere else found nothing to suggest the killer was hidden down there. Isn't that right, constable?'*

'Yes, sir,' he quickly answered, his face turned to the Chief Inspector, who was staring out of the window and thinking what a beautiful day it was, more lovely than any day he'd known since his wife died; the view he realised. A day of light and shade and birdsong as he had never thought to hear again. It was if time was suspended; caught in the thrall of its beguiling, winter enchantment. One that looked in loathing on the sight it found in that pretty room.

'The house stands in two acres or more of prime land, most of it to the rear of the property beside the river,' he continued, pointing to the sparkling, mist hung, snow covered garden with a broad sweep of his left hand and sounding, and he again realised he did, like the worst kind of estate agent he had ever met. But most definitely not like the spiv who sold him his own bijou dwelling. A steal at four hundred and twenty-five pounds, the lying bastard had said. Describing it as, an attractive labourer's cottage with many original features and with a charming country pub within easy walking distance of its gabled front door. Yeah, of course it was. Everything a couple mortgaged up to the hilt on less than twelve pounds a week and with four hungry mouths to feed, could dream of owning. By which, he meant in his own bollocky way of saying these things, it was a near derelict, two up and two down, end terrace so close to the only pub in the village - the Greyhound, he could hear the drunks spilling out of it at ten forty every night, and sometimes did himself, if he could find a ten bob note his wife hadn't already spent. *'It's enclosed at the front and on both sides by a high stonewall, probably eight or nine feet high, less maybe, it's difficult to say with all this*

snow and by the garden and the river to the rear, as I just said. The front wall stands about twenty feet from the house and is continuous with the two adjacent, occupied properties, which like this one is protected on the top by a vicious row of broken glass and iron spikes. The only way into the property that I can see from the Lane, by foot or by car, is either through the wooden carriage gate on the uphill end of the property or through the small, wooden gate that opens at the downhill end, which was locked. The uphill gate, as you saw when you drove in, opens onto a substantial cobbled drive-in front of the lofted, double garage and the main entrance to the house. Parking for five or six cars at a pinch, I should think, though the Casterbrook's appear to own just two, the British racing green, 1959, Jaguar XK 150, sports car, which is locked in the garage, which Mrs Hussey says belongs to Mrs Casterbrook ....'

'That's right, Chief Inspector, Violet bought it new as she did all her cars and was a very keen driver since long before the war, wasn't she Edna, wasn't she Daphne? Since the late twenties, when she learned to drive in India, where the old General was stationed for many years; Burma, too and Tibet, I remember her saying.' Interrupted, Gloria Hussey, who, when the Chief Inspector, first arrived hoped to impress him with her account; she hadn't. Her voice a highly contrived nasal confection of stunted vowels and stretched consonants, she hoped captured the quality of Kay Kendall's effortless diction in the film, *Genevieve*. A Yorkshire woman born and bred, she was astonished to read in a magazine - *ABC Film Review, Flix* or was it *The Listener,* she couldn't recall, but without a trace of an accent and sounding more Home Counties than

the Queen. Which, despite her gorgeous blonde hair, which men adored better than the brunette she was, no matter how she wore it, and she wore it up today in a loose twist, was the leitmotif of her life. And for no better reason than Kay was the quintessentially, elegant English woman of breeding she strived to be. And so effortlessly played in *Genevieve,* which more than any film she had seen showed her the life she longed to have; a life that might now be hers. If her useless prick of a near bankrupt husband inherited Violets considerable house and fortune before that jumped up tosser of a Jonny-come-lately, Lionel Casterbrook did, which she hoped and prayed the gods in heaven he would and why not, they both deserved it.

'*Exactly,*' he said, watching the firelight bathe her face in a soft yellow glow that showed no trace of sorrow or regret in the sculpted lines of her upturned face; nor any attempt to show there was. A flint hard bitch and he had met plenty of her sort in his time. A woman to watch, though he doubted she wielded the blow that killed her friend, though she might know who did with all her money to be had. *'A grey, with silver trim 1957, Wolseley, 15/50 saloon he drives every day.'* Again, something Gloria Hussey was quick to confirm behind the cloud of cigarette smoke that blew from her mouth, the second cigarette she had smoked since he arrived.

'*Yes,*' she answered with a smile of appreciation she was, at long last, included in his growing more tedious account, which told her nothing she didn't know or hadn't already guessed, that gave him a more perfect look at her elegantly crossed legs, which she turned towards him with a confidence that knew how to impress a man like him. Any man for that matter. And her long and shapely legs beneath her burgundy, pencil skirt were as much a compliment to her beauty as the daring plunge of her neckline beneath the white, pleated silk blouse she wore. Which, gathered at the neck in a simple ruff above the collar of her stylishly tailored, winter coat, flattered the imperious arch of her neck and diamond drop earrings better than anything Daphne Plant could ever wear, and she wore everything so well. Much to Sydney's boastfully preening delight and her spoilt, but beautiful stepdaughter's sulky sullen dismay.

'Thank you, Mrs Hussey, you are most kind, but to continue, if I may,' he patiently said, turning on his heels face his Chief Inspector, who, now half turned from the window watched her all too obvious attempts to seduce his Sergeant with a look she found hard to read; as did his Sergeant.

Disapproval certainly, but was there a hint of jealously pique, she wondered in those ever-watchful eyes? A question he quickly answered, she was dismayed to see, with a second mirthless look, which, seeming to read her coquettes, wanton mind, said a most emphatic no there wasn't.

'The front door is substantial by any stretch of the imagination, as you no doubt saw when you came in, sir, as is the back door and both of them locked, as was the back gate, as I said, when Ruby left the house at approximately 12.30pm. And her mistress still very much alive to remind her to pick up Mr Casterbrook's dry cleaning on her way back from her lunch, on the Tarvin Road. A bit of a hike out of her way in this weather, but not so far it would take her almost two hours; but it did?'

Once again, he pointed with his finger their approximate locations, much to the bagman's amusement, who urged him on with a sniggering look that was enjoying every minute of his interrogation. That even then knew the husband had done his wife in.

'*Go on Sergeant,*' said the Chief Inspector, seemingly pleased with his report and not in the least inclined to hurry him, his face returned to the window and the robin that had just landed on the nearest of the snow topped, Tibetan cremation urns to stare at Violet's body. A messenger from the gods come to bear witness to her murder and to promise the killer it would not go unpunished. A nonsense of course, but a pretty thing that made a promise of sorts on that mournful day.

'*An odd looking house from the outside, don't you think sir, what with the long sides running parallel to the Lane and the river, can't say I've seen anything like it before, but as secure as the proverbial drum as far as I am able to judge,*' he replied thinking to lighten the mood a little.

'*Perhaps,*' said the Chief Inspector, turning again to look at the three women seated beside the fireplace. A look that gruffly said they shouldn't be there! A look they returned with equal certainty they were going nowhere, but would hear his nice, Sergeant's report to the very end.

'*Mmm, it just struck me as a strange way to build a house, when you have all this land to play with, but maybe that's the way they did things back in 1863,*' he said, seeing his look and knowing he should have insisted they should sit in the morning room, as he twice urged them. But they refused.

Mrs Scullion with a tearful sigh, Mrs Hussey with that scowl she reserved for oiks like him and Mrs Plant with a deep throated sob that would never leave the others.

'1863?' Asked the Chief Inspector, thoughtfully. Heartened, though he didn't show he was by the thoroughness of his report, which he had so far enjoyed, a mental appreciation of the facts, as known to someone else taught to him by an old friend, whose experience of such things was legend.

'Yes, sir, the date it was built, I think. It's written on the stained-glass transom window just above the front door with the name of the man who owned it or perhaps the architect who designed it. Mr Byron Blisset, July 1863', he replied, pleased he had seen that very small detail when he came in, and he hadn't. Or had he? He now wondered seeing the small smile crease his face.

'Gettysburg, Sergeant,' was his enigmatic reply. A name of sorts he vaguely knew from a film he had once seen. Or was it a book he had once read, he couldn't remember, which? Nor think how to reply to him with anything other than the quizzical look he now gave him. *The Red Badge of Courage,* with Audie Murphy, perhaps, he lamely thought. Little knowing the Chief Inspector had a fondness for all things, American, not least their war torn, selfishly savage revolutionary history, since he worked with their Military Police in the latter part of the War. The Nuremberg war trials, being his last and least fondly remembered attachment to their white helmeted, Snowdrops before his return to the UK in November 1946. A late, but very welcome return home from

more than six years' active service that saw his promotion to Sergeant delayed until 1950, despite he was a Major when he left the army and lesser men, including his ambitious, Chief Superintendent, promoted long before him. And only made Chief Inspector on the back of the work he did for the Special Branch in the Malaya Emergency in 1956. But a promotion he none-the-less owed to Lieutenant Colonel A A Dent, late of MI6 who was his commanding officer back then and a man who had taught him everything he knew. A friend he visited as often as time would allow, and when last, he did, only last week, introduced to his charming lodger, as she rushed out of the front door. To a date, he rightly guessed by the flushed look on her happy face. Astonishingly beautiful and alluring young, French woman called, Valeria, who smiled at him with such a saucy mischief in her eyes, he almost lost his heart to her. Would have lost his heart to her had he been twenty-five years younger.

'Sir?' He asked, seeing the amused half smile come to the Chief Inspectors distracted face.

'Nothing, Sergeant, but I suspect the architect had a greater concern for the narrow sandstone bluff this house and all the other houses on this side of the hill are built upon, the gardens steep fall to the river and the turning circle required for a carriage and four, which the substantial garage was surely built to accommodate, when he put the front entrance where it is.'

'Oh,' was all he could reply, as Gloria Hussey glanced a smirking, though not inconsiderate smile at him, impressed by the Chief Inspector, who for the first time glanced at her with anything, but the stern look he had so far given her. An oddly boyish smile she rather liked, but one that too much remembered, Valeria and not for her, who he would love to see again.

'But the name on the transom window is most certainly the proud owner of this commodious accommodation and not the architect, who, I suspect, by the rather grand design of the four Corbel turrets at each corner, is none other than the celebrated Victorian architect, Sir George Gilbert Scott. Whose name, though now a little obscured by the ivy and lichen is carved just below the apex of the roof at the front, but had it not been, would have been revealed by the boastfully decorative chimney stacks, which though hardly visible from the front drive, are easily seen from the Lane. A Gothic revival much in tune with his twee Victorian renaissance pretensions, which rise quite unnecessarily, in my opinion from the middle of the two longer sides of this ugly, if fascinatingly impressive house, to overlook the Lane and gardens below.'

'Yes, sir,' he answered, thinking him a cocky, clever sod, but more than a little discomfited by his obvious lack of knowledge and doubly cautioned not to underestimate him again.

'But no matter, I doubt it advances our investigation a jot to know any of that useless twaddle, but it makes for an interesting diversion, don't you think, Constable Williams? You were saying, Sergeant Fasthead,' he asked before the eager young man could offer his own opinion.

'Yes, sir. It seems the front gate is locked shut every night and opened every morning by Mr Casterbrook, before he leaves for work at 8.30am. As it was this morning, though he left a

little before that because Ruby said he and his wife had a row and he left in a huff at about eight.'

'Interesting', he's the Headmaster of Love Street Secondary Modern, if I'm not mistaken?' Said the Chief Inspector, knowing full well he was. A man he had several times met and several times disliked for the pompous, overblown humbug he was! A barking mad bully like all his kind, as he well-remembered from his own school days, though the City Grammar was his alma mater. But a fine, Olympic class sportsman he had many times heard it said.

'Yes, he is, sir, I sent a man over to the school to fetch him just before you came. He should be back with him in the next few minutes, I should think. Though his secretary, a Miss Paget, said she would have to call him on the Tannoy as he wasn't in his office. But she confirmed he was there. Seems he wasn't too long back from a practice gala they are having at the swimming baths where he'd been since late that morning and in full view of most the school.'

'Good, see he's met at the door when he gets here and don't let him see any of this when he comes in, take him straight away to the morning room where we can talk. That screen might help? Put it here, he pointed a spot three feet from the door and twelve from the body. *That's your job, Williams,* he said with a grim smile that had more threat in it than the warmth he supposed.

Yes, sir, answered Constable Williams, surprised the screen was as heavy and as cumbersome as it was and almost collapsing beneath its weight when he tried to manoeuvre it into its new position.

'Steady Constable that screen probably worth ten years of what we pay you,' said the Chief Inspector.

'Sorry sir.'

'No other way in, Sergeant'

'Not really. But to cover all bases there's an iron grated, coal hole, which opens onto the pavement outside, which drops into the basement. The door, as I previously said, is just below the stairs by the telephone,' he pointed. *Anyway, the door was locked from the outside when we checked it, but as I said we had a look just to make sure no one was lurking about in the dark down there. Well Constable Williams had a look, didn't you, Williams and saw nothing of any note?'*

'Yes, sir,' he again confirmed he didn't. But unsure if the door was locked or not but remembering the fear he felt when he took his first few tentative steps into that dark place, the light of his service torch casting a thin beam that barely saw anything in that junk cluttered, black hole.

'So, given no one has come in through the coal-hole, which require a set of purpose made levers to lift it up more than an inch or two, or came in through the garden, and by the pristine look of it and the terrace, no one has,' he said pointing to the mantle of white snow that covered them, *'it's my guess whoever murdered her came in through the front door. Either forced his way in when she opened it, which I doubt he did, she's a very big woman, as you can see and formidable, too, from what Ruby has told me of her forcefully fierce character. She being the daughter of a General and not the sort of woman to be daunted by threats of violence at the front door of her home. Not by anyone. But very much the sort of woman who would put up a terrific fight if*

she was threatened by a stranger and there are no signs she did, not in the vestibule entrance, the hallway, or in here. Whoever it was, she knew and trusted. And because she did, he came up behind her when her back was turned and hit her savagely on the back of her head, not once, but twice by the thin splash of blood on the carpet and then fell headlong through the door. Perhaps was trying to escape him, knowing that was the only way to get out of the room?'

'Perhaps,' answered the Chief Inspector.

'So, it seems likely to me whoever it was talked his way in. A salesman or street vendor, door knocking his way up the Lane. Or someone who pretended he was? Or, if not a stranger, then someone she knew or was in some way acquainted with, a tradesman perhaps? Though maybe not one she regularly uses, but someone she no less trusted? Someone from MANWEB or the Gas Board? Or said he was? But if it wasn't someone, she opened the door, too, it has to be someone who had a key because there is no sign of a forced entry at the front or back door, sir.'

'Are you certain the windows were all securely locked, Sergeant, if this was a two-handed robbery gone wrong, then a man might easily be lifted through a downstairs window to let the second man in whilst she was upstairs? And no one to see them from the Lane behind that wall if they darted through the gate?' Said the Chief Inspector, his tone mild and not at all disapproving.

'Certainly, sir, all the windows are vertically opening sash windows with a screwed in wooden jam at the top and bottom that prevents more than three inches of upwards or downwards slide, so there's no way in through them and no sign a jemmy was

used to force them, either. Not down stair or upstairs. Whoever it was they came through the front gate and door!

Mmm, he remembered, was his disappointing reply, as he cast a first critical look at Mrs Edna Scullion, the most distressed of the three women, as she had been since he arrived. A tall, thin, bob-cut, bespectacled woman, whose Chapel-certain-she-was-always-right, harshly unforgiving face, was crumpled into floods of tears beneath the misty lenses of her blue, butterfly-winged spectacles, which more than anything else appeared to confirm her innocence; that and she was the last to arrive. Whose dour, almost comical appearance in sensible-for-the-weather, still-wet-on-her-head, tight-tied-at-her-neck, pink plastic hat, loose belted *Camel Wrap* coat, powder-blue woollen twin set, baggy grey, thick-buttoned-from-waist-to-hem, Herringbone skirt and horribly unfashionable utility zip-up, fur lined, brown suede ankle boots, was such a hapless contrast to her two immaculately dressed companions, she looked the image of *Martha Longhurst* in the television programme that was all the rage just then.

Mrs Plant, half her age at barely twenty-five, whose five feet six inch, neatly curved, size fourteen, quietly confident frame, was immaculately dressed in a crystal-fox, full-fur, Russian hat and matching three quarter length, fur-trimmed-at-the-collar-and-sleeve, expensive tan-brown suede coat, André Courrèges, sharply tailored black trousers, she bought on her Paris honeymoon, just two years before and all the more so in her elegant, knee length, brown leather boots.

An ensemble Gloria Hussey, so chic and so expensively

elegant in her own persuasive choice of tight skirt and fashionably cut, red leather coat, envied, no less than her age and her husband's wealth, though he was a thoroughly ugly old trout who had more than once tried to touch her up!

'*Good*', said the Chief Inspector, '*anything else I should know about before we get on?*'

'*There were no recognisable footprints or tyre prints in the snow outside when we arrived, sir, which wasn't surprising given the much heavier fall of snow, we'd had in the last hour and the tread and slush marks made by the three cars already parked there, Mrs Hussey's, Mrs Plant's and Mrs Scullion's. Nor, as I previously said, was there any sign of a violent struggle anywhere in the house. It seems she was taken completely by surprise, struck on the head from behind with the blood stained golf club lying beside her left shoe, which was almost certainly taken from its canvas bag under the stairs*', he pointed to the fallen, barrel shaped, leathered bound, canvass bag and the spill of seven or eight clubs that fan-like were fallen beside it. '*The first blow was struck about there,*' he pointed to the just visible droplets of blood on the corn-coloured carpet, just beyond the now open screen. '*But not hard enough to stun or kill her, it would seem. You see,*' he pointed a second time, '*there is hardly any blood until she reaches the French window, three or four paces away, when she was probably hit a second time just after she unlocked the door and then several more times after that and this time very much harder by all the blood you can now see,*' he said, crouched beside the blood that spattered the carpet by the sill. Splashes of which he pointed on the wall, the sea-blue and gold, taffeta curtains, the sill, the gloss white wooden frame, the door and windows and even the ceiling above them.

'*Mmm,*' sighed the Chief Inspector taking in every detail.

'*The motive, and I know this is speculative, appears to have been an opportunistic robbery, which went horribly wrong with evidence several easily transportable items were stolen from the downstairs.* He paused hoping he might agree; he didn't appear, too. *A carriage clock from the mantelpiece in the sitting room next door, a silver cigarette box and lighter from in here and a small but very expensive, so Ruby said it was, watercolour from the wall over there and set of gold napkin rings from the dining room. And though she is far from certain, she thinks Mrs Casterbrook's jewellery box and possibly a substantial quantity of cash; fifty pounds at least, were taken from her bedroom. Though she may have returned her jewels and money to the safe after she left, which is very cleverly hidden in her fitted wardrobe and locked shut.*

'Could be? But let's keep an open mind, just for now, Sergeant, who's to say what this afternoon or tomorrow will bring? And the maid, Ruby found the body soon after she returned, you said?'

'Yes, it was Ruby who found the body at 14.20 and soon after that called Mrs Hussey in from her car, as she turned into the drive, the 1962, Jaguar E type, red, two door coupe, parked in front.'

Nice. I wondered who owned that. He answered, to the smirking approval of Gloria Hussey, who fixed him with a haughty, told-you-so, sort of gaze as she lit another cigarette from her lighter.

It was Mrs Hussey who phoned 999, five minutes before Mrs Plant and Mrs Scullion arrived by separate cars and in that order, Mrs Scullion driving the white, 1959, Mini, Mrs Plant the beautifully restored, azure blue, 1937, Triumph Dolomite Roadster, one of several vintage cars her husband owns.' She agreed, with a faint nod of her head, wanting to catch the Chief Inspectors eye, which she did, impressing him she was not only attractive, but thoroughly reliable, too.

'*Good work Sergeant, anything else, I should know,*' he answered ignoring Gloria Hussey's want of attention.

'*Yes, the perimeters secure. Forensics and photographer are on their way, as is the duty Home Office pathologist, Dr Marcus, who said he was busy, but would be sure to arrive before you left. Said you were not to touch anything before he says you can, sir. Nor should you leave before he's had a word with you, seemed most particular about that. A bit high handed I thought.*'

'*He is.*' Grunted the Chief Inspector, who knew him of old and despite his curt and sometimes deliberately obnoxious manner, liked and respected him, as he liked and respected him.

Chapter 20

Monday December 17, 1962
Roy Orbison: Dream Baby

Yes, he knew, alright. knew he had called the doctor, he smiled, turning to catch the eye of Gloria Hussey, who quite suddenly realised she knew him, though not to speak too, though she hoped that might be rectified when this terrible business was over, 'should be here soon, sir.'

'Good,' he answered.

'Mmm,' grunted Gloria Hussey, spinning on her stiletto heels to throw her half smoked cigarette waspishly into the fire before sinking into the settee opposite her companions in a disgruntled heap that still managed to look sophisticated and sexy, 'where the devil is that bloody woman, Ruby, she was supposed to bring us a large brandy and soda ten minutes ago,' she seethed.

'She's upset, Gloria, you know how she dotted on Violet,' said Daphne, kindly, her near finished cigarette elegantly posed in a three-inch-long, black cigarette holder, a look once again in vogue after Audrey Hepburn's, fabulous performance as quirky, *Holly Golightly* in the film *Breakfast at Tiffany's* last year. A woman much like her, she dared to think. A woman who had escaped a troubled past for a better future, though Sydney and his pampered and too much indulged, daughter, the monstrously selfish Linda were not the future she truly intended for herself.

'He's here now, sir,' called a respectful, Constable Williams, hearing the front door opened to the grumbling voice of the notoriously bad tempered police pathologist, a voice that grew louder as he kicked the snow from his heavy, black shoes and removed his battered Homburg from his head in an irritation he was called from his precious mortuary on so cold a day as this.

'Touched, nothing I hope, Tomon.' He barked in a middle European accent he refused to identify, as he rudely pushed his way past, Constable Williams. His diminutive five feet four inches of bristling authority commanding the scene until he said otherwise, an authority he took very seriously and would brook no challenge. An authority he relished because his trade in dead bodies was a speciality of singularly profound, not to say onerous merit, and his temper always frayed to a rag by the difficult and precise work he had done these thirty-five years and more.

'Nothing, doc,' answered the Chief Inspector with a polite deference, pointing to the meagre trail of blood spots that spattered the carpet to the open window.

'Sergeant,' said Dr Marcus, to Tomon's bagman, who was standing on the other side of the screen beside the cello. A man he had known since the late 1920's and saw promoted by Captain Horden to the rank of Detective Sergeant in 1934, the first there ever was. A position confirmed by Major Becke the following year and then again by Mr Banwell in 1946, his friend from the war, though he proved no friend to Major Tomon Hughes on his return. A man he liked, who was now just weeks away from his well-earned retirement, a retirement that would see the end of an era in British policing and one he greatly disapproved. It was discipline that was needed in this world, not the freedoms promised by books, television and film. A thin sort of freedom that set the labouring proles against their masters as never before, and no good would come of it, when the likes of Sergeant Wilding were gone. When he was gone as he soon would be.

'This the weapon, Tomon?' He demanded, his mood downcast by the thought of his going, no less than the sight of Violet's surreal, half-buried body, pointing to the blood soaked, golf club that rested on the carpet beside her well shod in a sensible brown brogue, left foot. An 1899 *Joe Anderson*, hand forged, smooth faced mashie, the old General had purchased when he was posted to Scotland before the Great War, as he had the other clubs that were spilled from their dried out leather bag in a fan, its metal head, yellow dappled with age, powerfully flexible Hickory shaft and worn, black leather grip soaked in an ooze of clotted blood.

'Seems likely,' said the Chief Inspector, knowing the fussy old Jew was a stickler for form and convention and would challenge any unsubstantiated claims he might make in public, though he was open and welcoming to any well-grounded opinion in private, and all the more when he had a large glass of malt whiskey and soda in his fat little fist, which he every night did.

'Yes, it does,' he parodied his caution. A thin and knowing smile parting his lips as he deeply inhaled the smoke from the stub of the fat cigar he was never without. Expensive Partagas or Bolivars that took an age to smoke and cost him a fortune to buy, but a cigar he was never without. 'Seems most likely, indeed, I'll grant you that, Tomon, but we'll see, hey? We'll see.

'Just as you say, sir,' answered the Chief Inspector, mildly. A non-smoker himself, he had detested the habit from when he was a boy and Marcus knew he did. Knew he hated the stream of smoke he deliberately blew in his direction but was too much of a gentleman to say he did.

We'll need photographs, of course, so mind your size elevens don't disturb my crime scene until I say they can and that includes the rest of you gawping clowns,' he growled, turning his rheumy old eyes on Sergeant Fasthead for the first time. A tall, athletic, muscularly strong man with a line of three colourful war ribbons on his chest, he knew only by sight. Who to his surprise was standing directly in front of the three women on either side of the fire, who with varying degrees of curiosity, watched him with an eager anxiety like the Chorus in some ancient Greek Tragedy? Euripides' Electra, he conjectured, such was the hopeless look of sadness on all their faces for the woman who lay prostrate and broken on the floor beside him. A woman slain in some cruel passion; but was it sacrifice or revenge that brought her to this bitter and bloody end? Was she the ill Fated, Iphigenia, slain in innocence to appease the gods or the guilty Clytemnestra, who so richly deserved her vengeful end? And was it Agamemnon or Electra, who did this terrible wrong? He wondered, doubting his metaphor would carry him much further than that pitifully weak and doubtful conclusion. 'And that mostly means you, Wilding, who stood unmoving beside the cello, as he had done since he first walked into the room.'

'Sir,' said Wilding, with that incongruous fondness that so often grows between men of intellectual distinction, if not physical prowess and the hardy, uncomplaining foot soldiers they think to command. Each recognising in the other the deficiencies they too little care to name.

'Sam's on his way with his trusty *Kodak* as we speak, doc,' said the Chief Inspector and forensics are fast on his heels, if I am to believe my Sergeant, which I am happy to say I do.' And he said it with a smile of appreciation and approval not lost on him, his bagman or Dr Marcus, who acknowledged the anointment of his new man and neither of them disapproved his choice.

'It's a *Praktica FX3,* if I'm not mistaken, which I rarely am,' replied Dr Marcus. 'But leaving that small detail aside, important thought it is to get things right and not merely suppose one is right, who is this poor woman?' He asked, kneeling down beside Violet and marvelling there was so little blood to be seen, but realising it was most probably drained into the gravel terrace beneath her head and chest. The quiet of the garden several times broken by the squawk of some unseen bird, a Magpie or Crow, though certainly not the red breasted Robin that watched him from the balustrade with such a fixed eye, he suddenly shivered his oddly nervous fright.

'Cold, doc?' Asked the Chief Inspector, his lips breaking into a broad smile, Gloria Hussey marvelled to see as she lit a cigarette; appearing more handsome than she had first realised.

'Not a bit, you?' He asked accusingly.

'A little perhaps, but not enough to complain to you I am, sir,' he answered with good natured humour from beneath the heavy overcoat and snap-brimmed fedora hat he wore at such a racy slant. Some remarked was reminiscent of the American Detectives, he so liked on, Television, men who reminded him of the soldiers he served with during the war. *Dragnet's Detective, Joe Friday,* perhaps? Whose gruff manner was his trademark. But though they did, they were wrong, it was ever his style to wear a hat from when he first became a detective twelve years before, as it was the style every other detective he knew. But if there was a comparison to be made, he hoped they would consider the inimitable, *Fabian of the Yard,* or radios, *Sexton Blake,* who he first read as a boy in *The Sexton Blake Library,* British detectives through and through. 'How long has she been dead? Can you pin it down? A guess would do, for now?'

'You want me to guess?' Asked Marcus, his cigar hovering at his sardonically smiling mouth.

'If you would. It would be a help. I make it a little after 15.15pm, now and she was found by the maid at 14.20pm, almost an hour ago and was last seen alive by her at about

12.30pm this afternoon, so a window of opportunity of less than two hours, if we are to believe her? But earlier if she is mistaken? Or is confused or lying to protect herself or someone else? A possibility?'

'I doubt I can get much closer than that, Tomon, not in this ball freezing cold and given her size and weight, what five feet ten inches tall and eighteen stone, maybe more? And then we have the prone position of her body, all of it adding to the morbid confusion? But, I'll know more when I get her back to the morgue,' said Marcus with peerless certainty. 'The city morgue, not the Infirmary by the way Tomon, we have the painters in. The first time since thirty-seven and still they're painting us the same horrible bilge green. Where do they get that paint from? Must be gallons of it left over from the war, enough to paint us green until the end of the century?'

'Will I have something this evening? Asked the Chief Inspector.

'You'll have my report when it's done, Chief Inspector and not a minute before,' he grumbled, his voice an affable sotto voce, 'but I can give you a rectal temperature before we bag her up, which should narrow the *window* of your investigation to within half an hour or so within and without the parameters we already have, if my esteemed colleague, Professor Keith Simpson is to be relied upon. Which I have never doubted he is. It's the best I can do until tonight and we have her deep liver temperature to confirm or deny it, which we will, I assure you.'

'That's good enough for now, sir. I'll let you get on,'

answered the Chief Inspector, with a curt, barely discernible nod to Sergeant Fasthead to bring the women into the morning room.

Chapter 21

Monday December 17, 1962
Leonard Bernstein and Stephen Sondheim: Maria

'You going back to school, Judy? You Gerry?' Asked a breathless, Ronnie, furiously rubbing her short, uncommonly thick, mousy brown hair dry with her towel. Her hitched-up skirt and wet spotted blouse already zipped and buttoned to avoid their searching stares, which never failed to notice, nor ever failed to comment on her sadly unimpressive breasts, which she every day hoped would grow, but didn't, just hinted they would in the smallest possible way. The three of them having so long delayed their return to school after Cod-Eye called a stop to their practice swim at 2.35pm, when Fay almost drowned in the deep-end at the start of the relay Judy won by a mile and Hilda came a surprising second, it hardly seemed worth their bother, now. Well not for the poetry of John Donne with Joe Fisher, who was so easy to tease they had long ago lost all interest in his immature, easy to find, red faced blushes, though he was quite good looking beneath his soft curls and spoke so posh he sounded like someone off the telly or the radio, though no one like the American *Moondog* on *Radio Luxembourg's, Jamboree,* they all three adored. Her favourite programme, though it was every week spoiled by Ted, who danced around the radio like he was Elvis Presley or Chuck Berry and insisted she dance with him, much to her mum's amusement, who didn't seem to care he was a perve, even when he grabbed her like a guy shouldn't grab a girl, feeling her up like she liked it. Which Judy said was a sure sign Joe was a virgin and because he was, liked him in that odd way she took to some people and not others, Madame Doucet for instance, who she disliked. Though she suspected her dislike was paper thin masking an admiration she feared to say.

'Nope,' answered Gerry, fabulously naked to her waist in the luxurious wrap of her soft white bath towel, which fell from the flat of her belly to her ankles like a sarong, as she nimbly applied mascara to her eye lashes, her nose almost pressed to the wall length, rectangular mirror; 'you?'

'Not sure. Might. Don't really know. What time is it, anyway?' Answered Ronnie with a flip blasé she didn't feel, who despite her want to be hip and cool like them, like any girl would, hated they were so mean to Madame Doucet like and admired, but didn't dare say she did.

'Five past three,' she answered, glancing at her distinctive, gold plated, heart-shaped, bracelet watch, which like her gold, hooped earrings sparkled in the electric light. 'What about you, Judy, you going back?' She asked, knowing what her answer would be, as she turned her head a fraction to look at her friend of so many years, standing naked beneath the frosted window smoking a cigarette, her back pressed to the apple-green, glazed tiled wall in a careless languor that knew no fear. So beautiful and so perfectly formed she looked like a Greek goddess, if a goddess ever looked like Sophia Loren, which she did better than anyone she knew.

'Na, I'm going home, I've had enough of all this fucking about for one day, I really have, my arms ache like you wouldn't believe. Fuck, I don't know why I let that fucking arsehole, Cod-Eye bully me into swimming all those races the way he does? Always touching me up, too, like I don't know he wants to fuck me seven ways to Sunday with that monster knob of his. As if I'd have that fucking pervy twat inside me, makes me want to puke just thinking about it.'

'Ha,' laughed Gerry, her face turned to the mirror, so streaked and foggy she could hardly see.

'I mean, did you see the size of him this morning, Gerry, jacked up like a monster when that stupid twat, Greta stripped off and looking more like a boy than, little Cocky does, it's not fucking natural? Doesn't he bleedin' know we can all see him bursting out of his shorts like he's deformed or something?' He should be locked up for the fuck he is!' She spat her contempt, drawing deeply on her cigarette. The lean and graceful curves of her tall, athletic body bristling with rage he, of all people - or any man for that matter, would dare think she would want him? That a woman, any woman is a docile cow to be taken, used and abandoned by them?

'Yeah, he's a fucking wanker and no bleedin' mistake,' giggled Gerry. 'But you know what if it was anyone else, but him, I might give him go, it would be nice to know what it was like to have a really big one in there. Better still if he knew how to use it, which I doubt he does,' she sighed, pretending the experience she didn't have, as she returned to her artful makeup.

A remark that brought a silent sneer of contempt to Judy's lips she could say such a stupid thing. Could believe a man, no matter how big he is, could make a woman happy and contented as she longed to be. Believing any woman who thought like that was no better than brainless whore deserving the contempt of men and the women they so easily betray for their pleasure.

'Fuck,' she impatiently groaned, her gaze turned to her happily distracted friend. *Why is it*, she asked herself, *so many beautiful and sexy young women like her with everything to live for conspire and collude with men in the ruin of their lives? Like Cocky's and Tinker's mum's, did, who for years had whored for Clooney Barron and without the least shame they did? Is that what she wanted? To be like them? Any mans for the price of a good time in their pockets?*

'What about, Casterbrook?' Asked Ronnie, struggling, as she always did, to brush her hair into something presentable in the mirror directly behind, Gerry, her jealous eyes instinctively drawn to the elegant curves of her fabulous, gorgeously round breasts and the pert hard of her pink nipples, as her hand moved with angry, well-practiced strokes. Hair which though it was thick and short above her ears was, despite she thought otherwise, a remarkably attractive feature of her wide-eyed good looks and better by far than the shaggy mane of hair she wore last term. Which in a fit of temper she had cut almost to the scalp just a few months ago and now hated for the mess it was, but it wasn't a mess and could easily be curled to look quite sexy. Hair so unlike Gerry's expensive upturned cut and Judy's impeccably stylish hair, which even when wet and dishevelled, as it now was, looked fantastic; like it was meant to be like that. Like she should be on the cover of a magazine advertising it was like an Italian movie star. Or Miss Langford, whose photograph she was determined to find, though she wasn't sure why?

'Shit,' she cursed, much to Gerry's sniggering amusement, who she watched in the mirror, her face distorted in the fog of steam. A face that would haunt her in the days to come; as if, in that very moment, she was already gone, had somehow passed from this life into the next.

A very bad hair-cut she had to admit that was entirely her fault, her mother, who dotted on her, as most mothers do their only child - if not quite as much as she once did, now, skiffle-boy Ted was so firmly on the scene, had rescued as best she could and said with a heartfelt love she truly meant, gave her the gamine good looks of Leslie Carron. Whatever that meant, but in *An American in Paris,* her favourite film ever, she was at pains to say, not *Gigi,* which she never took, too, because Louis Jourdan was such a sod to think he could take Gigi for his mistress, a courtesan as the French like to say, pretending it is something other than it was; a high class prostitute. But a cut, Ted teased her made her look like Ingrid Bergman in *Joan of Arc*.

A backhanded compliment because she was every bit as beautiful as Ingrid, but one that slyly hinted she was a lesbian, which she wasn't. Well didn't think she was. Which was his stupid way of saying she needed a fuck. Which she probably did. But not from him. Not from anyone like him! The hatefully vulgar, two-timing twat of a skinny-arsed lazy chancer, who wanted to have her and her mum and she, not for a moment realising he did. Never guessing he did and leaving her alone with him every evening until she got home from work and him now wanting her so much, she was afraid to go into the house until she was safely back. Couldn't take a bath or dress or fall asleep in peace knowing he was waiting his chance to fuck her. Would unless she could find a way to stop him better than the old chair, she every night fixed under the handle her bedroom door, which since August, had a dozen times stopped him.

'What about Casterbrook, Ronnie? Has he been sticking his fat knob into your leg like he does mine? Like he thinks it's a magic wand that will wet my cunt, like it does Carol Paget's?' Spat Judy with a giggle that wondered if he really was shagging that dim-wit secretary of his. A woman so stupid and up for it even that retard, Tinker thought she wanted to fuck him. Was every day prowling her office hoping she would grab his knob; and maybe she had?

'No, he hasn't, Judy' moaned Ronnie, with exaggerated distaste, knowing he had tried it on with dozens of girls, but never with her. But then, why should he, she looked like the scarecrow, *Worzel Gummidge.* 'What I meant to say was, won't he mind us not going back to school? You know what he's like about stuff like that? How much he wants you to be the poster girls he's made you out to be for the gala on Friday, what with the mayor coming and all that palaver?'

'I don't care if he does; I'm not going to swim for him or for anyone else. They can't make me if I don't want too. No one can. I'll do as I fucking well, please and he and Cod-Eye can hang themselves. And if they do, I'll play it like *Smith* did in that film. What was it called Gerry? Yeah, *The Loneliness of the Long-Distance Runner* and come last. That'll take the smirk of his face.'

'But you won every race, Judy, crawl, butterfly, backstroke, breaststroke and both the freestyle and medley relay races and even saved, Fay. You were wonderful, everyone said you were. Better even than Anita Lonsbrough,' groaned Ronnie, recalling her fabulous success at last month's British Empire and Commonwealth Games in Perth; Perth a place she longed to see.

'I know,' she answered, ever so slightly mollified as she carelessly blew a ring of blue smoke through the pouting hollow of her butterfly lips; she was good and knew how good she was.

'Casterbrook has been telling everyone you're certain to be picked for the county squad next year and who knows, you could even make the British Olympic team with a bit more practice.

'Maybe?' She replied.

Maybe nothing, Judy, you're a dead cert, you really are. I can't imagine there is anyone half as good as you? Not anywhere,' gushed Ronnie. 'Think about it Judy, you could be in the next Olympics games and me and Gerry could come to Tokyo with you. Wouldn't that be the best thing ever and you'd be on the telly, on *Grandstand* with David Coleman and us, too, maybe?'

'Sounds good to me,' said Gerry. 'We could make a holiday of it, like we were film stars?'

'Yes,' said Ronnie.

'Could I suppose, but I'm still not swimming on Friday, poster fucking girl or not. He can just fuck off. Nor am I going back to school this afternoon, not for an hour of Joe Fisher's boring romantic twaddle, like he believes all that tosh. No, I'm going to the Wimpy for an espresso?' Want to come, Gerry?' She asked, offering her half-finished cigarette to her now outstretched, blindly searching fingers, her manicured nails polished to a lustrous red to match her red lips.

'No, got no time.'

'What do you mean, got no time, what the fuck are you up, too, anyway dressed like that?

'Got me a hot date with a hot man who wants to fuck me like a real man wants to fuck a woman and maybe I'll let him,' she answered, with a snake-like shimmy that left no doubt she would.

'Have you? And who would that be with then? Like I don't know who you've been seeing behind my back, you, horny little tart and he ain't fucked you yet? Well, well, well, ain't he the slow one to let you off the hook so easy. Or have you been teasing him with your virgin ways.'

'Can't say, Judy, it's a secret between me and him,' she giggled, expertly shaping her cornflower blue eyes with an Italian flick at each corner, an effect made all the more alluring by the smoky black eye shadow she had just applied.

Greta eat your heart out, 'cos you ain't never going to look as good as this, she cooed, thinking what a sad little twat that scary girl was, even if the scary witch frightened the life out of her as no one ever had. What was it about her?

'It's him, isn't it?' Said Judy.

'I don't know who you mean?' She laughed.

'Like fuck you don't know? You dirty cow,' said Judy, her right hand easily untying the half knot of her towel, which she dropped to the wet floor as she parted her legs with her knee.

'Maybe I do,' teased Gerry, as Judy's fingers began to plough the lips of her moist vagina to find the hardening swell of her clitoris in a wriggle of pleasure, she was only too eager to enjoy.

'You be careful,' she softly whispered in her ear. 'I don't want you to be hurt by that Welsh fucker like so many girls are, he may think he's god's gift to women, but I don't trust him. And I don't trust, Terry Mack he's an evil little sod. Do you hear me?' She urged, finding her lips with a gentle kiss, Ronnie was utterly startled and bewildered to see, never realising just how intimate they were. 'Promise me, Gerry,' she begged, pushing her fingers deep into her vagina and feeling as she did the moist of her own growing lust as she arched and groaned to let her deeper in. 'He hurt you last time you went with him. Remember, you, silly mare, he hurt you? You said you weren't going back to him, not ever? So why are you going with him now?'

'Don't know,' she hoarsely whispered, her buttocks sliding up and down the wet tiles to better find the pleasure in Judy's deliciously strong, well-practiced fingers, which more than any boy, knew how to love her in that special ways girls do, but not now. Not now she wanted Dylan so much she couldn't sleep or eat or think but dreamt of him as she never dreamt of her in that way. 'But this time it'll different, I know it will. He said he loves me; really, he said did.'

'My arse he did?'

'He did, Judy, really' she lovingly sighed, caressing the hair from her face and kissing her ears, her eyes, her, her lips and her neck in the growing more urgent swell of her pleasure. 'And he's going to love me all the more when he discovers, I'm so virgin tight down there his balls are going to explode when he comes. Boom like a bomb going off,' she giggled and gasped.

'Will he?'

'Yes.'

'And will you come better than I can make you? Gerry or will he tease you like he likes to tease all the girls. Like his wife wouldn't be shagging that sad old cunt Casterbrook if he was half the man he pretends to be. Fucking them quick or fucking them slow, but all the time getting off watching them trying to come. Begging him not to stop and thinking all the time he won't; but he does. All the time wanting them to want him like the perve he is more than he wants them. Like he hates them because they want him. Like he'll hate you, Gerry when he's done.'

'He won't, Judy, he won't, I promise,' she moaned, her left leg now draped around her hip. 'Ooooh, baby, please,' she gasped, as she pushed deeper and deeper inside her, her thumb so deliciously hard against the silky moist of her clitoris she almost fainted with the rising thrill of it.

'Like that, cow?'

'Yes, like that, bitch.'

'You love it don't you?'

'Yes, I love it, bitch,' she squirmed, kissing her throat.

'Don't go, please, Gerry?'

'I want too, I love him.'

'But you love me, too.'

'Yes, but not in the same way, not like you want me, to love you baby.'

'Please, baby?'

'No,' she sighed, rising to kiss her on her lips, their bodies so passionately entwined, Ronnie blushed, feeling cheated and betrayed they had kept this secret; a secret that was never for her to know.

'No.'

'No.'

'No, well, what about this? Do you like this you fucking horny tart?'

'Aaaaaaah, you, fucking twat, Judy, that really hurt me,' she squealed, as Judy pinched her labia with her fingernails. 'Fuck, Judy that really hurt me. Look you've made me bleed. Fuck!'

'Did I? Well, it serves you fucking well right you, brainless tart,' she spat, taking the nearly finished stump of her cigarette from her fingers. 'He's dangerous, Gerry, she hissed. 'How many times must I tell you he's out of your league and dangerous like you wouldn't believe a sweet talking, handsome man like him can be dangerous to a woman like you. He's a perve on the make; don't you see that? A perve no better than Terry Mack or Casterbrook or any man for preying on girls like you, just better looking than they are. No better even than Hussey and Lomas, who are drugged off their heads. Don't you see that? And he will hurt you worse than I have because his type always does. They hate women, like my dad hated me and they hate us all the more for loving them, like the love we give to them is some sort of poison. And he will hurt you, believe me, but not with a pinch on your fanny, he'll break your heart forever.'

'He' won't, he loves me, he said he did,' she whimpered, as Judy pressed her to the wall.

'My arse he loves you, Gerry, he's been fucking Doucet so why would he want to fuck you? And she's a stylish, sexy woman. A French woman who could have anyone one she wants.'

'He's not. He told me he's not,' she whimpered.

'He is,' she snapped, 'I heard Pauline Fisk say he was just last Friday afternoon. They had a row, but they're back together now and him talking about leaving his wife to be with her.'

Judy, please, let me go, you're hurting me. Judy, please you, bitch you really have hurt, me' she cried, pushing herself clear of the wall and crouching to reach her towel, fallen at her ankles.

'Course it hurts. Serves you right for wasting your cherry on that twat,' she spat her contempt. 'You do know he tried it on with me before he ever looked at you? Yeah, he did. But I told him to fuck off and when I did, he turned and punched me in the face. Did you hear that? He grabbed me by the throat and punched me hard in the face, like man punches a man in a fight.'

'I know, you already said,' she sullenly answered.

'You know nothing, he's a dangerous shit and you would do well to stay well clear of him. Fuck, Casterbrook is all the time groping me and Cod-Eye stares at me like I'm his fucking wet dream, but I'm certain neither of them would hurt me like that fuck did. Have never once raised a hand to me no matter how much I curse and cheek them and Cod-Eye least of all, who I know likes me and would never hurt me, or you. I'm telling you he's mad, Gerry. Mad, bad and bloody dangerous to women, so you watch out for that sweet talking Welshman, Dylan Lloyd-Thomas'

'No,' she fumed, dabbing the blood on her towel

'Like fuck, no! And tried it on with every girl in the school with tits, ain't that right, Ronnie?' She cried her bitter frustration, as she drew a long last drag on her cigarette before flicking it into the drain where it smouldered to ruin. 'Tried it on with Angela Dee and that evil cow, Linda Plant, before he ever thought of you, tried it on with everyone who looked at him more than once, but they had the good sense to walk away and both with dads he wouldn't mess with.'

'Not sure,' said Ronnie, her towel pulled to her chest.

'No, he didn't you jealous, cow, he's never looked at any of them. Not Angela and not Linda. Told me what a scheming slut she is, just because her dad's minted, she thinks she can have everything she wants. But she ain't had him, even if she's always mooning around his class.'

'Course he has, you, silly mare.'

'No,' she cried, one last time, trying to sooth the pain in her labia with the dab of her blood spotted towel. A pain that was even now swelling to a livid bruise. A bruise Dr Marcus would ponder into the night no less than the horrible wounds that will so very soon ruin her body.

A reproach Judy hardly noticed as she turned to find the slatted bench beside, Ronnie and when she had watched her dress in a brand new, very expensive, pure lace, see through black bra, pants and suspender belt, so sexy and pretty, no man could resist her, so perfectly did they hug her lithe and sensuous body beneath the simple, smock-like blue dress she now draped over her shoulders.

'Will you take my school bag home, Ronnie?' She asked, as she slipped into her black, patent leather, four-inch, spike-thin, high heeled shoes, stubbornly ignoring, Judy as she did. 'I'll pick it up later tonight or if not tonight, tomorrow morning, first thing. Depending on what time I get in,' she slyly smirked. 'You'll be up until late, won't you? What with Ted shagging your mum and keeping you up all hours. A handsome bloke, you should try him yourself if only for the practice?' She cooed her bitchy remark, as she turned to the mirror one last time to put her lipstick on and tease her hair into place. 'Nearly done,' she sighed, turning her head this way and that and dabbing a drop of *Yardley* perfume to her wrists before she tripped out of the changing room, clutch bag in hand and with never a backward glance at Judy, who watched her go with a sullen, spoiling rage to hurt her even more than she already had. Would, too, and no mistake if she ever got her hands on her. Would slap her face silly! Slap her so hard it would hurt!

''Course I will, Gerry,' answered Ronnie, angry she said what she did, as she watched her go, wondering how she managed to produce that slight, but ever so sexy, rotating flick of her heels as she did. A motion that synchronised so perfectly with the gentle roll of her pert, well-shaped bum it was truly poetic, and knowing only too well it was, Mr Dylan Lloyd-Thomas she was going to meet and wondering if the rumours about him and Madame Doucet were true?

*

'**W**hat are you two girls doing here, you should have left half an hour ago with the rest of the school?' Barked, Miss Langford, swathed in a gorgeous fluffy white towel, which covered her from her breasts to her mid-calf, a pink plastic cap and with a large green washbag in her hand.

'Just going, miss. Sorry miss,' said Ronnie, gathering up the two bags she now had to carry, and carry so far in the snow that had begun to fall once again she would be late home, but not that late, she shivered. Not late enough to avoid, Ted trying to feel her up; would feel her up!

'Good and see you take yourself straight back to school, I'll check with Mr Fisher in the morning you did, and I won't be best pleased if you have bunked off home. No, indeed I won't be.'

'Yes, miss,' she answered, as she stood to go.

'Nearly done, miss,' said Judy, shamelessly standing to meet her poker-faced stare and urging Ronnie to go with the merest arch of her elegant brow, 'I just need a quick shower before I change, the chlorine makes such a mess of my hair I can barely get a brush through it. Do you mind if I join you, it's a bit spooky in here on your own and there's no telling the boys won't come running in to catch a look at me tits, when they know you've gone, miss? Hussey and Lomas most likely, but who knows who else is hiding out there hopeful of getting a look me nips?'

With a sigh, Miss Langford dropped her towel and washbag onto the bench and stepped beneath the nearest of the twelve, chrome shower heads, which lined the two facing walls of the shower cubicle and no sooner had she, then she was drenched in a bracing cold that was reminiscent of every camp she had ever been on. A sight that better even than that morning, reminded Ronnie, she had seen her naked before, or someone very much like her, in one of Ted's magazines.

A cold that turned to sudden desperate hot when Judy roughly and so unexpectedly, it left her dizzy with fright, pressed her to the wall and kissed her so hard on her refusing lips she almost fainted with the fierce, astonishing exhilaration of it, her left hand gripping her hair so tightly she could hardly move, didn't want to move though it hurt her so much she wanted to scream. 'No,' she moaned, in sudden surprise, as she savagely prised her legs apart with her muscular thigh and after a moments tantalising delay, a heartbeat that fluttered the merest, ghost-like caress on her swelling vagina found its melted open with the tips of her fingers, a gentle searching touch that left her twitched and shivering with pleasure she would never have believed possible. 'No, please, Judy, stop, I can't,' she begged, her voice a breathless whisper, only to find she was gagged to a thankful silence by a second kiss. But a kiss so sweet and so languorous tender she pressed her own urgent lips for more. The first kiss like this she had ever known. 'Please,' she whimpered, tasting the bittersweet tobacco in the warmth of her open mouth, their bodies pressed so tightly together, Cod-Eye, seeing Ronnie hurrying off and thinking her the last to leave the changing room, saw them in a startled wonder through the billowing steam. Which like the swirling mist in the enchanted forest of his imagination made their barely glimpsed, liquid slow, growing more passionate pleasure, a poetic dance of sinuously erotic joy and held him so utterly enthralled behind the wall that hid him, he sighed like a schoolboy.

A schoolboy he would have punished without compunction for doing such a thing, as he had been punished as a boy, as all boys since the dawn of time had been punished for their wrongdoing. But a joy that in a fleeting whisper of his long-forgotten past, reminded him for the second time that cold winter day of who he was, who he had once been, but who he must become again, an emotion so overwhelming he felt a stab of pain in his chest that pierced him to his heart.

'*Stop?*' Tempted Judy, speaking to her as if she was an untutored child, her voice a husky, though less assured sound than it was just moment ago. Her frustrated desire, smothered to nothing by Gerry's want of someone else more than her, rising in the deep well of her, like a fast-gathering wave. A wave more certain now of its eventual course than it had ever been before. A certainty that made her weak and wanting of the beautiful young woman who now held her so tight she would never let her go, who she had so disliked and who she had hoped to tease and shame for the power it would give her. But who, she now urged with all the sensuous power she possessed to love her back as hard as she would now tenderly love and want her? To love her as no one had ever loved her. Not her mother and not her father, who she hated.

Chapter 22

Monday December 17, 1962
Bobby Vinton: Roses Are Red (My Love)

Valeria sat at her cluttered desk the low static of the still switched on *Tannoy* adding to her serene sense of disconnection and after a brief hesitation that hoped she could resist its sweet taste a little longer, lit a cigarette from the packet on her desk, the growing dark of that cold, late afternoon, dimming her unlit classroom to a gloom that exaggerated the dizzying, wind danced slant of snow outside her classroom window to a hypnotic blur. A dreamy blur which like the impressionist paintings she so adored, Monet's, *Sunset on the Seine at Lavacourt* - in winter and in summer, coming instantly to mind, leaving her again, astonished the world could be so changed by the merest hint of light and shade. The low dark roof scape and the river he painted from Vétheuil appearing much like the scene she now saw of the city as it fell to the meadows and with the same brooding melancholy and orange-pink sunset that lit his canvas to such a dazzling perfection A sunset that found its likeness in the twinkling yellow-orange glow of the street and window lights to produce an effet de neige as charming as any she had known.

Lifting her knees almost to her chest she rested them on the curved, wooden arm of her thinly cushioned, ladder-back chair and drew heavily on her cigarette, the first she had smoked all day; though not the last. The hem of her tight, pencil skirt pulling carelessly high on her thighs to expose an inch of bare skin above the red clip and bow of her gartered stockings. Her peep toe, sling back, high heeled, black satin shoes so chic and so utterly *Roger Vivier* lying on the polished parquet floor beneath her desk in a carelessly contrived symbolic abandon that matched the sublime, dreamlike detachment she felt from the world, which now pressed so heavily on her heart she felt utterly confused and adrift. Fuck-me shoes, Dylan once called them without realising they were named for the then daring style of shoe Joan Crawford made famous in the 1945, film noire, *Mildred Pierce.* Shoes with a red polished cleavage every bit as teasing as her neckline. A woman hurt by the people she loved and trusted, as she had often been,

A mood so enchanted, so completely enraptured and diverted by the singular thing that had happened, she barely acknowledged the presence of the small group of excitedly laughing children coming out of Arno's classroom in the corridor outside her own, tight shut door or the heavy, muffled shut of the swing doors that took them to the stairs a moment later in a delicious gush of mischief that was glad their day was at last done. Instead, her heart beat a gentle flutter of excitement as she recalled her midday tryst in the storeroom. A memory that warmed her skin, which blushed her cheeks to a glow, which caught her breath on her moist, full red lips, which tingled every fibre of her being in a heady thrill she hardly dared believe. So much had it left her limp and longing for more of the love she had so unexpectedly found in the arms of the *boy* who had come to her from nowhere. A love so blissful in its passion it had no equal in her life before.

Mmm, she sighed her guilty secret, wondering who he was and if she would see him again, but knowing she would. Though his face was now as vague to her as it was beautiful the memory of him like a picture painted on a rushing stream now churned by the rocks of her desire?

'Bah,' she groaned, enjoying her cigarette far too much, as she always did, as every addict did their cravings, but longing to give them up, just the same, as she had a hundred times promised she would. Hating she smoked and never during the day, she reminded herself with an impish, rather guilty smile, as she inhaled the smoke again. And now only with AA, who was not only delightfully interesting company, but an incorrigible temptation to all her bad habits. Smoking and drinking too much red wine and Cognac, being just two of them, which she almost every night now she did, she mused, savouring its strong, sweet, soothing taste in her mouth.

AA, who had become such an unexpected friend and confidant in the weeks of heartache and misgivings she had experienced after she and Dylan so spectacularly fell out –

though friend and confidant hardly expressed the intimacy that now existed between them. Who exerted a powerful, but nevertheless charming, almost, but not quite, fatherly influence over her and who, in his intuitively thoughtful, English way had brought a calm to her troubled mind? A calm she had not felt since Étienne's death. A death like Camus - the man he longed to be the man who was their friend. A death he could not have better planned and a betrayal he would have approved, she could hardly bring herself to think about, let alone talk about, as her mother, said she must. Preferring instead, Flaubert's view of things: *la morte n'a peut-être pas plus secrets a nous reveller que la vie;* saying little, if anything, to anyone, of the hurt she had known.

Whose death in the arms of his long-time lover, her older sister, Madeleine, had been such a bitter turning point in her life. A death that knew better than even the free spirited and effortlessly sensual, George Sand said, there is only one happiness for a woman; to love and to be loved. Il n'y a qu' un bonheur dans la vie, c'est d'aimer et d'être aimé. And then, and only then, she felt sure, by the man you first love, the sweetest love of all, the man you will love forever.

But smoke she now did and with a relief that knew the worst of that awful time was now over. That despite the demons of despair that still haunted her - that so often came unbidden into her mind, her life, whatever it had been, could begin anew. She would go home to Paris, the city of her birth, if not her childhood, the city she loved. Would leave this awful place before Christmas, barely more than a week away. Would go this coming weekend; come what may.

*

She had waited for Dylan long after their twelve o'clock *rendezvous;* so long, it was after one when he eventually came – perhaps ten minutes after, so long, she despaired he would ever come and despised herself she did. Three times leaving her desk and the thin sliced *Gruyère de Comté* cheese and tomato on rye bread she nervously nibbled to search the empty corridor for him.

The first time, walking on tentative, hopeful-not-to-be-heard, tiptoes out through the double swing doors that closed so firmly on cushioned rubber, the corridor behind her onto the small, railed square of landing that overlooked the twice turning stairs. That on deep worn concrete treads led to the cheerless empty ground floor below, the only way in or out of the annex, except through the fire doors? Where, careful not to be seen, she cautiously, peeped over the wood and wrought iron balustrade like a lovelorn Juliet to search in vain for her Romeo. *'O Romeo, Romeo, where fore art thou Romeo?'* She whispered, a nervous mocking reproach he wasn't there. But worse, knew she was weak and foolish to wait so longingly for a man who had no love for her, nor she for him; she would now readily admit. Whose every mean hurt to her wounded woman's pride; she had greeted as if it was some sort of challenge. A challenge she would meet blow for blow until she bested him, as she knew she must; knew she could.

Perhaps, she idly thought, by denying him the pleasure of her body – a faint hope as she knew it was, as *Lysistrata* and the women of Athens denied their men their bodies? As he had three times amazingly denied her. *Yes, she could do that,* she thought, though she almost swooned he had promised to fuck her until she ached, and she so wanted him to fuck her like that. Would taunt him like the Spartan herald until he begged her to lift the *burden* of his desire, which she might, but not until he had had hers, which he would. This time there would be no silly games!

Or better still enslave him with better sex than he had ever known before. As Barbara, his wife, and all his many lovers, the Chinese girl in the red bikini, he last Thursday drunkenly boasted about, never had. As *Ishtar* the daughter of sin had enslaved all the men she had favoured with her *love,* though not, she recalled, the mighty, *Gilgamesh,* who refused to marry her. As *Phryne* enslaved her accusers with her nakedness. Which men both fear and desire as nothing else and because they do, are rendered weak and foolish and despise they are so easily unmanned. And because they are, want to dominate, control and hurt women; to have them for their own and strike out at those they cannot have. Not that she wanted Dylan as a husband! Definitely not. But she would like to wipe that self-satisfied smirk of his handsome face; just once.

A thought that quite suddenly and quite unaccountably reminded her of one of her favourite childhood stories, *Les Malheurs de Sophie,* the little girl who preferred to be bad rather than be good – a choice we can all make, within the limits of our biological disposition to behave in certain ways. As her mother so often urged her to be, Sophie's mother that is, not her own. Who cared for no one, but herself? Was that it? Was this silly, sordid affair with Dylan no more than that. A want to be bad? As bad as her mother and sister were? Who cared nothing for what she and others thought of their selfish and often cruel behaviour, which was always so hurtful?

Or was she punishing herself for the wrongs she had, in some inexplicable way, done to them? As they had many times alluded, she had and never more so than when they were forced to leave their beautiful home on the famous Boulevard de Cimiez in Nice, when she became ill with pneumonia. Though it always seemed odd to her they left the healing warmth of the south of France for the cold of the north. Madeleine most of all, whose life there had been so wonderful, she never wanted to leave; and hated she had? A perverse, self-loathing worthy of Freud or Lacan, though, perhaps Lacan better than Freud, whose weekly lectures at the Sainte-Anne Hospital, the famous psychiatric institute on the Rue Cabanis, she had often gone too. Who, though, dense and inscrutable in everything he said or wrote, appeared to like and admire women, which he doubted Freud did? A fixation, she was certain, with *his* mother, Amélie? For why else would he have dreamt up his impossibly stupid and irrational, *Oedipus Complex* if he wasn't? As Dylan was fixated on his mother though he was to hurt by her to see he was.

But did she have the willpower of *Lysistrata,* the cruelty of *Ishtar* or more importantly the bravery of *Phryne* to deny herself the pleasure she too much wanted as all women want sex? She doubted she did. But then why should she? She liked Dylan, perverse and hopelessly absurd though her liking for him was - as Camus, the champion of the absurd would say it was, and she knew he liked her. Liked her more than he was prepared to say; perhaps never would? A thought that made her suddenly shiver, but not from the fierce cold that filled the stairs from the quarter open door below, but from the tendril of some long forgotten memory that just then crept into her mind and when it had, left, leaving only it's trace and the regret it always did; as it had a hundred times before. Something too painful to know that was now gone, the merest hint of it haunting her subconscious mind like a troublesome, tiresomely familiar ghost in an empty house.

It was then, listening to the wind banging and blowing at the door below in a staccato of empty sound, no less irritating than the *Tannoy,* which even there, filled the void with its strange, otherworldly presence, she realised, and with a sudden fear that was quite out of character, how utterly deserted and quiet the annex building was that miserably cold, Monday lunch time; she was utterly alone. Hardly surprising, she scolded herself, returning on defiantly clicking heels to her cheese sandwich, with so many children and teaching staff attending the headmaster's extended until two-thirty, rehearsal for next Friday afternoons annual swimming gala.

Something she remembered with a bristle of exasperation she was ordered to attend and couldn't refuse, though she hardly knew why she must? Having no interest in going to the meet or the events that were to follow. The mayor's reception, the end of term prize giving and the evening disco in the school's main hall, which poor Joe Fisher had been planning since his arrival. But go she would if only to keep the peace and avoid the fuss Casterbrook would make if she didn't.

When next she got up from her desk, a tediously long five minutes later it was to peer squint-eyed through the frosted glass window of Arno's deserted classroom in a seemingly idle curiosity that pretended a useful, if yet unknown purpose, should Dylan suddenly appear behind her.

The only other classroom on that desperately lonely corridor, which was testimony, as hers decidedly was not, to the austere discipline and public utility the school both boasted and encouraged. Its walls bare of any colour or distraction, except for the framed print of Pietro Annigoni's extraordinarily elegant, marvellously painted, 1954, portrait of the young and beautiful queen Elizabeth II, which was hung above the horizontally sliding, chalk board in pride of place. A constant, if far from subtle reminder to every child who saw it of their lowly place in Britain's still, archly, class dominated by unfair aristocratic privilege, social and public life.

And, as if to emphasise their bleakly regimented life the outside windows of that grim, forbidding room were painted a creamy-white from top to bottom, much like hospitals, sanatoria and public toilets, are, as no others were, so no curious eye would gaze onto the street, park and river below. And where every desk and every chair were fixed in its place in a rigid, military formation, no one would dare alter, except that morning when the whole school experienced a sort of mass, riotously anarchic, bedlam when the *Tannoy* system couldn't be switched off and Casterbrook and Carol Paget appeared to lose their minds. He apparently masturbating in his office, and she could think of no other reason for his erotic grunts and moans and she trying to explain it away with some creatively garbled message it was a comic radio show.

A classroom so unlike her own she marvelled any French was taught there, except the rote, grammar they learned in choir-like recitations they would never remember, nor ever understand. His classroom being the only other working classroom in that now sadly neglected building, empty since the builders hurriedly left, the two of them forming what Arno grandly called *his* language suite. A poseur's title that ignored the headmaster thought him and the subject he taught, a useless waste of time and money and because he did, consigned them to that dingy place. An echoingly desolate place, she now realised, having never thought of it like that before of cluttered corridors and empty paint flaked classrooms. No place to be alone at night, she thought, glad she never was, that her nemesis, Mr Eldred, the school caretaker or Mrs Wiśniewski's were always there to lock up when she left, and she was always the last to leave.

'J'en ai ras le bol,' she cursed, walking to the locked fire door at the far end of the corridor and looking out of the rime stained, snow flaked window onto the metal fire escape the back yard below, hopeful she might see Dylan's car parked there, or better still, see him arrive. But saw only Terry Mack's 1955, *Ford Popular 100E* only just arrived by the fresh made tyre marks that curved an elegantly round, almost ninety-degree circle in the snow from the narrow back entrance to the high wall, it now faced, its engine still smoking its soot black exhaust.

Disappointed, she stood for a long while, her arms hugging her breasts, never for a moment thinking Dylan and Terry were watching her through the snow frosted back window of his car, their faces a sneering smirk of boyish, greedy pleasure, as she gazed at the leaden sky above the park and the glassy water of the river it ran, too. A place more beautiful in snow and ice than she thought possible and one she felt certain, Monet would have delighted to have painted.

Turning slowly on her heels she stopped a moment beside the deeply recessed entrance into Arno's back store room, which unlike her own, opposite, which was without obstacle, except for Mr Eldred's refusal to open it to the light of her inspection - refused her even a key, which she had many times asked him for, was mounted with a waist high, red painted, brass fire reel. Which, to her sly, growing bored and mischievous amusement, dangled a foot long, two-inch-wide, length of brass-tipped-to-a-bulbous-nozzle, red rubber hose stitched with seams of purple thread over the two red fire buckets of cigarette poked sand that stood at her feet. In the middle of which a foam-filled-for-electrical-use-only - so the yellow triangular label said, cone-shaped fire extinguisher stood waiting its moment of panic. One that would surely see everyone burnt to a crisp before they ever escaped the permanently locked fire door it protected.

Sighing she slowly traced her index finger over the curve of the pipe, which, limp with expectation, hung before her in a sullen promise it would one day rise to do its important work – a cliché she knew and an all too obvious one at that, she blushed like a schoolgirl she was so silly. A Freudian allusion that made her smile a very wicked, tongue licking, lascivious smile as she walked back to her classroom, never seeing, Dylan was crossing the yard behind her his feet deep in the snow and Terry was waiting his chance to follow and with such a lustful hate in his black, twisted heart he had long forgotten the risk they were taking. A risk too much he had several times cautioned his friend, but better by far than anything Clooney Barron could offer him.

Entering her classroom and still hopeful he would come, though it was now five past one, she made one last, absurd check on the storeroom she had so shamelessly prepared for his arrival and with such a care she hardly knew why she bothered. So swaggeringly cool and indifferent to her frustrated feelings was he when he did eventually come and with a *Lipton's* plastic carrier bag hanging from his gloved hand to excuse his lateness. A lateness that would guarantee her protection, he mockingly cooed into her ear with an earthy good humour that was confident he would not be turned away, as he showed her his barber shop purchase with an intimacy that dared to know her every want better than she knew herself, a packet of *Durex* condoms.

It was a drab and dingy room with the damp and dusty smell of long neglect – despite the lemon, aerosol freshener she daily used, that was in every part the antithesis of all she had hoped their *love* affair would be it wasn't. Twelve feet deep its walls were the same polished-red and yellow brick every wall in every corridor of the school was made of. A brick so cold and bare it looked like a prison, or an asylum, or worse still, a municipal toilet - a humiliation she now realised she deserved, so blindly confident and self-regarding had she been of her power to seduce him. To master him. To change him from the pig he was to the lover he might be.

A room so dimly lit by the forty-watt bulb that hung without a shade from the ceiling like noose and the sash window that cut a deep rectangle in the back wall so grimed and streaked with age and covered in a mottle of diaphanous snowflakes, it threw little more than a mote filled square of mournful light onto the large, ink stained, wooden desk that stood like an altar beneath it, she had to strain and blink her eyes to see the mountain of clutter it contained. An oak brown, wooden cabinet, six feet high, two feet deep and eight feet wide stuffed so clumsily full of lever arch-files, cardboard boxes, dun-brown folders and tottering heaps of yellow, curling paper it every day threatened to fall on top of her, divided the room from just beyond the end of the window. A false partition, as it turned out, that did little to hide the two thirds of the room it closed, where stacks of tubular metal and canvas chairs bent aslant reached almost to the ceiling, where near tottering pillars of Victorian flip-up wooden desks menaced her every attempt to find the door they blocked, where gun grey metal filing cabinets, book and paper filled cardboard boxes and tea chests spilled their contents onto the floor in slippery heaps. Beneath the window and behind the desk that would be their *lit de l'amour* a stout, olive-green, cast-iron radiator was fixed to the wall and on the adjacent wall beside it and directly behind the turning arc of door she now held firmly held open against the pull of its pneumatic piston – surprised, as she always was it, never made the least sound when it was opened or closed, not so much as a hiss, squeak or locking click, was a wardrobe-sized, grey metal cabinet where she hung her coat. And beside it a small, white porcelain, half- sink, above which a rectangle of faded mirror was screwed onto the wall. A personal space she had made her own with a soft blue towel, a matching blue flannel, a cake of perfumed French soap by *Rigaud of Paris*, a rose printed spongebag and her most important possession of all; her make-up-bag.

'Mon Dylan chéri que j'espère que vous n'avez pas oublié le peu de plaisir nous avons arrange, il seriez des tels déchetes, un gaspillage si terrible de ce qui pourrait avoir été. Ce que nous pourrions avoir partagé ensemble, vous et I,' she gasped in her impatient frustration he was so late. Remembering, she had prepared the room with a thrill of anticipation that quite made her blush, so wanton and hungry for her lover's touch had she become – like Zola's love starved, *Thérèse Raquin,* though she doubted she would ever become the murderously tormented, guilt ridden, suicide she became, a silly girl. Who waited for her lover, the lazy and cruel, *Laurent* in her cheerless bedroom above the *Passage du Pont-Neuf* with an insane passion for his ardent touch - a parallel that quite suddenly stung her heart; knew was only too true?

Dressing the windowsill with the small posy of wildflowers she had earlier found with such a delighted and astonished surprise, on Hilda's chair beneath her desk, as if she had left them there for her to find. But gave no sign she did when she left, and she might have overlooked them had she not seen them by the merest chance through the corner of her eye. A red anemone, a purple withy, a pink and white asphodel and a yellow narcissus, the same small posy of five, flowers she once, long ago, when she was a student just a few days arrived at the Sorbonne, found in a bistro in the Rue Mouffetard. And all of them so ridiculously fresh she almost believed she saw dew on the petals, they were surely grown in a hot house by an expert, but by whom, she wondered, knowing she was an orphan in the care of the council. The smell of them more beguiling than any perfume she knew? Better even than anything conjured by the Noses at *Rigaud* or *Chanel;* each incomparable. Flowers which shimmered in the thin dapple of iridescent sunlight that pierced the gloom from the window. A small touch of elegance in that awkwardly uncomfortable room that did little to soothe the eye but cheered her spirit as she cleaned and tidied what little she could, singing as she did, *Roses are Red my Love,* which she heard on *Pick of the Pops* only yesterday afternoon. But sang it in French, which was so much better.

And to make certain of their privacy placed a large rectangle of plain white cardboard on the frosted glass window of the door, knowing the picture of Notre Dame Cathedral and the Ile de la Cité on the other side was quite enough to deter any prying eye, though she knew her classroom door would be securely bolted against any intrusion, and, who, but Arno would look, anyway?

A room for all its size was little better than the cramped

car he had now twice fucked her in and always in a careful hurry that ignored she had her own place, where, had he wanted, they would have been safe and warm in her gorgeously comfortable bed, though AA may have been surprised and shocked by what she did, because she knew, as women do, he loved her a little. A place he refused to visit excusing his hesitation with blandishments she now saw for what they were. A ruse that had no love or care for her pride! A ruse that only wanted to make a tart of her! A *chair a plaisir* for his wounded ego; an ego she had all too willingly and so dangerously satisfied in her blind and greedy need for him. Any man who would love her just a little!

To Be Continued...